George Edmundson

Milton and Vondel

A Curiosity of Literature

George Edmundson

Milton and Vondel
A Curiosity of Literature

ISBN/EAN: 9783337202958

Printed in Europe, USA, Canada, Australia, Japan

Cover: Foto ©Andreas Hilbeck / pixelio.de

More available books at **www.hansebooks.com**

MILTON AND VONDEL.

"Evenwel indien gij eenige bloemen op den Nederlandschen Helicon pluckken wilt, draeg u zulks, dat het de boeren niet mercken, nochte voor den geleerden al te sterck doorschijne."—VONDEL.

MILTON AND VONDEL:

𝔄 Curiosity of 𝔏iterature.

BY

GEORGE EDMUNDSON, M.A.

LATE FELLOW AND TUTOR OF BRASENOSE COLLEGE, OXFORD,
VICAR OF NORTHOLT, MIDDLESEX.

" C........ ...: .... l.......... "

LONDON:

TRÜBNER & CO., LUDGATE HILL.

1885.

𝔅𝔞𝔩𝔩𝔞𝔫𝔱𝔶𝔫𝔢 𝔓𝔯𝔢𝔰𝔰
BALLANTYNE, HANSON AND CO
EDINBURGH AND LONDON

CONTENTS.

PAGES

CHAPTER I.

INTRODUCTORY   1–12

CHAPTER II.

MILTON AND VONDEL .   13–30

CHAPTER III.

THE LUCIFER   .   31–87

CHAPTER IV.

JOHN THE MESSENGER   .   .   88–123

CHAPTER V.

REFLECTIONS ON GOD AND RELIGION .   124–135

CHAPTER VI.

PAGES

ADAM IN BANISHMENT 136-157

CHAPTER VII.

SAMSON 158-192

APPENDIX 193-223

MILTON AND VONDEL.

CHAPTER I.

INTRODUCTORY.

THE "Paradise Lost" of Milton is now, by universal consent, numbered among those few productions of rare poetical genius whose supreme merit assures them an immortality of renown. Yet its record has not been one of unbroken triumph. The poem, when published, did not take public opinion by storm. Its popularity was at first of slow growth, and when at length it had won its way to that position of acknowledged pre-eminence, which it has since retained, its very originality and inspiration began to be vehemently questioned. In the eighteenth century a perfect storm of controversy arose as to the supposed sources from whence its author derived not merely the rudimentary ideas, but even the very details both in plot and imagery of that "adventurous song," which, in the poet's own words, was "to pursue things unattempted yet in prose or rhyme." Voltaire was the first who threw out the suggestion that the conceptions of Milton might not be entirely original. In an essay on Epic Poetry, written in English and published in the year 1727, he remarks

A

"that Milton during his year's sojourn in Italy saw at Florence the performance of a Scriptural drama by an Italian writer named Andreini, entitled 'Adamo,' and dealing with the subject of the Fall of Man, and that he (Milton), piercing through the absurdity of the representation to the hidden majesty of the subject, took from that ridiculous trifle the first hint of the noblest work the human imagination has ever attempted."

The careless suggestion did not fall to the ground; it was seized upon by critics and commentators with the avidity peculiar to their kind. The question, "Was Milton a plagiarist?" opened out a field for curious research too tempting to be neglected. Bookshelves and catalogues were ransacked, and the dust shaken from many a forgotten volume in the laborious search that was instituted in quest of the *prima stamina* of the Paradise Lost.

It is not necessary to enter into any detailed account of this curious episode of literary history; the more curious because its result, so far from detracting from Milton's fame, has rather served to establish his reputation as being one of the most learned and well-read men of his time. It will be sufficient for our purpose to mention the malicious attempt made by William Lauder, who undertook to prove that Milton in writing his poem had made the freest use without acknowledgment of the works (principally in Latin) of a number of poets and poetasters, English, Scotch, Dutch, and German. Lauder published in 1750 a series of essays upon the subject in the pages of the *Gentleman's Magazine*, supporting his argument by copious quotations. These essays were afterwards collected in a volume under the title of "Milton's Use and Imitation of the

Moderns in his Paradise Lost," and secured the impos-
ing sanction of the then all-powerful literary dictator,
Dr. Johnson, who contributed a short preface.

The effort of Lauder was to some extent successful,
for he had undoubtedly discovered many similarities
between passages of the Paradise Lost and others
which he had brought forward ; as, for instance, from
Sylvester's Du Bartas, [1] and the "Adamus Exul" of
Hugo Grotius. But he was not content with adducing
such resemblances as really existed. He deliberately
forged lines of his own and interpolated others, which
were taken from a Latin translation of the Paradise
Lost by a certain William Hogg, and assigned them
to authors whom he professed to quote.

His triumph was, however, of short duration. The
barefaced forgeries were ere long detected by the acute-
ness of Mr. Bowle, a tutor of Oriel College, Oxford ; and
a clergyman, Mr. (afterwards Bishop) Douglas, under
the form of a letter addressed to the Earl of Bath,
revealed to the public the gross imposition which had
been practised upon them. Lauder's shameless attempt
to cast a slur upon Milton's fame by false representation recoiled upon himself and ignominiously collapsed.
His fabrications were exposed, himself discredited, and,
as a natural result, a certain amount of obloquy and
disparagement has since attached to that " Inquiry into
the Origin of Paradise Lost" with which his too noto-
rious name is associated.

But surely there are two points of view from which
to regard this interesting chapter of literary criticism.
A critical inquiry into the construction of his great

[1] See on Milton's debt to Du Bartas, Dunster's "Considerations on
Milton's Early Reading and the *Prima Stamina* of his ' Paradise Lost.'

Epic *need not be* carried out in a spirit of hostility to
Milton. It is one thing to go to work in the spirit of
Lauder, who bluntly asserted to Dr. Newton[1] "that
he could prove that Milton had *borrowed the substance
of whole books together,* and that there was scarcely a
single thought or sentiment in his poem which he had
not *stolen* from some one or another." It is quite
another thing to study the Paradise Lost with loving
and curious care for the purpose of a discriminating
investigation of the hoarded treasures which it contains, drawn from the best literature of all previous
times,—an investigation which should lay bare that
prodigious store of learning with which the mind of
the poet was full to overflowing, and which in the
plenitude of his power he wielded and moulded at will.

Mr. Masson[2] speaks with some contempt of any
"Inquiry into the Origin of Paradise Lost," which he
stigmatises as "for the most part laborious nonsense."
But while fully admitting with him that "it is utterly
preposterous" to say "that in any or all of the books
which critics have" *as yet* "brought forward is to be
found the origin of Paradise Lost in any intelligible
sense of the phrase;" yet Mr. Masson surely ought to
be the very last, he who has devoted so many lengthy
volumes to the "History of Milton and his Times," to
desire to put on one side, contemptuously, as "laborious
nonsense" anything that throws light upon the studies
and mental proclivities of his favourite author.

The judgment, indeed, which should be passed upon
such an "Inquiry" depends entirely upon the meaning
which is assigned to the phrase "Origin of Paradise

[1] Todd's "Milton," vol. i. p. 205.
[2] "Milton's Poetical Works," vol. i. p. 39.

Lost." Something, doubtless, trivial or otherwise (possibly, as Voltaire suggests, Andreini's "Adamo"),[1] did first draw Milton's attention to the subject of the Fall of Man as well adapted to poetic treatment. The organisation of the mind is so subtle and its susceptibility so great, that the very slightest inciting cause may give the first impulse to the most considerable effects, as in the well-known stories which assign such commonplace ORIGINS to the great discoveries of Newton and Watts. But if we mean something much more than this; if by saying that in such and such a work or writer is to be found the "Origin of Paradise Lost," we do not refer to any chance hint which may have stirred the poet's fancy with a sudden inspiration, but to a prompting influence which has struck its roots deep into his mind and entwined itself around his imagination; then we must allow that any "Inquiry" into the operation of such an agency (if it exist) in fashioning the conceptions of a Milton ought to have a very real interest for every student of English literature. It is to such an inquiry as this that the present volume proposes to direct the attention of its readers.

The beginnings of Paradise Lost are veiled in no mystery. They have been disclosed to us by the Miltonic MSS. in the Library of Trinity College, Cambridge, in a manner singularly full and complete. Here are to be found one hundred drafts in Milton's own hand of subjects suitable for tragedies, written when he was about thirty-one years of age, and immediately after his return from Italy. A certain number of these were taken from Early British History; but the mind of Milton was already inclining towards a Scrip-

[1] See Scolari's "Saggio di Critica sul Paradiso Perduto."

tural subject, as is shown by the fact that no less than sixty of them are drawn from the Bible. Foremost among these stands, even at that early date, the now famous title of " Paradise Lost." Four drafts containing schemes for dramas upon the episode of the Fall of Man exist among this interesting collection, indicating the hold which this particular subject had, from the first, upon his affections.

But our acquaintance with the growth of the Poem, in what may be called its embryonic stage, extends farther still. The great idea, though early conceived, was for many long years slowly matured before it issued from the Poet's brain in its full perfection of form and beauty. The mind of Milton was for some time undecided as to the important question of dramatic or epic treatment. His writings contain many passages of great autobiographical interest bearing upon the engrossing subject of his thoughts. " Time serves not now," he wrote in 1641, " and, perhaps, I might seem too profuse to give any certain account of what the mind at home, in the spacious circuits of her musing, hath liberty to propose to herself, though of highest hope and hardest attaining—whether that epic form, whereof the two poems of Homer, and those other two of Virgil and Tasso are a diffuse, and the Book of Job a brief model, ... or whether those dramatic constitutions wherein Sophocles and Euripides reign." [1]

We know also on the authority of Edward Phillips, the nephew of the Poet, that a few lines of Satan's Invocation to the Sun at the beginning of the fourth book of Paradise Lost [2] were already penned as the

---

[1] " Reason of Church Government," book ii. Int.
[2] Paradise Lost, iv. 32–41.

commencement of a tragedy on the Fall of Man fifteen or sixteen years before the EPIC poem was seriously undertaken. Thus it is clear that this poem occupies a position unexampled among works of imagination, that of having been planned a quarter of a century before it was written, during the whole of which time the author was (to use his own words) " by labour and intent study " gradually preparing himself for the great task which he had set before him. He deliberately trained himself for his vocation of poet. The work which it was his lofty ambition to achieve " was not to be raised from the heat of youth or the vapours of wine, like that which flows at waste from the pen of some vulgar amorist or the trencher fury of a riming parasite, nor to be obtained by the invocation of Dame Memory and her siren daughters, but by devout prayer to that Eternal Spirit which can enrich with all utterance and knowledge, and sends out His Seraphim with the hallowed fire of His altar to touch and purify the lips of whom He pleases. To this must be added *industrious and select reading,* steady observation, insight into all seemly and generous arts and affairs." [1] After such revelations as these, any " Inquiry into the ORIGIN of Paradise Lost," if we use the words in their ordinary and literal sense, seems, indeed, superfluous, for not only have the rough drafts of the poet's first tentative imaginings been handed down to us, but, as in this last quotation, the very secret springs of his method are exposed to view. We seem to behold the growth and development of the work from its first germ to its glorious completion in the hidden depths of the creative mind.

---

[1] " Reason of Church Government," book ii. Int.

At the time of the composition of the Paradise Lost, by these long years passed "in intent study," by the ever-increasing acquisitions made by his " industrious and select reading," Milton had become one of the best-read men of his time. He had familiarised himself with the literature of both ancient and modern times. He had absorbed into his memory and made part of himself the choicest thoughts, the aptest metaphors and images, to be found in the writers of his own and all preceding ages. His memory indeed was simply prodigious, though not exact. He had not the gift of accurate verbal recollection, and was never fond of making quotations. He assimilated, as it were, into his very being the ideas and phrases which specially impressed him at the time of reading, so as to reproduce them almost unconsciously whenever, at a later period of poetic travail, they attuned themselves to the complex harmony of his lofty verse, or fitted themselves in, as subordinate embellishments, to his magnificent imaginings. The Paradise Lost is consequently not only in style, in diction, and in plan, one of the supreme creations of the human intellect, but it is also unique as a learned poem and for the wide range of literature which it places under contribution. Every portion of the poem is studded with quotations and allusions, but these, like the jewels upon one of the *chef-d'œuvres* of a Van Eyck or a Memling, add indeed richness to the effect, but nothing to the dignity of the conception or to the subtlety of the execution.

The spirit of the Poet broods over the whole of his work. Milton undoubtedly borrowed materials, freely, from this man and from that, but, with the skill of a master-architect, he so appropriately builds in each piece of carved stone and polished marble as to enhance its beauty by making it a component part of the stately edifice he is rearing.

But is not this plagiarism? Were Lauder and other detractors from Milton's fame justified in the charges which they brought against him? The answer to these questions depends entirely upon the definition which we give to the word plagiarism. Milton himself lays it down that "borrowing, if it be not *bettered* by the borrower, is accounted plagiarie." But this is far from satisfactory. If the borrowing be itself clandestine or otherwise illegitimate, the mere "bettering" cannot remove the stain which rests upon the original act. The German aphorism is more complete, "In der Kunst, der Diebstahl nicht erlaubt sei, wohl aber der Todschlag," and the latter expression is amplified in the explanation that the borrower must be "nicht der Sklave, sondern der frei schaltende Herr des Materials."[1]

In other words, he who ventures to make use for his own literary work of the language or ideas which he finds ready made to his hands in the writings of others, must, if he would free himself from the charge of plagiarism, fulfil two conditions. He must be to such an extent supreme over his materials, that in the consuming fire and fervid glow of his imagination each foreign ingredient becomes, as it were, fused with the native ore, so that from their union a totally new substance is formed. And at the same time he must never attempt to pass off an alloy for pure metal. There must be no concealment. A coin which bears Cæsar's image and superscription, though it may contain a certain proportion of baser metal, should be no

---

[1] Stern's "Milton und seine Zeit," vol. i. p. 236.

counterfeit. It is inevitable that a great writer should utilise the rich stores of knowledge which he has accumulated, and that at times he should blend ideas and thoughts derived from study in indissoluble fusion with the creations of his own mind, but it is none the less a dishonest act if he, without acknowledgment, place the stamp of his personality upon that which is clearly not his own.

For who is to adjudge the question as to whether such and such a writer borrows from his *inferior*, or *betters* what he borrows? Obviously each one would decide for himself according to his own estimate of his merits, and the way would be thrown open to an indefinite amount of literary pilfering. To take the case of Milton, the charges which have been brought against him amount to little more than this: he was far better acquainted than most men with those books, with which every student ought to be acquainted. His mind was peculiarly receptive, and its retentiveness was as characteristic as its originality. Consequently, when he drew upon his richly furnished brain for fresh images wherewith to give expression to his daring conceptions, phrases, expressions, metaphors came crowding thick upon him from the pages of the favourite authors to whom he had devoted so many studious hours. We find, therefore, numberless reminiscences of well-known writers in Milton's works, more especially of Euripides and Virgil among the Ancients, of Dante and Tasso among the Italians, and of Spenser, the Fletchers, and Sylvester's Du Bartas among the English poets. But these writers were all well known; their works had become, so to speak, public property. Had Milton largely appropriated either their language or ideas, he would have been at once discovered. So far from being a defect or a crime, this wealth of literary allusion constitutes one of the chief charms and merits of the Paradise Lost.

But Milton did not confine himself to classical or familiar authors. His use, for instance, of the Latin poems of Hugo Grotius and Masenius (proofs of which can be found in the essays of Lauder), from the very fact that these were slight and trivial productions was perhaps scarcely justifiable, if viewed by the code of strict literary morality. But here, undoubtedly, the plea can be put forward that no plagiary was committed, because Milton "borrowed, but *bettered* in the borrowing;" and we admit its force.

All these things indeed show what may be called the besetting tendency of Milton's mind, but so far nothing has been proved against him which could be held in the slightest degree to cast a stain upon his reputation as a man, or his merit as a poet. Had the controversy as to the originality of the Paradise Lost ended here, there would be little need for any farther "inquiry" upon the subject.

Mr. Masson, who, as we had occasion to mention above, exhibits such a strong distaste to this branch of Miltonic criticism, owing, as we think, to a misapprehension as to its aims and to a diffidence as to its results, contents himself in his Introduction to the Paradise Lost with the briefest *resumé* of the subject, and refers the reader, in a footnote,[1] to Mr. Todd's chapter for fuller information. He concludes with a remark, which first led the writer to make the investigations, which are contained in the present volume. It runs, as follows: "This chapter of Todd is the most

---

[1] Masson, "The Poetical Works of Milton," vol. i. p. 39.

complete compilation on the subject, *save that* it omits the Dutch Poet, Joost van den Vondel, from the list of Milton's creditors. The claims of this poet have been urged in Antwerp and elsewhere since Todd's chapter was written."

Curiosity prompted an examination of the omitted Poet's writings, and of the literature bearing upon their supposed influence upon the composition of the Paradise Lost, and the results have been in many respects so interesting and so remarkable, that we make no apology in placing them before the public in the following pages.

CHAPTER II.

MILTON AND VONDEL.

IN the year 1654, four years before Milton commenced his Paradise Lost, the great Dutch Poet, Vondel, published a drama entitled "Lucifer," whose main theme deals with the story of the rebellion of the angels and their overthrow by Michael at the head of the armies of God. The possible indebtedness of Milton to this play escaped the notice of all the keen-eyed INQUIRERS INTO THE ORIGIN OF THE PARADISE LOST, the history of whose researches into the nooks and corners of many a library is given in the chapter upon the subject in Todd's "Milton;" the cause of this curious oversight being doubtless their ignorance of the Dutch language and literature, which already in the eighteenth century, after a short-lived outburst of extreme brilliancy, had rapidly fallen into a state of torpor and decadence. It was not until quite recent times that the attention of students was turned to Vondel's drama, and that a comparison was instituted between it and the Paradise Lost. This comparison, however, as will be abundantly shown in the sequel, has been of a most cursory and superficial character. Moreover, with the "Lucifer" the labours of these latter-day inquirers have begun and ended. We shall proceed to justify a farther and more detailed discussion of the subject by proving, not only that the language and imagery of the "Lucifer" exercised a powerful and abiding influence on the mind of Milton, and have left indelible traces upon the pages of the Paradise Lost, but that other writings of Vondel can be shown to have affected in no slight or inconsiderable degree all the great poems of Milton's later life.

In 1661 the Dutch writer published an Epic poem in six books upon the subject of the Life and Death of John the Baptist.[1] The plan and descriptions of this Poem will be discovered to have a strong affinity with certain portions both of the Paradise Lost and the Paradise Regained.

A drama of Vondel's entitled "Adam in Banishment,"[2] published in 1664, and intended as a sequel to the "Lucifer," although its general outline has much that is in common with the Paradise Lost, and the materials for the plot are necessarily the same, differs widely both in language and character from those earlier books of Milton's Poem which were composed before it was published, but offers some remarkable coincidences with the ninth and tenth books, which were probably written after its appearance. Again, a number of passages from a didactico-religious Poem of Vondel's,[3] of the date 1661, which bears the name "Reflections on God and Religion," are almost reproduced in portions of the eighth book of the Paradise Lost.

Lastly, in 1660 Vondel composed a drama entitled "Samson, or Divine Vengeance."[4] This work, written a few years previous to the "Samson Agonistes," has in

[1] "Joannes Boetgezant."
[2] "Adam in Ballingschap."
[3] "Bespiegelingen van God en Godsdienst."
[4] "Samson, of de heilige wraak."

disputable claims to be regarded as its literary parent.
Those features of the English drama, which have hitherto
been regarded as so peculiarly its own, are all to be
found in its Dutch predecessor.

We shall proceed to verify these assertions *seriatim*;
but, before doing so, one step is essential as a preli-
minary. We must establish the fact that the works
of Vondel were accessible to Milton; that he was able
to understand the language in which they were written;
and that there was a strong *à priori* probability, apart
from the internal evidence contained in his poems, that
he would be acquainted with them.

We will take first the all-important question as to
Milton's knowledge of the Dutch language. Milton
was a great linguist. He was perfectly familiar with
the ancient classical tongues and with Hebrew, and that
not merely from the literary point of view: he could
speak and understand, as well as read them. He is
also known to have been proficient in several modern
languages, more especially in the Italian. The account
given by his nephew, Edward Phillips, of the manner
in which, after he became completely blind (about April
1652), he employed his daughters and others to read
aloud to him books in various languages is well known [1]
and has been often quoted. "Those he had by his first
(wife) he made serviceable to him in that very particular in which he most wanted their service, and supplied his want of eyesight by their eyes and tongue;
for though he had daily about him one or other to read
to him—some, persons of man's estate, who of their
own accord greedily catched at the opportunity of

---

[1] Phillips' Memoir of Milton, prefixed to the English edition of
"Letters of State," 1694.

being his readers, that they might as well reap the
benefit of what they read to him as oblige him by the
benefit of their reading; others of younger years, sent
by their parents to the same end—yet, excusing only
the eldest daughter by reason of her bodily infirmity
and difficult utterance of speech, which, to say truth,
I doubt was the principal cause of excusing her, the
other two were condemned to the performance of *reading and exactly pronouncing of all languages of whatever
book* he should at one time or other think fit to peruse,
viz., the Hebrew (and, I think, the Syriac), the Greek,
the Latin, the Italian, Spanish, and French. All which
sorts of books to be confined to read *without understanding one word* must needs be a trial of patience almost
beyond endurance." This authentic record of Milton's
habits of study after his blindness, and during the
period when his great Epic was being gradually composed, proves that during all this time his appetite for
new literature in all languages was ceaseless and con-.
stantly gratified. Phillips' information being derived
from the daughters, who confessedly did not understand
a single word of the books which they read, does not
make the omission of the Dutch language, from the
list which he gives, a fact of great importance. If it
can be proved from other sources that Milton could
understand Dutch, then the evidence supplied by the
extract above makes it morally certain that Dutch
books would be included amongst those which "at one
time or other he should think fit to peruse."

The proof, we require, is given to us in a manner
singularly direct and unimpeachable. It is contained
in a letter written by the celebrated Roger Williams
(the founder of the State of Rhode Island), at Provi-

dence, July 12, 1654, to his friend John Winthrop at
Pequod.[1] The following statement (from Jared Sparks'
Library of American Biography) gives us all the information we require.[2] Williams visited England on business of the colony in 1651 and remained till 1654.
During his residence in London " he formed an intimate
acquaintance with Milton, who was then Latin Secretary to the Council, and already rapidly rising to the
zenith of his renown as a statesman and a poet. The
Paradise Lost had not been written, but the repub-
lican bard had sung many of his sweetest sonnets, and
had published in prose some of those noble vindica-
tions of liberty of which all Europe rang from side to
side." " Younger than Williams by more than nine
years, he was now in the freshness of early manhood
and the full vigour of his great powers. The infirmities
and disasters of his later life had not yet darkened the
hopes or damped the ardour of his spirit. In their
frequent companionship, with the interchange of con-
genial views and the expression of common principles
and aims, they appear to have mingled the studies of
languages and literature ; and FOR THE DUTCH, *which the
Poet acquired from the teachings of Williams*, he opened
in return the rich stores of his varied learning in many
different tongues ; " or, to quote Williams' own words,
" It pleased the Lord to call me, for some time and
with some persons, to practise the Hebrew, the Greek,
Latin, French, and Dutch. The Secretary of the Council,
Mr. Milton, for my Dutch I READ him, read me many
more languages. Grammar rules begin to be esteemed
a tyranny. I taught two gentlemen, a Parliament

---

[1] This letter is given in full in Knowles' "Life of Roger Williams,"
pp. 261-264.   [2] "Life of Roger Williams," pp. 150-151.

man's sons, as we teach our children English, by words,
phrases, and constant talk." Nothing can be more
clear than that Milton, who was already blind in 1652,
learned to understand Dutch, orally, from the conversations and readings of Williams, and that in the year
immediately preceding the appearance of the "Lucifer."

The further question remains, what were the in-
ducements to Milton to pursue his Dutch studies, and
what his facilities for intercourse with Holland and
for acquaintance with its literature? The whole of
the fourth book of Masson's "Life of Milton," which
deals with the period (1649–54), is full of evidence
upon this point. Its pages are crowded with references
to Holland, its statesmen, ambassadors, professors, and
writers. It was the period of the Dutch war, the
period of the famous controversies with Salmasius and
Morus. As Secretary for Foreign Languages to the
Council of State, it was Milton's duty at audiences of
envoys and ambassadors to act as interpreter and to
translate into Latin all the correspondence. Now, "of
the foreign relations of the Commonwealth through
1652 and part of 1653, by far the most important were
those with the Dutch Republic."[1] During those years,
in which was waged a fierce naval war between the two
Commonwealths for the supremacy of the seas, constant
negotiations were going on, and many eminent Dutch-
men, who came to London as special envoys, were
brought into the closest relations with Milton. Among
these was the Pensionary Cats, the "Father Cats,"
whose poetry is still so popular in Holland.[2] More-

---

[1] Masson's "Life of Milton," vol. iv. p. 371.

[2] Masson's "Life," iv. 353. Mr. Masson says that "there is a very
credible tradition that Milton," in his official capacity, "was allowed
a weekly table for the entertainment of such foreigners of distinction
as came on embassy business."

over, during these same years that the Dutch and the
English were contending in the Channel, Milton was
engaged in those bitter controversial struggles against
Salmasius and Morus which first gave him a European
reputation. Now both these opponents, though the one
was of French, the other of Scotch extraction, were resi-
dent in the United Provinces. Salmasius (Claude de
Saumaise) was professor at Leyden ; Morus (Alexander
More), pastor and theological professor at Middleburg.
The reply of Milton to the first, his celebrated " Pro
Populo Anglicano Defensio," was published in 1651 ;
the " Defensio Secunda," an onslaught upon Morus, in
1654. Now, these works not only made Milton's
name a household word in Holland, but they brought
him into the most intimate connection with Dutch
booksellers and correspondents. A perusal of the latter
pamphlet will speedily prove how minutely Milton
had been supplied with the gossip of the Hague and
the petty scandals of Leyden. The way he obtained
his information was no doubt largely through the
agency of a group of friends, whom Mr. Masson calls
the " Hartlib connection." [1] These consisted of Samuel
Hartlib, John Durie, John Pell, Theodore Haak, March-
mont Needham, and others ; [2] and they might quite
as appropriately have been called the Dutch connection. Needham started in June 1650 a weekly
journal called the *Mercurius Politicus*, and on January
1, 1650–51, associated Milton with himself as "censor,"
or supervising editor. Now this paper (copies of which
during the period of Milton's censorship are to be
seen in the British Museum) had regular Dutch corre-

---

[1] Masson's " Life," iv. 329, 449, 452, 459, 462 *et sq.*
[2] Stern's " Milton," ii. 266 *sqq.*, iii. 27 *sqq.*, 191, 278, 282, iv. 20 *sq.*

spondents at the Hague, so that from this source alone
information at first hand was accessible to Milton of all
the passing events of interest across the water. Letters
to Milton from Durie at Amsterdam are extant.[1] Pell
had been a professor both at Amsterdam and Breda.
Haak was a Dutchman. Hartlib, whose activity in
literary matters was of boundless capacity, was the
medium through whom Milton was brought into correspondence with a certain Ulac, a bookseller at the
Hague. This Ulac was a very shrewd man of business.
He had, after the success of the pamphlet against
Salmasius, been anxious to obtain a promise from Milton through Hartlib that he should print for him.
Milton had replied that he had nothing at present for
publication. Meanwhile the manuscript of the attack
against Milton, the " Regii Sanguinis Clamor," had been
placed in his hands; so, desirous at once not to refuse
an opportunity for doing some trade, and at the same
time to keep on excellent terms with a possible good
customer, he undertook to publish the hostile pamphlet,
while he " informed Hartlib of what was coming, and
sent over to him, week by week, the single sheets of
the book *wet from the press*, making tender inquiries at
the same time as to the state of Milton's eyes, and
hinting that, if Milton should write an answer to the
book, he would be happy to print the foreign edition." [2]
This is such a very remarkable proof of the facility
with which books printed in Holland could find their
way to London, that it is superfluous to accumulate
further evidence. Negotiations with Dutch envoys,
controversies with Dutch professors, intercourse with
a circle of quasi-Dutch friends, correspondence with

---

[1] Masson's "Life," iv. 631.   [2] Ibid., iv. 466.

Dutch residents, quarrels with Dutch booksellers, all conspired to familiarise Milton with Dutch affairs, and to make him only less well acquainted with the events and intrigues, nay, the very gossip of the chief centres of Dutch life, than with the current topics of London.

If this be so, it is well-nigh impossible that Milton should not speedily have learned so interesting a piece of news, to a man of letters, as the appearance in January 1654 of Vondel's " Lucifer," and the storm of ecclesiastical enmity which it evoked. For Vondel was no young or unknown man, and had long ere this established his fame, as the foremost of the many brilliant writers who flourished during this, the Golden Age of Dutch literature. He was now at the zenith of his fame. His position of supremacy had just (20th October 1653 [1]) been recognised at the celebration of the Feast of St. Luke at Amsterdam. As if in antici- pation of the masterpiece which was so soon to be given to the world,[2] above a hundred poets and painters and lovers of the arts, assembled on this occasion, saluted the aged Vondel as their chief, and one of their number, in the guise of Apollo, solemnly placed on his head the Laureate's crown. This was a literary event which, amidst the other items of intelli- gence from Holland, was almost certain to reach the ears of Milton, and to stimulate him to inquire after the works of so celebrated a writer, even had they been entirely unknown to him before. There is, how- ever, no reason to suppose that this was the case. The

[1] Brandt's " Leven van Vondel," pp. 74-75; Van Lennep's " Vondel," vi. 376-384.

[2] The " Lucifer " was already complete in MS. Thijm's " Portretten van Vondel," p. 135, &c.

two most famous productions of Vondel's pen previous to the appearance of the "Lucifer" were undoubtedly the two plays entitled the " Palamedes," and the "Gysbrecht van Amstel." With both of these it is, at least, strongly probable that Milton was acquainted.

The former, written in 1625, under the form of a Greek story, is a political allegory, and perhaps, as a sustained piece of trenchant satire, has never been surpassed for delicate irony and richness of allusion. It holds up to obloquy and public resentment the motives and the conduct of the political and religious party, who had rewarded the patriotism of the great Advocate Barneveldt by a death of shame, and had condemned to lifelong imprisonment the young and illustrious Hugo Grotius.[1] The daring author barely escaped from paying with his life the penalty for his temerity. Summoned before the court at the Hague, some staunch friends that he had upon the Town Council of Amsterdam pleaded the privileges of the city, and refused to surrender him to other jurisdiction. He was tried, therefore, before the two sheriffs of Amsterdam, and mulcted in a heavy fine. This, as might easily have been foreseen, "served only "—to use the words of the friend and biographer of Vondel, Brandt—" to make the book better known and men more curious. It is also certain," he adds, "that there is no means to make books more sought after and read than to forbid them . . . and punish the writers; because this awakes much notoriety, and many, who otherwise would have never thought about such writings, wish to see them. It is the right sauce to make such fare tasty." The first edition was sold out in a

---

[1] Brandt's " Leven," pp. 24-32 ; Van Lennep's " Vondel," ii. p. 520, &c.

few days, and within a few years more than thirty fresh editions were issued.

Such a sale as this, it is scarcely necessary to point out, was something quite extraordinary at the beginning of the seventeenth century, and signified not only an almost universal dispersion of the book in Holland, but that a considerable number of copies must have found purchasers in other lands, and made the name of Vondel known even to some, who were unable to read his works.

Now the subject of the drama was one which was likely to be of special interest to Milton. The story of the death of Barneveldt and of the Synod of Dort must have been the subject of frequent converse in a Puritan household like that of the elder Milton, who was not only a religious precisian, but a man of learning and education, to whose care his son, in the first instance, owed his early acquaintance with the "humane letters," and through whose encouragement, while yet a boy, he pursued his studies with precocious energy. For Holland was, in the reign of James I., the house of refuge for those who fled from religious persecution in England, and there was no lack of communication between the "Separatist" congregations[1] at Amsterdam, Leyden, and Rotterdam and their sympathisers on the banks of the Thames.

Moreover, the fate which befell the literary hero of his age, Grotius, the man of universal and dazzling genius, can scarcely have failed to stir the chords of pity and sorrow in the youthful heart of one who in

---

[1] From these refugees in Holland came the Pilgrim Fathers, who sailed in the "May Flower" from Plymouth two years after the death of Barneveldt. See Masson's "Life," vol. ii. pp. 538–542.

after years (1638), during his brief visit to Paris, sought, as a special favour from the English ambassador, an introduction to the great Dutch statesman and scholar, then residing as Swedish Envoy at the court of Louis XIII.

This admiration for, and personal intercourse with Grotius, on the part of Milton is in fact one of the valuable personal links which connect him with Vondel. For Grotius had been the friend and protector of Vondel from the time when he first emerged from obscurity, and was his instructor[1] in acquiring the Latin and Greek languages; and their esteem for one another, which commenced thus early, continued throughout life. Many letters from Grotius are extant expressing the strongest admiration for Vondel's poetical powers, and a number of Vondel's compositions were written in honour, praise, or defence of his friend. Of one of these we shall have occasion to speak more particularly anon.

Before doing so, we must point out that the man, who at the time of the publication of the " Palamedes," used his utmost influence to have Vondel dragged before the Fiscal at the Hague to be tried for his life, was none other than Adrian Pauw, then Pensionary of Amsterdam, afterwards Grand Pensionary of Holland, and twice envoy-extraordinary of the United Provinces to England. He was the son of the Burgomaster Reinier Pauw, who had sat in 1618 as one of the members of the tribunal which condemned the Advocate Barneveldt to death, and had thus special reasons for being incensed at the reflections which were cast by Vondel upon his father. He appeared first in England to plead for the life of Charles I., and afterwards, in the

[1] " J. Vondel," &c., par l'Abbé A. Stillemans, p. 10.

beginning of 1652, he was dispatched to make every effort to avert the then impending war. Of this visit Milton himself speaks in his "Defensio Secunda," and says that the Envoy, whom he calls "the honour and ornament of Holland," sent him "frequent assurances of his extraordinary predilections and regard."[1] Even had they no opportunity for friendly converse, the assailant of Vondel was here brought into close relation with Cromwell's Latin Secretary, and it is evident that they regarded each other with feelings of mutual esteem and respect, which could only have arisen from knowledge of their respective lives and characters.

The circumstance proves nothing, but the collocation of names is again interesting and suggestive. We have already, in alluding to the story of the publication of the "Palamedes," pointed out how strong was the probability that Milton, through friendship with Puritan refugees in Holland or otherwise, may have heard, *at the time*, of the sensation, which Vondel's brilliant satire had caused throughout the United Provinces, and have hinted the possibility that a copy may have come into his hands. Had this been so, there could be no insuperable difficulty for so skilled and accomplished a linguist to decipher the Dutch text, even though the language might not be familiar to him. There is, indeed, no direct evidence to show that Milton did in this manner and at this time make acquaintance with Vondel's play, but the resemblance between the imagery in a famous chorus of the "Palamedes" and certain portions of the "Allegro" and the "Penseroso" is of such a nature as to lend force to the supposition. The similarity is not close enough to justify us in making

---

[1] "The Prose Works of John Milton," vol. i. p. 178, Bohn.

the assertion that the one passage has supplied the motive for the others, but sufficiently so to give it plausibility.[1]

With regard to the "Gysbrecht van Amstel," the other play of Vondel's mentioned above, and the one of all his dramas which has retained the strongest hold upon the affections of his countrymen, a curious coincidence of dates makes it extremely likely that this too, at the time of its first appearance, may have been brought to the cognisance of Milton. This play was specially written for the opening of the new theatre[2] at Amsterdam, and was the first piece performed on its stage (Christmas Day, 1637). It was dedicated to Grotius, who sent to the poet from Paris a letter of acknowledgment,[3] a portion of which we quote : "I have always most highly esteemed your gifts and your works. If I should say of this work what I feel, then would suspicion be aroused as to whether I were willing to recognise the honour which has befallen me through the dedication thereof, the which I neither by this nor by other methods see that I could do according to my satisfaction. To others I shall speak highly of the happy choice of this truly realistic, but, by you, beautifully embellished story, peculiarly belonging to the town of Amsterdam, where this work is produced and represented ; the very pleasing arrangement of all parts from the first to the last, the wise teaching, tender emotions, flowing yet well-knit verses. To yourself I shall say no more than that I should hold Amsterdam

---

[1] The translation of this chorus is given in the Appendix. It is taken from the "Batavian Anthology" by John Bowring.

[2] Van Lennep, iii. 319, &c.

[3] Brandt's "Leven," p. 54.

as fortunate should there be many who can esteem this work according to its value. The ' Œdipus at Colonus ' of Sophocles, the ' Supplicants ' of Euripides, have never afforded Athens greater honour than Amsterdam herewith enjoys."

This is a specimen of several other letters from Grotius to Vondel on works which the poet had submitted to his judgment and approbation, and it can be shown that their language of eulogy was not dictated by merely friendly courtesy or complaisance ; for certain letters from Grotius to the eminent scholar Gerard Vossius have come down to us, containing comments on Vondel's writings couched in the very same strain. One of these letters contains a lengthened notice of the " Gysbrecht," a single sentence of which is sufficient to prove, that the play had commended itself to his critical judgment, and that he felt really pleased at its dedication to him : " Vondel has done me an act of friendship by dedicating to me, as a man having some taste in such matters, a tragedy of admirable import, wellordered symmetry, and overflowing eloquence."[1] Now the letter of Grotius to Vondel just quoted bears the date May 28, 1638, and it was in this very month of May 1638 that Milton, setting out on his journey to Italy, came to Paris, and asked the English Ambassador to give him an introduction to Grotius. The introduction was given, and Phillips tells us that the distinguished Dutchman " took Milton's visit kindly, and gave him entertainment suitable to his worth and the high commendations he had heard of him." Thus, at the very time when Milton was enjoying Grotius' hospitality, his host was writing to express his obligations to

[1] Brandt's "Leven," p. 56.

Vondel for the dedication to him of the "Gysbrecht," and doubtless the newly-arrived play occupied the place of honour upon his library table, and was the subject of conversation between himself and his literary guests.

But it is time to return from these digressions to that play which is the more special object of our investigation. Already on that 20th October 1653 when Vondel was crowned at the Festival of St. Luke, the manuscript of the "Lucifer" was complete,[1] and was shortly afterwards placed in the printer's hands. It was published and brought upon the stage at the commencement of 1654, but, after two representations only, was withdrawn, owing to the violent hostility which it aroused among the more extreme Calvinistic preachers. They proclaimed from the pulpit that it contained " unholy, immodest, idolatrous, false, and very bold things, too cunningly devised for human brains," and brought the matter at once before the Church Council. From the account of the proceedings contained in the "Protocol," bearing the date 5th February 1654, it appears that a remonstrance was addressed to the authorities of the town " against a play written by Joost van den Vondel, named Luisevaer's Tragedy, about the Fall of the Angels, treating the high matters of the mysteries of God in a carnal manner," and much more to the like import.[2]

The result was an official inhibition of the " Lucifer," a result on which Brandt makes the comment—" The opposition awakened so great a curiosity to read that

---

[1] Thijm's " Portretten van Vondel," pp. 135-137.

[2] See Van Vloten's edition of the " Lucifer," in the Klassiek Letterkundig Pantheon Series, under the heading " Kerkelijke Tegenwerking," pp. 92-98.

which was forbidden to be played, that the entire impression of 1000 copies was in eight days' time sold out, so that the publisher brought out the tragedy again from the press."[1] As twenty-nine years before with the "Palamedes," the enemies of the poet had "scourged him with a fox's tail,"[2] and the effect of persecution was increased popularity.

Vondel was not the man to submit tamely to his fate. The lampoons and travesties, which greeted the appearance of his play, roused him to reply in a series of vigorous retorts, full of that biting wit and pungent satire, which he knew so well how to use, to the discomfiture of his foes. The fame of "Luisevaer's Tragedy" was spread far and wide, and the victory of its writer in the paper-war of reprisals was doubtless the subject of discussion and amusement in every literary coterie throughout Holland.

At this very time, Milton in England was busily writing and gathering materials for his attack upon Alexander Morus, then pastor at Middleburg and professor at Amsterdam, whom he imagined to be the author of the Royalist pamphlet entitled "Regii Sanguinis Clamor ad Cœlum." He actually published his "Defensio Secunda" in May 1654. We have already pointed out that in this piece we find that Milton displayed a remarkable acquaintance not merely with the general course of events in Holland, but with the subcurrents of rumour and scandal, with the tittle-tattle and innuendos of private spite. It is impossible to glance at the contents of the pamphlet without seeing that the writer is perfectly at home with all that was passing in

---

[1] Brandt's "Leven," p. 76.
[2] Met een vossenstaart gegeesselt.

Amsterdam, Leyden, and the Hague; and we may assume as a certainty that the fame of the "Lucifer"
would be speedily transmitted to him through some
of his friends and correspondents,[1] and that he would
be eager to make every inquiry after a drama dealing
with the very subject on which his own thoughts had
been fixed already for many years.   Further, as we
have already shown, he had just been learning the
language, in which it was written, from the conversation and readings of Roger Williams, and his teacher
did not leave England till the early summer of 1654,
or some months at least after the appearance of the
"Lucifer."[2]   We can easily imagine that Milton would
be desirous before the departure of his friend to make .
acquaintance with this play, which all Holland was
reading; and thus it is at least possible that it was
from the lips of Williams himself that he first heard
the rhythmic lines and learnt to appreciate the poetical
power and fine imagery of Vondel's masterpiece.

[1] Among others, Durie was in Amsterdam in the spring of this year,
corresponding with Milton, Hartlib, &c.

[2] Knowles' "Life of Roger Williams," p. 260.

CHAPTER III.

THE LUCIFER.

IT is now full time to pass on from the consideration of the probability that Milton *may* have studied the Lucifer to the actual proofs from internal evidence that he *must* have done so. No adequate or exhaustive comparison of the Lucifer with the Paradise Lost has ever yet been undertaken,[1] and the judgments, which have been passed upon the subject, have too often been based on second-hand and unsifted evidence, or at the best on a thorough knowledge of only one of the two poems.

[1] The essay by Mr. Gosse, "Milton and Vondel," in his volume entitled "Studies in Northern Literature," is a good instance in point. The essay is simply an essay upon Vondel; a number of vague generalities comprise all that bears upon the subject which the title suggests. Mr. Gosse has given an excellent analysis of the plot and action of the Lucifer, and he has translated into English verse (we should be sorry to say *travestied*) a number of specimen excerpts, which may have been chosen as illustrative of the Dutch Poet's style and manner, but have certainly not been happily selected for the purpose of Miltonic parallelism. The representation which they give of the remarkable similarities between the Paradise Lost and the Lucifer in language and turn of thought is both incomplete and misleading. Mr. Gosse gives prominence to many passages which are irrelevant to his purpose, while he omits most of those which have an important bearing upon the comparison he institutes; the vein of burlesque, moreover, which runs through the renderings gives an altogether wrong impression of the nature of Vondel's splendid poetical gifts.

Mr. Pattison, in his admirable and scholarly little work upon Milton,[1] has expressed in a very clear and concise manner his views upon the question of the obligations of Milton to Vondel. He does not pretend to speak from personal investigation; he evidently assumes the claims of Vondel to have been put forward in their strongest form (by Mr. Gosse and others); he weighs their arguments and delivers sentence accordingly. We will, therefore, take his statement as an unbiassed summing-up of the case as heretofore presented, and point out how unsound are the foundations on which it rests. False premises have produced false conclusions.

Mr. Pattison writes as follows:—"The Dutch drama turns entirely on the revolt of the angels and their expulsion from heaven, the fall of man being but a subordinate incident. In Paradise Lost the relation of the two events is inverted, the fall of the angels being there an episode, not transacted, but told by one of the personages of the Epic. It is, therefore, only in one book of Paradise Lost, the sixth, that the influence of Vondel can be looked for. There may possibly occur in other parts of our Epic single lines of which an original may be found in Vondel's drama, . . . but it is in the sixth book only in which anything more than a verbal similarity is traceable. . . . Vondel is more human than Milton, just where human attributes are unnatural, so that heaven is made to seem like earth, while in Paradise Lost we always feel that we are in a region aloft."[2]

Now, no one who reads this passage would imagine, what is actually the case, that in the Dutch drama the

[1] English Men of Letters Series, pp. 202–206. [2] Ibid., p. 203.

conflict in heaven only occupies a portion of the fifth act, and that there, as in the Paradise Lost, it is "not transacted, but told by one of the personages" of the drama. Again, it is not "in the sixth book only of the Paradise Lost that the influence of Vondel can be looked for;" as a matter of fact, this influence shows itself in every one of the first nine books of Milton's poem, and notably in the first, second, fourth, and ninth.

Once more, though "the incident of the fall of man" is undoubtedly "subordinate" to the main action of the Lucifer, yet Mankind, its privileges and its fortunes, gives the keynote to the leading motive of the play. Throughout the drama MAN is the continual subject of angelic discussion, and jealousy of MAN is the determining cause of the revolt in heaven. Nor does Vondel confine himself to allusion. As we shall see later, the Lucifer opens with a description of Paradise and its inhabitants which is rich in coincidences with that portion of the Paradise Lost, which deals with the same subject, and it closes with an account of the Council of the Lost Angels in Hell and of Lucifer's plan of revenge, resulting in the temptation and fall of man, which, though very briefly sketched, shows a remarkable outline resemblance to Milton's more elaborate and more highly-wrought picture of the same events.

Lastly—for we quarrel with Mr. Pattison's statement throughout—we do not consider that his criticism upon Vondel's treatment of the subject is quite fair to the Dutch Poet. Vondel was compelled to be "more human" than Milton; he was obliged to make "his heaven seem like earth" from the very fact that he wrote a DRAMA which was intended for the stage, and

c

was indeed actually represented, and not an EPIC POEM. The exigencies of the case demanded a more human treatment. Had Milton carried out his first intentions and written a tragedy, even he would have had to clip the wings of his imagination and materialise his conceptions. The Satan of Milton would be utterly impossible, as a dramatic personage.

Without entering into any detailed analysis of the plot of the Lucifer,[1] we shall find it sufficient for our purpose to give the author's own short account of its contents. It runs as follows :—

"Lucifer, the archangel, proud, ambitious, blindly selfish, envied God's unlimited greatness, and man also, who, being created in the image of God, held sway in his luxuriant Paradise over the whole earth. He envied God and man the more when Gabriel, the herald of God, declared all the angels to be but ministering spirits, and revealed to them the mysteries of God's future Incarnation, whereby human nature, exalted above that of angels and united truly with the Divine, might expect equal might and majesty ; whereupon the proud, envious spirit, attempting to place himself upon an equality with God and to keep man out of heaven, through his abetters incited to arms innumerable angels, and lead them against the host of Michael, the heavenly commander, but was defeated. Enraged at his overthrow, he swore revenge, and tempted man into disobedience against God, for which he and all his hosts were plunged into hell and doomed to eternal perdition."

---

[1] For this see Mr. Gosse's Essay ; also Stilleman's " Dichter Joostvan den Vondel," pp. 34-47 ; and Van Lennep's " Vondel," Introduction to the Lucifer, vol. vi. p. 201 *sqq.*

In this outline of Vondel's play we find the entire scheme of the Paradise Lost indicated; the salient features of the two poems are identical.

And not merely so. The chief defects on which the earliest critics of the Paradise Lost dwelt were these:—That Milton brings his story to a conclusion by representing hell and sin and death as triumphant, and that he has so delineated the character of Satan as to make him in reality the hero of the poem.[1] Now these were precisely the charges brought against the Lucifer. Here also it was argued that the drama should not issue in "de triomf der Hel;" here also objections were made to "de karakterteekening van den hoofdpersoon, Lucifer, als toonbeeld van den hoogmoed zelf."[2] Again, as regards this latter point, it is at once curious and interesting that critics should have regarded either poem as being to a certain extent an historical allegory upon the events of the English Rebellion, and the character of Satan in the one, and of Lucifer in the other, as being framed upon that of the great Rebel, Cromwell.[3]

The evidence that Vondel, at any rate, deliberately intended in the creation of his Lucifer to present a counterfeit of the famous English leader is very strong, and there can be little doubt that to Cromwell, specially, the closing sentence of the introduction to the drama was intended to apply. "We are the more eager to bring 'Lucifer' upon the tragic stage since he, stricken at last by the thunderbolt of God, is thrust down to

[1] Addison in the "Spectator," Essay 297, &c. ; Dryden, Dedication to his translation of the "Æneid."

[2] Van Vloten's Inleiding, p. xv. (Klassiek Letter Kundig Pantheon Lucifer).

[3] See Stern's "Milton und seine Zeit," vol. iv., p. 79, &c.

hell, as a signal example to all thankless and ambitious persons, who audaciously dare to rise up against consecrated powers and majesties and lawful authorities."

The language of certain pieces, in which Vondel from time to time assailed the revolutionary party in England with fierce satirical invective, makes this quite clear. One, for example, runs thus (in free translation):—

To the Regicides of England.

Dissembling Lucifer made Parliament his tool
To seize his Sovereign's sword, in Church and Court to rule;
And that Anointed Head, by many a bloody coil,
To buy with Judas' blood, the scum of Scottish soil.
When Royal neck and crown beneath his axe lay prone,
Then raise in th' English (angel's) realm the Hellish Host
    his throne.[1]

After these prefatory and general considerations we shall now produce the evidence of the play itself, and for this purpose have made a careful selection of those

---

[1] Aan de Koning-dooders van Engeland.

Vermomde Lucifer had door zijn Parlement,
Den Heer het zwaard ontrukt, de Kerk en 't Hof geschend,
En dat gezalvde Hoofd, na 't bloedig t'zamen rotten,
Gekocht van Judas-bloed, den droesem van de Schotten,
Als hij de moordbijl klonk door 's Konings hals en kroon.
Zoo bouwt het Helsche Heer in 't Engelsch rijk zijn troon.

The play in the last line is upon the word **Engelsch**=English or Angelic.

Another passage occurs in the " Morgenwekker der Sabbisten :"—

    " Uw scepter-stormen, geen hervormen,
      Volgt Lucifer's banier in 't stormen," &c.

In the best known of these pasquinades (that entitled "Protecteur Weerwolf," and commencing "Milord Isegrim, van den boozen Geest bezeten ") the following lines seem to refer to Milton's writings against Tyranny :—

    " Hij ontvangt, in spijt van *blinden* en zienden,
     Kostuimen en schipgelt, vrijbuitgelt en tienden."

passages which appear the most important for the purpose of comparison, and shall place them side by side in their English garb [1] with parallel passages from the Paradise Lost, those from the less-known work being placed in continuous order, with the design of indicating thereby the sequence of events, and drawing attention to the more salient points of Vondel's plot.

The first act of the play opens with the return of Apollion, the messenger of Lucifer, from a mission of discovery upon the newly-created earth. Belial and Beelzebub stand on the brink of heaven watching the upward flight of Apollion. Belial addresses his companion—

> "*Lord Beelzebub, Stadholder's counsellor!*
> *He riseth steep, with many a wheel, in view;*
> *Outstrips the wind, and leaves a track of light*
> *And splendour after him, where his quick wings*
> *Winnow* [2] *the clouds. And now our air he scents*
> *In brighter light and more resplendent sun,*
> *Whose sheen is mirrored in crystalline blue.*
> *The heavenly globes gaze on him from below,*
> *As he upsprings, the cynosure of each,*
> *Astonished at his speed and godlike shape,*
> *Which seems no angel, but a flying fire;*
> *No star so swiftly shoots.*"—Act i. 10–21.

---

[1] The translations have all been made with scrupulous and literal accuracy into English blank-verse. This metre has been chosen in preference to the rhymed Alexandrines of Vondel, because the latter are unfamiliar to the English ear and uncongenial to the English tongue, accustomed by the usage of Shakespeare and Milton to the cadence of (what Milton in his Preface to the Paradise Lost calls) " English heroic verse without rime." It is obvious, likewise, in this special case, that this course at once enables the renderings to be given with far greater verbal exactness, and makes the comparison with parallel passages from Milton's works clearer and more trustworthy. The original Dutch of all the quotations will be found in the Appendix.

[2] Lit. break.

On reading this finely-conceived passage, our thoughts at once turn to Milton's description of the descent of the Archangel Raphael into Paradise; and upon examination we shall find here some very remarkable coincidences between the two poets—

> " Down thither prone in flight
> He speeds, and through the vast ethereal sky
> Sails between worlds and worlds with steady wings ;
> Now in the polar winds ; then with quick fan
> Winnows the buxom air, till, within soar
> Of towering eagles, to all the fowls he seems
> A phœnix, gazed by all as that sole bird."
> —*P. L.*, v. 266-272.

In addition to the actual similarities of language, the ideas involved in these two passages are almost identical.   In the one case, as Raphael nears the earth, the fowls each and all gaze on him as a rare bird; in the other, as Apollion speeds upwards, the globes gaze after him as a strange and glorious star.

The whole of this passage of the descent of Raphael will again come under our notice in the chapter upon Vondel's " Johannes Boetgezant."

Turning to Milton's[1] account of the journey of Satan from hell, we find that after his interview with the Anarch Chaos the fiend—

> "Springs upward, like a pyramid of fire,
> Into the wild expanse."—*P. L.*, ii. 1012.

To the Anarch old peering into vast abyss he would appear precisely as did Apollion to the gazing spheres—

> " *A flying fire.*"

---

[1] All the Miltonic extracts are taken from the " The Poetical Works," edited by David Masson.   London : Macmillan & Co. 1874.

And when, at the close of his adventurous voyage, he descends from the sun to the earth, he

> "Throws his steep flight in many an aery wheel."
> —*P. L.*, iii. 741.

The comparison to a shooting-star, which occurs in the last line of our quotation, is somewhat amplified by Vondel in another passage. Michael is described as

> *" Warned from on high*
> *By Heaven's messenger, who downward flew*
> *Yet swifter than a star, which shoots through air."*
> —Act v. 1739-1740.

In the Paradise Lost Gabriel is warned by Uriel, who

> " Came, gliding through the even
> On a sunbeam, swift as a shooting star."
> —*P. L.*, iv. 556-557.

Again, just as Vondel makes Apollion, as he approaches heaven, to enter a region of purer air and brighter light, whose more resplendent sun is mirrored in the depths of the blue crystalline, so Milton when he describes the work of creation on the second day—

> "And God made
> The firmament, expanse of liquid, pure,
> Transparent, elemental air. . .
> . . . .
> . . For as Earth, so be the world
> Built on circumfluous waters calm, in wide
> Crystalline ocean."—*P. L.*, vii. 263-271.

Lucifer is represented in the play, as the Stadholder of Heaven, the deputy of the Almighty, in the same sense as William of Orange had been the deputy of

Philip of Spain in the government of the Netherlands. Beelzebub is addressed by his companion by the title of "the Counsellor of the Stadholder of Heaven," and throughout the drama he appears as Lucifer's chief adviser and abetter in his ambitious and rebellious projects.

Now it is interesting to note that this is the very position assigned by Milton to the Beelzebub of the Paradise Lost, who is "next" to his chief "in power and next in crime,"[1] and whose lineaments are thus portrayed—

> "Deep on his front engraven
> Deliberation sat and public care,
> And princely counsel in his face yet shone."
>
> —*P. L.*, ii. 303.

But we must pass on. Our next Vondelian citations are all taken from Apollion's narrative of his voyage of discovery and of the wonders that he saw upon the new-created world, except the first, wherein Beelzebub expresses his admiration of a golden bough which Apollion had brought with him from Paradise in these terms—

> "*I see the golden leaves
> Laden with silv'ry dew, ætherial pearls.*
>
> .   .   .   .
>
> *The sight allures the taste. Who would not long
> For earthly luxuries? He who can pluck
> The fruits of earth disdains our clime above,
> And heavenly manna.*"—i. 29, &c.

With these we take the following lines, which were spoken to Adam by the Archangel Raphael; they occur

[1] Paradise Lost, i. 79.

very shortly after the lines which we have already
quoted from the description of Raphael's descent to
Paradise—

> " Though in Heaven the trees
> Of life ambrosial fruitage bear and vines
> Yield nectar—though from off the boughs each morn
> We brush mellifluous dews and find the ground
> Covered with pearly grain—yet God hath here
> Varied His bounty so with new delights
> As may compare with Heaven ; and to taste
> Think not I shall be nice."—*P. L.*, v. 426, &c.

Next let us hear Apollion's narrative—

> *" My flight I pass in silence, not to tell*
> *How swift down-swooping through nine spheres I sank,*
> *Which round their centre whirl with arrowy speed.*
> *The wheel of thought cannot so quick revolve*
> *Within our mind, as I below the moon*
> *And clouds swept down, then stay'd on hovering wings*
> *The eastern tract and landscape to survey."*—i. 44, &c.

For a parallel passage we once more turn to Raphael's
conversation with Adam. Adam had been inquiring
about the celestial motions; the Archangel thus replies—

> " The swiftness of those circles attribute,
> Though numberless, to His omnipotence,
> That to corporeal substances could add
> Speed almost spiritual. Me thou think'st not slow,
> Who since the morning hour set out from Heaven,
> Where God resides, and ere mid-day arrived
> In Eden—distance inexpressible
> By numbers that have name."—*P. L.*, viii. 107, &c.

The sequence of ideas involved in these two passages is
identical. Curiously alike in their astronomical beliefs,
as in so many other points, the two poets here agree
in their adherence to the old Alphonsine or Ptolemaic
system with its nine consecutive revolving spheres.

But, as we shall see later, while using for poetical purposes the old conceptions, they were each of them
acquainted with, and had at least partially accepted, the
new Copernican theory.   Another passage, which tells
of the descent of the Son of God to Paradise after the
Fall, must likewise be quoted for its close analogy with
the above—

> " Him Thrones and Powers
> Accompanied to Heaven-gate, from whence
> Eden and all the coast in prospect lay.
> Down He descended straight ; the speed of gods
> Time counts not, though with swiftest minute winged."
>
> —*P. L.*, x. 85, &c.

We left Apollion "stayed on hovering wings to survey
the eastern tract and landscape " extending below his
ken. So likewise Satan, after emergence from Chaos—

> " Weighs his spread wings, at leisure to behold
> Far off the empyreal heaven, extended wide."
>
> —*P. L.*, ii. 104-105.

Apollion next tells what was the prospect which met
his eyes—

> " *From hence I saw a lofty hill emerge,*
> *Whereout a waterfall, source of four streams,*
> *Foams down a glade.   Precipitant I strike*
> *My oblique course headlong, and come to rest*
> *Upon the mountain's brow, from whence one gains*
> *A prospect clear far o'er the nether world,*
> *Her happy fields and rich luxuriance.*"—i. 52, &c.

In the third book of the Paradise Lost Milton describes the fiend as having attained to Heaven-gate,
and looking down with wonder and delight upon
the new-created universe, the object of his painful
search—

" At sight of all this world beheld so fair,
Round he surveys, ...
. . . and without longer pause
Down right into the world's first region throws
His flight precipitant, and winds with ease
Through the pure marble air his oblique way."
—*P. L.*, iii. 554, &c.

The coincidence of language here is so remarkable
that we almost seem to be reading an amplified translation of Vondel's graphic lines—

" Wij streken steil en schuin
Voorover met ons hooft."

The rest of the passage is likewise reproduced in the
two following Miltonic excerpts. All allowance should
be made for their common Biblical origin. The reader
will judge how far this accounts for the similarity—

" Southward through Eden went a river large,
Nor changed his course, but through the shaggy hill
Passed underneath ingulphed. . . .
. . . . Thence united fell
Down the steep glade, and met the nether flood,
Which from its darksome passage now appears,
And now, divided into four main streams,
Runs diverse."—*P. L.*, iv. 223, &c.

And again—

" Yet higher than their top
The verdurous wall of Paradise upsprung,
Which to our general sire gave prospect large
Into his nether empire neighbouring round."
—*P. L.*, iv. 142, &c.

Evidence, however, accumulates when we find that
not an isolated line here and there, but that the WHOLE

of Apollion's narrative appears to have been placed under contribution; for the messenger thus proceeds—

> " *The mountain rises in the midst, whereout*
> *The fountain gushes, which divides in four*
> *And waters all the land, refreshing trees*
> *And fields, whence many a brook wells forth, as clear*
> *As crystal, which reflects no mirror'd face.*
> *The streams are rich in ooze, which feeds the ground.*
>
> .   .   .   .
>
> *In these Dame Nature sowed a galaxy* [1]
> *In stones, which pales our stars.   Here glitter veins*
> *Of gold, as if she wished to gather up*
> *Her varied treasures in one single lap.*"—i. 60.

Compare with this [2] the following, taken from the very same descriptive passage in the fourth book of the Paradise Lost which we have just been quoting—

> " For God had thrown
> That mountain, as His garden mould, high raised
> Upon the rapid current, which through veins
> Of porous earth with kindly thirst up-drawn,
> Rose a fresh fountain, and with many a rill
> Watered the garden.   .   .   .   .
> .   .   From that sapphire fount the crispèd brooks,
> Rolling on orient pearls and sands of gold,
> With mazy error under pendent shades
> Ran nectar, visiting each plant, and fed
> Flowers worthy of Paradise, which not nice Art
> In beds and curious knots, but Nature boon
> Poured forth profuse.   .   .   .   .
>
> .   .   .   .   .   .
>
> .   .   Meanwhile murmuring waters fall
> Down the sloping hills dispersed, or in a lake,
> That to the fringed bank, with myrtle crowned,
> Her crystal mirror holds, unite their streams."
> —*P. L.*, iv. 225, &c.

---

[1] Lit. constellation.

[2] Compare also Paradise Lost, v. 294–297.

Milton is here, as would be expected, fuller and more diffuse; and too great stress should not be laid upon the many points, in which the fancy of the two poets shows such close agreement, for they both fill in the same Biblical outline. Nevertheless it is singular, if accidental.

The unusual imagery of Vondel's lines (68, 69) seems to find an echo in

> "A broad and ample road, whose dust is gold
> And pavement stars, as stars to thee appear
> Seen in the galaxy."—*P. L.,* vii. 577, &c.

Apollion tells of the luxuriant produce of the earth—

> "*Then swells the bosom of the field with herb*
> *And colour, shoot and blossom, flowers and scent*
> *Of every kind, by dew each night refreshed.*"—i. 75, &c.

When "the bare earth is with verdure clad" in the Paradise Lost—

> "Then herbs of every leaf, that sudden flowered,
> Opening their various colours, and made gay
> Her bosom smelling sweet."—*P. L.,* vii. 317, &c.

While Milton, like Vondel, follows the account of the Book of Genesis, when he concludes—

> "From the earth a dewy mist
> Went up and watered all the ground and each
> Plant of the field."—*P. L.,* vii. 333, &c.

Apollion, after telling of the natural beauties of Eden, speaks next of the animals he saw there, and of their submission to man—

> "*The lion gazed upon his lord and wagged*
> *His tail. The tiger laid his savageness*
> *Aside before his master's feet. The ox*
> *Bowed low his horns, the elephant his trunk,*
> *The bear forgot his fierceness.*"—i. 91, &c.

These details seem a little grotesque and undignified, but almost unaltered they make their appearance clothed in Miltonic apparel—

> "About them frisking played
> All beasts of the earth, since wild, and of all chase
> In wood or wilderness, forest or den.
> Sporting the lion ramped, and in his paw
> Dandled the kid ; bears, tigers, ounces, pards,
> Gambled before them ; the unwieldy elephant,
> To make them mirth, used all his might and wreathed
> His lithe proboscis."—*P. L.,* iv. 340, &c.

We now come to Vondel's portraiture of our first parents. Apollion still speaks—

> "*No creature hath on high mine eyes so pleased,*
> *As these below. Who can so deftly soul*
> *With body knit, and twofold angels mould*
> *From clay and bone ? Their body's shapely frame*
> *Proclaims the Maker's art, which in the face,*
> *The mirror of the mind, is chiefly shown.*
> *Each limb with wonder strikes, but in the glance*
> *I saw the image of the soul revealed.*
> *Their form displays each loveliness that here*
> *One singly finds. From human eyes a gleam*
> *Divine darts forth. The face's lineaments*
> *Express the reasoning soul. While the dumb beasts,*
> *Of reason void, look downward to their feet,*
> *Man proudly lifts alone his head to Heaven*
> *In lofty praise towards God, who made him thus.*"
>
> —i. 104–117.

These ornate and finished lines (even under the disguise of a somewhat bald translation) offer to us a fair specimen of Vondel's poetical skill and imaginative power. The rhythm and the diction alike would impress the most careless reader as not unworthy of comparison with, and as showing a more than passing resemblance to, the mingled dignity and luxuriance of the Miltonic style. We shall prove further that the resemblance is more than superficial, and extends to actual coincidence of thought and phrase. With this object we would willingly give the whole of Apollion's glowing delineation; but in order to avoid unnecessary diffuseness we shall content ourselves with two more brief extracts to complete the picture.

> " *Both man and wife are shaped with equal grace,*
> *Perfect from head to foot. Adam of right*
> *In valour's traits and dignity of form*
> *Excels, as ruler of the earth elect.*
> *But all a bridegroom lists in Eve is found—*
> *Fineness of limb, a softer flesh and skin,*
> *A kindlier tint, and eyes of ravishment.*"—i. 151-157.

> . . . .

> " *There shines no seraph bright in heavenly courts*
> *Like Eve amidst her hanging hair, a screen*
> *Of golden beams, which from the head streams down*
> *In waves of light, and falls upon her back.*'
> —i. 168-171.

At this point we hold our hand, and, amidst a wide field of choice, we once more exercise a needful discretion, and bring forward only those passages of Milton which are the most important for exhibiting the analogy we seek to establish. We cite first the well-known description in the fourth book of the Paradise Lost—

> " Two of far nobler shape, erect and tall,
> Godlike erect, with native honour clad
> In naked majesty, seemed lords of all,
> And worthy seemed ; for in their looks divine
> The image of their glorious Maker shone.

> . . . .

> Not equal, as their sex not equal seemed ;

For contemplation he and valour formed,
For softness she and sweet attractive grace.

.   .   .   .

His fair large front and eye sublime declared
Absolute rule.

.   .   .   .

She as a veil down to the slender waist
Her unadorned golden tresses wore
Dishevelled, but in wanton ringlets waved."[1]
        —*P. L.*, iv. 288–292, 296–298, 300–301, 304–306.

We find in the same book the following lines in
Satan's soliloquy upon first beholding Adam and
Eve—

"Creatures of other mould, earth-born perhaps,
Not spirits, yet to heavenly spirits bright
Little inferior,[2] whom my thoughts pursue
With wonder and could love ; so lively shines
In them Divine resemblance, and such grace
The hand that formed them on their shape hath poured."
            P. L., iv. 360–365.

Our next and last citation comes from the account of
the work of the sixth day of creation—

"There wanted yet the master-work, the end
Of all yet done—a creature who, not prone
And brute as other creatures, but endued
With sanctity of reason, might erect
His stature, and, upright, with front serene,
Govern the rest, self-knowing, and from thence
Magnanimous to correspond with Heaven,

.   .   .   .

And worship God supreme, who made him chief
Of all His works."—*P. L.*, vii. 505–511, 515–516.

If any one will but take the trouble to examine

[1] See also Paradise Lost, iv. 496.
[2] Compare Paradise Lost, ix. 457.

carefully these two sets of passages, he can scarcely come to the conclusion that they have been written independently.

We must, at this point, draw attention to the criticism which we passed upon the statement that "the Dutch drama turns entirely upon the revolt of the angels and their expulsion from heaven. . . . It is, therefore, only in one book of Paradise Lost, the sixth, that the influence of Vondel can be looked for."[1] We said that we were prepared to prove that such a conclusion was entirely erroneous. We think that the fact, that at present very marked traces of Vondel's influence have been found in different parts of Paradise Lost, and particularly in the fourth book, while as yet not a single allusion has been made to the revolt of the angels, nor a single line quoted from the sixth book, offers ample and sufficient testimony in favour of our assertion.

We have yet one more sample to produce of Vondel's poetry from this first act of the Lucifer, and it is one important to our purpose. It is taken from the proclamation of God's herald, Gabriel. The Archangel announces the divine decree conferring supremacy on the human race. On this decree turns the whole future action of the play. Part of the angelic host resent the position of inferiority assigned to them. The seeds of dissatisfaction are sown, which ere long ripen into open revolt. Now, it will be remembered that Raphael assigns, in his discourse with Adam (in the fifth book of Paradise Lost), a similar origin to the rebellion of Satan—similar, but with an apparent difference. In the Lucifer, the jealousy is caused by the privileges promised to the newly-created human race; in the

[1] Pattison's "Milton," p. 201.

D

Paradise Lost, to the position of pre-eminence assigned to the Son of God. The two passages which
follow are therefore specially interesting, not only for
their parallelism, but because they enable us to bridge
over what seemed to be a discrepancy between the
plots of the two poems, and show us that in either case
it is the same supreme event, the future Incarnation
of the Son of God, on which the thoughts are fixed.
Gabriel speaks—

> *" Though spiritual Beings seem pre-eminent* [1]
> *Above all other, God decreed of old*
> *His purpose to exalt the human race*
> *Above th' angelic, and lead man up*
> *To light and splendour, differing not from God.*
> *Ye shall behold th' Eternal Word, when clad*
> *In flesh and bones, anointed King and Lord*
> *And Judge, pass sentence on the countless host*
> *Of spirits, all, angels and men alike,*
> *High seated on the throne of His bright realm."*
>
> —i. 217–224.

The passage is somewhat stiff and tedious, and in
this it resembles that portion of the Paradise Lost with
which it should be compared, the colloquy between the
Eternal Father and the Divine Son (in the third book
of Paradise Lost) concerning the Fall and Redemption
of man. Our extract from Vondel has been made as
short as possible; we take from Milton those portions
only which essentially concern the argument. The
Almighty speaks—

> "Well Thou knowest how dear
> To me are all my works ; nor man the least,
> Though last created, ...
>   .   .   .   whom Thou only canst redeem ;

---

[1] The scanning of this line follows that of Milton's Paradise Lost,
v. 402.

Their nature also to Thy nature join,
And be Thyself man among men on earth
Made flesh.   .   .   .   .

.   .   .   .
.   .   .   . Thy humiliation shall exalt
With Thee Thy manhood also to this throne ;
Here shalt Thou sit incarnate, here shalt reign
Both God and Man, Son both of God and Man,
Anointed Universal King.   .   .   .   .

.   .   .   .
When Thou, attended gloriously from heaven,
Shalt in the sky appear, and from Thee send
The summoning archangels to proclaim
Thy dread tribunal, ...
.   .   .   .   . Thou shalt judge
Bad men and angels ; they arraigned shall sink
Beneath Thy sentence."

—*P. L.*, iii. 276-278, 281-283, 313-317, 323-326, 331-333.

As the second act opens, the effect of the decree
upon the angels is quickly seen. We find Lucifer
indignant, Beelzebub inciting him to uphold the rights
of the Celestial Spirits against this new favourite of
Heaven, the upstart Man. He complains—

" *Should God a younger son, from Adam's loins
Begotten, raise above (great Lucifer)* I "—ii. 498.

We find in the same colloquy of the third book of
Paradise Lost, from which we have just been quoting, an
exactly similar definition of the relationship between angelic and human beings. Fallen man is described as—

" Thy creature late so loved, Thy youngest son."—iii. 150.

We have now reached a crucial point in our inquiry.
Apollion's narrative is only episodical; the second act
brings us face to face with the chief Personage of the
drama, and we scan with eager curiosity the lineaments

of Vondel's Lucifer, to see if we can trace therein any family likeness to the Satan of the English poet.

To assert that Milton's portraiture of the fallen Archangel stands by itself for grandeur and impressiveness amidst all the creations of the human imagination, is scarcely an exaggeration. The mind fails to grasp the Titanic proportions of the figure, and remains dazzled and overpowered by a vague sensation of colossal dignity and transcendent force. He, who should venture to say that such a conception was not *original*, would stand self-condemned by his own awestruck feelings in the presence of this dread Being, of immeasurable form and nameless attributes.

But, to take a parallel case, no one has ever challenged or impugned the *originality* of Raphael's great picture, the Sposalizio, which deservedly ranks as one of the master's best productions; yet a genuine work by Raphael's predecessor and instructor, Perugino, may be seen at Caen,[1] which treats the subject of the Betrothal of the Virgin in a manner so similar, that it does not require artistic training to recognise here the source from which was derived the primary conception of the pupil's more finished and perfect composition. Such an admission is in no way derogatory to the genius of Raphael; and similarly it need not be considered an aspersion upon Milton's fame, when we assert, that he was not the first to portray in heroic outlines the Leader of the Rebel Angels. The character of Vondel's Lucifer, though cast in a less stupendous mould than that of the Miltonic Satan, displays the same traits. Haughtiness, pride, ambition, inflexible will, implacable resentment, unyielding resolve are the

---

[1] Taken by the French from the cathedral of Perugia.

marked qualities which distinguish alike either imper-
sonation.

It has already been said that the second act of the
drama commences with a dialogue between Lucifer
and Beelzebub, in which the latter strives to rouse the
Stadholder's indignation against the proclamation of
Gabriel, and to incite him to active resistance. His
skilful arguments at length take effect, and Lucifer
announces his intention not to submit to any invasion
of his rights. We quote his words—

> " *Thou reas'nest well. Essential powers care not*
> *So easy to let slip their lawful right.*
> *Th' Almighty, first of all, by His own law*
> *Is bound. To change becomes Him least. Am I*
> *A Son of Light, a Ruler over Light ?*
> *My rightful claims I shall assert. To force*
> *I yield not, nor arch-tyrant's violence.*
> *Let yield, who will, I move not one foot back.*
> *My fatherland is here. Nor misery,*
> *Nor overthrow, nor curse shall frighten me,*
> *Nor tame. To perish or to reach this port* [1]
> *Is my resolve. Is't fated that I fall,*
> *Of rank and lustre reft, then let me fall,*
> *So that I fall this crown upon my head,*
> *This sceptre in my grasp, esteem'd by friends*
> *And all the thousands, who embrace my cause.*
> *A fall like that to honour tends and praise*
> *Imperishable. Rather would I be*
> *The first prince in some lower court than in*
> *The Blessed Light the second, or e'en less.*
> *My hap I comfort thus, and henceforth fear*
> *Nor hurt nor hindrance.*"—ii. 427-445.

It is scarcely possible to conceive language more

---

[1] "Dien hoek te boven komen." A nautical term. Lit. to weather
this cape.

expressive of concentrated pride and reckless determination. Every line breathes out scorn and defiance, and tells us of a fierce courage which is careless of consequences, and which gains fresh strength from despair. To bring forward parallel passages from Milton's poems is at once an easy and a difficult task; for it is the very spirit and tone of the Satan of the Paradise Lost, which speaks to us here through the mouth of Vondel's Lucifer, and the production of a few verbal coincidences can only inadequately represent how strong is the affinity which exists between the two personations. Our selection is rather varied than complete. It includes passages from the Paradise Regained and the Samson Agonistes, as well as from the Paradise Lost.

We take first a part of the speech in which Satan strives to stir up his followers to rebellion. It is an expansion of Vondel's lines (427–432)—

> "Will ye submit your necks and choose to bend
> The supple knee? Ye will not, if I trust
> To know ye right, or if ye know yourselves,
> Natives and sons of Heaven, possessed before
> By none, and, if not equal all, yet free.
>
> .   .   .   .
>
> Who can in reason, then, or right assume
> Monarchy over such as live by right
> His equal, .   .   . or can introduce
> Law and edict on us?"—*P. L.*, v. 787–792.

And as a further parallel to the same lines—

> "Yet more there be, who doubt His way not just,
> As to His own edicts found contradictory,
>
> .   .   .   .
>
> As if they would confine the Interminable,

And tie Him to His own prescript,
Who made our laws to bind us, not Himself."
—S. A., 300-301, 307-310.

Turning to the first book of Paradise Lost, we meet
with Satan in his most defiant mood—

"Yet not for those (arms),
Nor what the potent Victor in His rage
Can else inflict, do I repent or change,
Though changed in outward lustre, that fixed mind
And high disdain from sense of injured merit.

.   .   .   .

All is not lost—the unconquerable will
And courage never to submit or yield,
And what is else not to be overcome ?
That glory never shall His wrath or might
Extort from me."[1]—P. L., i. 94-98, 106-111.

And once more—

"Thou profoundest hell,
Receive thy new possessor, one who brings
A mind not to be changed by place or time.

.   .   .   .

Here we may reign secure ; and, in my choice,
To reign is worth ambition, though in Hell :
Better to reign in Hell than serve in Heaven."
—P. L., i. 250-252, 261-263.

The resemblance between this last line and Vondel's

" *Rather would I be*
The first prince in some lower court than in
The Blessed Light the second, or e'en less,"

is, despite the prominence given to it by writers upon
the subject, in our opinion no more, but less striking
than the resemblance between many other passages to
which we draw attention.

[1] Comp. Paradise Lost, vi. 293.

In Satan's closing speech to the hellish conclave we find—

> "I should ill become this throne, O peers,
> . . . . . if aught proposed,
> And judged of public moment, in the shape
> Of difficulty or danger could deter
> Me from attempting."—*P. L.*, ii. 445, 448-451.

The sentiment expressed in which has an unmistakably Luciferian ring.[1]

Here we leave the Paradise Lost, and two excerpts from the Paradise Regained will demonstrate that it was not only in Milton's greater Epic poem that the language of the Vondelian Archangel found an echo. The Saviour has announced to Satan—

> "My promotion will be thy destruction.
> To whom the Tempter, inly racked, replied :—
> Let that come when it comes. All hope is lost
> Of my reception into grace ; what worse ?
> For where no hope is left, is left no fear.
>
> . . . .
>
> I would be at the worst ; worst is my port,
> My harbour, and my ultimate repose ;
> The end I would attain, my final good."
> —*P. R.*, iii. 201-206, 209-211.

In diction and in subject-matter the two passages are closely akin ; but one fact alone is sufficient to establish their relationship. The peculiar nautical metaphor, which seems a little out of place and strained in Vondel's lines, has here an almost exact counterpart.

In the next book of Paradise Regained we come

[1] *Lucifer*, ii. 444-445, 450-451.

across two lines which recall Lucifer's assertion of his position, " Son of Light "—

> " The son of God I also am, or was ;
>   And if I was, I am ; relation stands."
> —*P. R.,* iv. 518-519.

The place of Beelzebub is now taken on the stage by Gabriel, who tries to dissuade Lucifer from his purpose by representing to him the inscrutable nature of the Divine Wisdom and the necessity of obedience to the decrees of the Almighty. The next extract forms part of his argument—

> *" Thus far it is permitted us to tell*
>   *The secrets of God's book. Much knowledge may*
>   *Not always profit bring, but sometimes harm.*
>   *The Highest but reveals what He thinks fit.*
>   *Th' excessive glare of light would Seraphim*
>   *With blindness strike. In part pure Wisdom would*
>   *Her plans keep under seal, in part disclose.*
>   *Submission and conformity to law,*
>   *This best becomes the subject, who stands bound*
>   *To serve his Master's will."*—ii. 483-491.

In the eighth book of Paradise Lost Raphael replies to Adam's questions as to the celestial movements—

> " To ask or search I blame thee not ; for Heaven
>   Is as the Book of God before thee set,
>   Wherein to read His wondrous works. . . . .
>   .   .   .   . The rest
>   From man or angel the Great Architect
>   Did wisely to conceal, and not divulge
>   His secrets, to be scanned by them who ought
>   Rather admire.   .   .   .   .
>
> .   .   .   .
>   Solicit not thy thoughts with matters hid :
>   Leave them to God alone : Him serve and fear."
> —*P. L.,* viii. 65-67, 71-75, 168-170.

When we add—

> " Dark with excessive bright Thy skirts appear,
>   Yet dazzle Heaven, that brightest Seraphim
>   Approach not, but with both wings veil their eyes,"
>   —*P. L.,* iii. 380–382,

the reproduction of Gabriel's words is almost complete.
So likewise with his rebuke of Lucifer which immediately follows—

> " *Content you with your lot*
> *And state and dignity derived from God.*
> *He raised you to the highest place of all*
> *Among Hierarchal Powers.   Yet not that you*
> *Should envious be of others' rising light.*
>
> .   .   .   .   .
>
> *Then bow before the high decree of God,*
> *Who all, that being hath, or e'er shall have,*
> *From nothing called and guides to certain ends.*"
>   —ii. 501–504, 509–511.

Contrast this with Abdiel's rebuke of Satan—

> " Words which no ear ever to hear in Heaven
>   Expected, least of all from thee, ingrate.
>   In place thyself so high above thy peers,
>   Canst thou with impious obloquy condemn
>   The just decree of God pronounced and sworn,
>   That to his only Son, by right endued
>   With regal sceptre, every soul in Heaven
>   Should bend the knee?   .   .   .
>
> .   .   .   .   .   .
>
>   Shalt thou give law to God?   Shalt thou dispute
>   With Him the points of liberty, who made
>   Thee what thou art, and formed the powers of Heaven
>   Such as He pleased, and circumscribed their being?"
>   *P. L.,* v. 810–817, 822–825.

We next take the last words of Gabriel and place

them side by side with the last lines of Raphael's answer
to Adam—

> " *Thus learn we by degrees God's wise designs*
> *To question with respect and lowliness.*
> *He step by step lays bare the growing light*
> *Of Knowledge and of Science, and desires,*
> *That at his station each before Him bow.*"—ii. 555-558.

> " Heaven is for thee too high
> To know what passes there. Be lowly wise ;
> Think only what concerns thee and thy being :
> Dream not of other worlds, what creatures there
> Live, in what state, condition, or degree,
> Contented that thus far hath been revealed
> Not of earth only, but of highest Heaven."
> > *P. L.*, viii. 172-178.

Still from the second act of the drama we select a portion of an argument between Beelzebub and Apollion—

> " *Apol. Derived Might to weigh in the same scale*
> *With Might Divine, the weight o'erbalances.*
> *Take heed betimes.   We poise too lightly far ;*
> *Beelz. So lightly not, should the issue hang in doubt*
> *At first.*"—ii. 612-615.

The same simile appears at length in the fourth
book of Milton's poem.   Possibly a well-known passage of Homer *may* have suggested it to both poets ;
but we must take this, not in isolation, but as one out of
a multitude of other places in which such coincidences
have been shown to occur.

The Almighty is represented as hanging forth in
heaven His golden scales—

> " Which Gabriel espying, thus bespake the Fiend :
> Satan, I know thy strength, and thou knowest mine ;

Neither our own, but given.   .   .   .
    .   .   .   For proof look up,
And read thy lot in yon celestial sign,
Where thou art weighed, and shown how light, how weak,
If thou resist."—*P. L.,* iv. 1005-1006, 1010-1012.

This corresponds closely with Apollion's words.
Beelzebub's reply has likewise its analogue—

"Who have sustained one day in doubtful fight;
    And if one day, why not eternal days?"
                                        —*P. L.,* ix. 423-424.

Apollion in this conference takes much the same line
of argument as the Miltonic Belial in the hellish conclave.   He does not believe success to be possible—

" *His (Michael's) duty is to watch.   On every place*
    He, trusty, keeps his watchful eye.   .   .
    .   .   .   .   *What arms,*
What engines of assault can venture make
'Gainst him, or o'erthrow the Heavenly bands?
E'en were Heaven's citadel to open wide
Its gates of adamant, it need not fear
Or guile, or ambush, or surprise."

The words of Belial are—

            " The towers of Heaven are filled
With armed watch, that render all access
Impregnable."—*P. L.,* ii. 130-132.

And again—

            " What can force or guile
With Him, or who deceive His mind whose eye
Views all things at one view?"—*P. L.,* ii. 188-191.

And Beelzebub continues shortly afterwards in the
same strain—

            " Nor shall we need
With dangerous expedition to invade

Heaven, whose high walls fear no assault or siege
Or ambush from the deep."—*P. L.*, ii. 343-346.[1]

It is instructive to compare the two descriptions of the evil spirit who in either poem bears the name of Belial. Vondel thus—

> " *His face, smooth varnish of deceit and craft,*
> *In its disguise misleads each passer-by."*

Thus Milton—

> " A fairer person lost not Heaven ; he seemed
> For dignity composed and high exploit,
> But all was false and hollow."—*P. L.*, ii. 110-112.

Our poets at times agree in conceptions and fancies, which are in themselves out of the way and extravagant. Thus Lucifer declares—

> " *My mind is bent .   .   .   .   .*
> *Upon a weighty stroke, that shall not miss.*
> *Its certain aim, to pluck the battle-plumes*
> *From Michael's wings."*—ii. 590-592.

Satan taunts Abdiel—

> " But well thou com'st
> Before thy fellows, ambitious to win
> From me some plume."—*P. L.*, vi. 159-161.

We now pass on to the third act of the Lucifer, which mainly consists of a controversial dialogue between the loyal angels and the Luciferists; Michael, Lucifer, Beelzebub, and others joining in it from time to time.

We make one quotation, which corresponds in a very remarkable way to a Miltonic passage, which contains the Vondelian imagery in all its quaint details—

---

[1] Compare also Lucifer, ii. 640 ; and Paradise Lost, v 254.

> " *You see the host of heaven in gold arrayed*
> *And set in files, alternate keep their watch,*
> *How this star sets and that ascends on high;*
>
> .   .   .   .   .   .
>
> *How this a smaller round, a larger that describes.*
> *Yet know in all these inequalities*
> *No discord, envy, strife.   The Voice Supreme*
> *Of their Conductor leads their measured song:*
> *To Him they listen, eagerly attent.*"—iii. 971–980.

Milton thus describes the occupations of the heavenly host—

> " That day, as other solemn days, they spent
> In song and dance about the sacred hill—
> Mystical dance which yonder starry sphere
> Of planets and of fixed in all her wheels
> Resembles nearest ; mazes intricate,
> Eccentric, intervolved, yet regular
> The most when most irregular they seem ;
> And in their motions Harmony divine
> So smoothes her charming tones that God's own ear
> Listens delighted."—*P. L.*, v. 617–627.

Two passages of identical import now claim our attention, for Milton has also two wherewith to compare them. Towards the close of the third act the Luciferist Chorus thus encourages its chief—

> " *Is it no help, that in your train you draw*
> *A third part of the spirits ?* "—iii. 1244–1245.

The spectre Death addresses Satan—

> " Art thou that traitor-angel, art thou he
> Who   .   .   .   .   .   .
> Drew after him the third part of Heaven's sons ?"
> —*P. L.*, ii. 692.

At the opening of the fourth act of the drama,

Gabriel announces to Michael the outburst of the revolt—

> " *The Heavens' third part e'en now hath fealty sworn*
> *Unto his standard, the false Morning Star.*"
> —iv. 1336–1338.

Milton thus describes the same event—

> "His countenance, as the morning star that guides
> The starry flock, allured them, and with lies
> Drew after him the third part of Heaven's host."
> —*P. L.*, v. 708–710.

In this same narrative of Gabriel's we find the description of the Divine reception of the news of the revolt—

> " *I saw the bliss of God by a dark cloud*
> *Of sadness overcast; then at the last*
> *Wrath, kindled, flame from eyes of Light.*"
> —iv. 1462–1464.

In the corresponding lines of Paradise Lost—

> "So spake the Sov'ran Voice ; and clouds began
> To darken all the hill, and smoke to roll
> In dusky wreaths, reluctant flames the sign
> Of wrath awaked."—*P. L.*, vi. 56–59.

Raphael in the play now endeavours to dissuade Lucifer from his attempt, his action and his language corresponding in the main to that assigned to Abdiel in the Epic, but drawn out to greater length. He depicts in vivid and glowing terms the splendour and privileges of that position which the "Stadholder of Heaven" was on the point of scornfully rejecting—

> " *Yea ! God His own similitude and seal*
> *Had on your hallowed head and brow impressed,*
> *Transfused with beauty, wisdom, grace, whate'er*

Flows forth in streams unmeasured from the source
From whence all treasures spring.   In Paradise
You shone before the beaming countenance
Of God, beclouded by fresh roseate dews;
Your festal robes stood stiff with pearl, turquoise,
And diamond, with ruby and fine gold."—iv. 1470-1478.

The description in Paradise Lost of the derived glory of the Divine Son has many points of connection with the above—

> "Thee next they sang, of all creation first
> Begotten Son, Divine Similitude,
> In whose conspicuous countenance, without cloud
> Made visible, the Almighty Father shines,
> Whom else no creature can behold ; on thee
> Impressed, the effulgence of His glory abides ;
> Transfused on thee His ample spirit rests."
>
> —*P. L.*, iii. 382-389.

And that also of the Son of God going forth to war. The Father declares—

> "Into Thee such virtue and grace
> Immense I have transfused, that all may know
> In Heaven and Hell Thy power above compare."
>
> —*P. L.*, vi. 703-706.

There is also a passage which deals with a different subject (the angelic recreations in heaven), and yet is strangely full of verbal reminiscences with the latter portion of our quotation.   Raphael is the speaker in either case—

> "Rubied nectar flows
> In pearl, in diamond, and massy gold ;
> .   .   .   .
> .   .   Where full measure only bounds
> Excess, before the all-bounteous King, who showered
> With copious hand, rejoicing in their joy.   .
> Now when ambrosial night with clouds exhaled

From the high mount of God,   .   .
.   .   .   And roseate dews disposed
All but the unsleeping eyes of God to rest."
           —*P. L.*, v. 633–634, 639–643, 646–647.

One more short extract from Raphael's dissuasive pleadings—

> *" Stadholder ! why dissimulate your thoughts*
> *Before the All-Seeing Eye ? You cannot mask*
> *Your plans or soothe the All- Wise One with wiles."*
>   —iv. 1541–1543.

We place by its side the lines which follow—

> " What can force or guile
> With Him, or who deceive His mind whose eye
> Views all things at one view ? He from Heaven's height
> All these our motions vain sees and derides,
> Not more almighty to resist our might
> Than wise to frustrate all our plots and wiles."
>   —*P. L.*, ii. 188–194.

Immediately before Lucifer had proffered the excuse of necessity—

> *" By high necessity compelled, I guard*
> *The holy right."*—iv. 1536.

Similarly Satan—

> " Public reason just
> .   .   .   .
> .   .   .   .   Compels me now
> To do what else I should abhor.
> So spake the fiend, and with necessity,
> The tyrant's plea, excused his devilish deed."
>   —*P. L.*, iv. 391–394.

The pleadings of Raphael are of no avail, though he offers pardon—

E

> " *Luc.   What boots it though one be forearmed betimes*
>   *To face the worst ?   There is no hope of terms.*
> *Raph.   I promise certain grace.*"—iv. 1631–1632.

Satan, in Paradise Regained, thus answers the Saviour—

> "Let that come, when it comes, all hope is lost
> Of my reception into grace !   What worse ?"
> —*P. R.*, iv. 518–520.

With the fifth act of the drama we come at last upon that narrative of the War in Heaven, on which Milton has based his sixth book of Paradise Lost. It will be remarked that this book has hitherto scarcely contributed to our list of parallel passages. It will now make amends for previous deficiencies.

Raphael, in what may be called the first scene, hears the loud shouts which greet the triumph of Heaven, and meeting Uriel, the shield-bearer of Michael, returning from the fight, obtains from him a narrative of what has passed. Thus, in each poem, it is an angel who tells the story of the battle.

We commence with the opening soliloquy of Raphael—

> " *The whole of Heaven, from base to topmost crown*
> *Of her chief palaces, rejoicing shouts*
> *At Michael's victorious trumpet's sound*
> *And waving banners.   The foughten field is won.*
> *Our shields shine splendid with the sheen of suns.*
> *From ev'ry sun-bright shield streams triumph forth.*
> *There Uriel, the shield-bearer, himself*
> *Comes from the fight, and sways the flaming sword*
> *That, sharp on both sides, whet with heavenly wrath*
> *And vengeance fierce, amidst the raging strife*
> *Through armour, shield, and helm of adamant*
> *Hath swept to right and left.*"—v. 1717–1726.

Milton thus describes the joy of the angels over Satan's first overthrow—

> "Amazement seized
> The rebel thrones. . . . . .
> . . . . Our joy filled and shout,
> Presage of victory and fierce desire
> Of battle ; whereat Michael bid sound
> The Archangel trumpet. Through the vast of Heaven
> It sounded, and the faithful armies sung
> Hosannah to the Highest."—*P. L.,* vi. 200–2c6.

The sword of Michael, according to Milton—

> "Smote and felled
> Squadrons at once ; with huge two-handed sway
> Brandished aloft, the horrid edge came down,
> Wide-wasting."—*P. L.,* vi. 250–253.

Again—

> "The sword
> Of Michael from the armoury of God
> Was given him tempered so that neither keen
> Nor solid might resist that edge."—*P. L.,* vi. 320–323.

The two extremely picturesque Vondelian lines, whose alliteration we have endeavoured to reproduce in translation—

> "On schilden schitteren, en scheppen nieuwe zonnen
> Uit elcke schilt-zon straelt een triumphanten dag,"

have, as might be expected, not failed to leave their impress on Milton's mind. Their counterpart appears in—

> "Two broad suns their shields
> Blazed opposite."—*P. L.,* vi. 305.

The following is taken from Uriel's narrative—

> "*Michael, the chief commander, from on high
> By the heavenly envoy warned, who downward flew*

More swift than star, which shoots athwart the night,
How Lucifer, the Proud, had openly
Rebelled against the high behest of God,

.　　.　　.　　.　　.　　.　　.

With help of trusty Gabriel quick donned
His coat of mail, and forthwith gave command
To all his leaders, heads, and officers,
In God's high name, to summon all their troops
In ordered ranks, that with united force
They may sweep clean away this perjured scum
From off the broad expanse of Heaven's pure sky,
And plunge in darkness all this demon host,
Ere unawares they take us by surprise."—v. 1739–1752.

He who wishes to see the full connection of this
whole passage with the Miltonic account must study
the two, side by side, for himself. It would be weari-
some to indulge in too lengthy comment. The descent
of the heavenly envoy in the opening lines has already
been compared with that of Uriel in the fourth book of
Paradise Lost.[1]

The passage of the sixth book in which God sends
out Michael and Gabriel to battle first claims our attention—

"Go, Michael, of celestial armies prince,
　And thou, in military prowess next,
　Gabriel; lead forth to battle these my sons
　Invincible; lead forth my armèd saints,
　By thousands and by millions ranged for fight,
　Equal in number to that godless crew,
　Rebellious. Them with fire and hostile arms
　Fearless assault; and to the brow of Heaven
　Pursuing, drive them out from God and bliss
　Into their place of punishment."—*P. L.,* vi. 44–53.

---

[1] *Supra,* p. 39. Care must be taken not to confuse the spirits who
bear the same names in the two poems.

A few lines farther on we find—

> "At which command the powers militant
> That stood for Heaven, in mighty quadrate joined
> Of union irresistible, moved on."—*P. L.*, vi. 61–63.

And the reason appears later—

> "The banded powers of Satan   .   .
> .   .   .   .   .   weened
> That self-same day, by fight or by surprise,
> To win the Mount of God."—*P. L.*, vi. 85–87.

Each incident and point of the Vondelian description has its place in Milton's more elaborated narrative.

The one metaphor that does not appear in the sixth book fully worked out has its place in Belial's speech at the hellish conclave [1]—

> "Could we break our way
> By force, and at our heels all Hell should rise
> With blackest insurrection to confound
> Heaven's purest light, yet our great Enemy,
> All incorruptible, would on His throne
> Sit unpolluted, and the ethereal mould,
> Incapable of stain, would soon expel
> Her mischief, and purge off the baser fire."
>   —*P. L.*, ii. 134–141.

Under a most striking and peculiar simile Vondel thus depicts the appearance of the advancing rebel army—

> "*It quickly grew, and, like a half moon waxed,*
> *Sharpened its points, and closed on us two horns.*"[2]

Nearly identical with this is a simile which Milton uses at the close of the fourth book of Paradise Lost.

---

[1] Compare Paradise Lost, vi. 271–275.
[2] Compare also Paradise Lost, i. 616.

Satan, discovered in Paradise, had just been led before
Gabriel. The Archangelic Guard rebukes and threatens
him, but his words only provoke a fierce rejoinder.
Satan in turn threatens, but—

> " While he thus spake, the angelic squadron bright
> Turned fiery red, sharpening in mooned horns
> Their phalanx, and began to hem him round."
>
> —*P. L.*, iv. 977–980.

Vondel next describes the uprearing of the Archfiend's
standard—

> " *The lofty standard, where his morning star*
> *Shone brighter than the day, Apollion*
> *Upheld behind him (Lucifer), bravely as he could,*
> *In its full lustre, set on high to view.*"—v. 1780–1784.

The English poet tells in fuller detail how Satan,
having summoned together his scattered host after
their fall—

> "Straight commands that, at the warlike sound
> Of trumpets loud and clarions, be upreared
> His mighty standard. That proud honour claimed
> Azazel at his right, a cherub tall,
> Who forthwith from the glittering staff unfurled
> The imperial ensign, which, full high advanced,
> Shone like a meteor streaming to the wind,
> With gems and golden lustre rich emblazed."
>
> —*P. L.*, i. 533–540.

We now compare the respective portraitures of the
adversary of God as he appears in pristine splendour at
the head of his army. From " Lucifer "—

> " *Surrounded by his green-clad staff-bearers,*
> *He, furiously impelled by his deep grudge*
> *Irreconcileable, in golden mail*
> *That gleamed upon the military vest*
> *Of glowing purple with a lustrous sheen,*

Mounted his chariot with its golden wheels
With rubies thick beset. The Dragon fell,
And Lion, harnessed and alert for flight,
With stars bespangled over all their backs,
By pearly traces yoked before the wheels,
Long'd for the fight and for destruction flam'd;
War-axe in hand, his glimmering orbèd shield,
Whereon with art his morning star was chased,
Confronting fate, upon his left arm hung."
—v. 1780–1788.

From Paradise Lost—

" High in the midst, exalted as a god,
    The apostate in his sun-bright chariot sat,
    Idol of majesty divine, enclosed
    With flaming cherubim and golden shields.

    .   .   .   .

    Satan, with vast and haughty strides advanced,
    Came towering, armed in adamant and gold."
        —*P. L.*, vi. 99-102, 109-110.

The description of Lucifer's arms is likewise transferred
to those of Michael—

" O'er his lucid arms
A military vest of purple flowed."—*P. L.*, xi. 240–241.

In this picture of the chariot Vondel has followed
the splendid imagery of the first chapter of Ezekiel,
though not so closely as Milton has done in the magnificent passage which tells how—

" Forth rush'd with whirlwind sound
The chariot of Paternal Deity."

He has, however, departed from his Biblical original in
two points. He says their bodies were set with eyes
as with STARS—

" As with stars, their bodies all
And wings were set with eyes."—*P. L.*, vi. 754-755.

And again he tells how the cherubic shapes took an active part in the onslaught upon the rebel host—

> " Every eye
> Glar'd lightning and shot forth pernicious fire
> Among the accursed."—*P. L.*, vi. 848–849.

So Vondel's monsters are

> " *With stars bespangled over all their backs.*"

And they also

> " *Long'd for the fight, and for destruction flam'd..*"

The motive, which drives Lucifer on, is the same to which Satan gives expression—

> " Never can true reconcilement grow
> Where wounds of deadly hate have pierced so deep."
> —*P. L.*, iv. 98–99.

With the last lines of our citation compare the Miltonic description of Satan's shield—

> " The broad circumference
> Hung on his shoulders like the moon."
> —*P. L.*, i. 286.

As Uriel proceeds, his listener from time to time interrupts him with exclamations of wonder and interest, recalling the celebrated scene in Scott's " Ivanhoe " where Rebecca describes to her wounded companion the prowess of the Black Knight. Stirred by the recital of Lucifer's aspect and demeanour, Raphael thus apostrophises his former friend and chief—

> " *O Lucifer ! thou wilt lament this pride,*
> *Thou phœnix 'midst the worshippers of God*
> *Above. How thou dost stand amongst the host*
> *With head, helm, shoulders proudly eminent !*
> *How gloriously thy arms become thy form,*
> *As if by nature forged to grace thee well !*
> *O chief of angels, yet no more, draw back.*"
> —v. 1800–1806.

We naturally look to Milton's splendid delineation of the " Archangel ruined " for coincidences with these lines. The spirit of them is contained in more passages than one ; for instance, in—

> "Oh, how fallen ! how changed
> From him who, in the happy realms of light,
> Clothed with transcendent brightness, didst outshine
> Myriads though bright."—*P. L.*, i. 84-87.

While in—

> " He, above the rest (the rebel angels)
> In shape and gesture proudly eminent,
> Stood like a tower,"—*P. L.*, i. 588-590,

we have an almost literal transcript of Vondel's words, The pleading of the last line is that of Abdiel—

> "Thyself, though great and glorious, dost thou count,
> Or all angelic natures joined in one,
> Equal to Him begotten Son.   .   .
>
> .   .   .   .
>
> .   .   .   Cease, then, this impious rage."
>
> —*P. L.*, v. 833-835, 845.

Uriel takes up the broken thread of his graphic narrative—

> " *Confronted thus they stood, troop after troop,*
> *Most perfectly on either side by files*
> *To their battalions linked.   When madding drum*
> *And strident trumpet join in clamorous sound,*
> *The noise sharpens each weapon and each hand,*
> *And mounts to holiest circles of pure light.*
> *A din at which forthwith a pregnant cloud*
> *Of darts, asunder riven, volleying, brings forth*
> *A fiery hail, a storm and tempest fierce,*
> *That strikes the heavens with fear, their pillars shakes.*
> *The spheres and stars, confounded in their course*
> *And orbit, are perplexed, and on their watch*
> *Bewildered, know not where to turn.*"—v. 1806-1817.

To the details of this vigorously sketched battle-piece Milton was largely indebted. His presentment of the struggle is fuller, but not more realistic. A long passage tells of the orderly array of Michael's legions—

> " On they move
> Indissolubly firm, nor obvious hill,
> Nor straitening vale, nor wood, nor stream divides
> Their perfect ranks."—*P. L.*, vi. 68–71.

At length the two hosts

> " Front to front
> Presented stood, in terrible array
> Of hideous length."—*P. L.*, vi. 105–107.

Then the Archangel's trumpet sounds and battle is joined—

> " Through the vast of Heaven
> It sounded, and the faithful armies sung
> Hosanna to the Highest ; nor stood at gaze
> The adverse legions, nor less hideous joined
> The horrid shock. Now storming fury rose
> And clamour such as heard in Heaven till now
> Was never ; arms on armour clashing brayed
> Horrible discord, and the madding wheels
> Of brazen chariots raged ; dire was the noise
> Of conflict ; overhead the dismal hiss
> Of fiery darts in flaming volleys flew,
> And, flying, vaulted either host with fire ;
> So under fiery cope together rushed
> Both battles main with ruinous assault
> And inextinguishable rage. All Heaven
> Resounded ; and, had earth been there, all earth
> Had to her centre shook."—*P. L.*, vi. 203–219.

It is impossible to believe that the imagery of these lines is not derived from a vivid recollection of the previously written passage. Even the Dutch poet's somewhat fantastic conceit as to the perplexity and confusion among the heavenly spheres has not failed to reappear in a slightly altered form as a Miltonic simile.

The duel between Michael and Satan suggests it; their meeting is—

> " Such as (to set forth
> Great things by small) if, Nature's concord broke,
> Among the constellations war were sprung,
> Two planets, rushing from aspèct malign,
> Should combat and their jarring spheres confound."
> *—P. L.*, vi. 310–315.

This episode of the battle shall furnish but two more extracts. They tell of Lucifer's desperate attempt to stem the fortunes of the day, and of the failure of his onslaught upon Michael—

> *" In fury Lucifer three times renewed*
> *The fight, and proudly stayed his faltering host ;*
> *As if the stormy sea were beaten back,*
> *Time after time, when surging on a rock,*
> *And can with all its efforts do no more."*—v. 1836–1840.

> *" Waz-axe in hand, on this side and on that*
> *He parries blows or breaks them on his shield,*
> *Till Michael in his glittering armour stands*
> *Before him, godlike 'midst a ring of suns.*
> *' Hence, Lucifer ! give God the victory ;*
> *Lay down your arms and standard ; yield to God ;*
> *Lead off this impious host, this wicked crew,*
> *Or else beware.'   Thus from above he calls.*
> *The grand Foe of God's name, stiff-necked, unmoved,*
> *And prouder at these words, repeats in haste*
> *His blow three times, to cleave with his great axe*
> *The shield of adamant stamped with God's name.*
> *But he, who Heaven provokes, feels wrath divine.*
> *Upon the sacred adamant his blade*
> *Shivers and into fragments splits."* [1]*—v.* 1908–1921.

---

[1] Compare also Paradise Lost, 785-798.

The first extract is specially interesting, as affording a very strong proof of the correctness of our thesis. The simile it contains is taken by Milton and reproduced almost verbatim; and it appears, not in Paradise Lost, but in Paradise Regained, and refers not to Satan in arms, but to the Tempter in the wilderness—

> " As surging waves against a solid rock,
> Though all to shivers dashed, the assault renew
> (Vain battery !) and in froth and bubbles end ;
> So Satan, whom repulse upon repulse
> Met ever, and to shameful silence brought,
> Yet gives not o'er, though desperate of success,
> And his vain importunity pursues."—*P. R.*, iv. 18-25.

The second is part only of a passage which deserves to be closely compared with the whole corresponding section of Book vi. of Paradise Lost, for the contrasts are as remarkable as the resemblances. We will content ourselves with pointing out how in both poems the sympathies of the reader are attracted to the side of the rebel leader, who dauntlessly upholds a desperate cause, and is defeated by no superior prowess on the part of his adversary, but entirely by his possession of charmed weapons.

We select the chief verbal coincidences—

> " Satan, who on that day
> Prodigious power had shown, and met in arms
> No equal, ranging through the dire attack
> Of fighting Seraphim confused, at length saw
> Where the sword of Michael smote. . . .
> . . . . Such destruction to withstand
> He hasted, and opposed the rocky orb
> Of tenfold adamant, his ample shield."
>
> —*P. L.*, vi. 246-250, 253-255.

The fierce challenge of Michael contributes the following—

> " Hence then, and evil go with thee along,
> Thy offspring, to the place of evil, Hell—
> Thou and thy wicked crew, there mingle broils
> Ere this avenging sword begin thy doom."
> —*P. L.*, vi. 275–278.

Vondel's description of Michael's state is transferred by Milton to Satan after the hellish conclave—

> " With pomp supreme
> And god-like imitated state, him round
> A globe of fiery Seraphim enclosed
> With bright emblazonry and horrent arms."
> —*P. L.*, ii. 510–513.

Uriel concludes his record with the transformation of Lucifer after his fall. Now upon a certain passage in the tenth book of the Paradise Lost Mr. Pattison makes the following criticism :—" Another of Milton's fictions which has been found too grotesque is the change (P. L., x. 508) of the demons into serpents, who hiss their prince on his return from his embassy. Here it is not, I think, so much the unnatural character of the incident itself, as its gratuitousness which offends." [1] The passage in question will be clearly seen to have its original in Vondel's lines, which are, like Milton's, *grotesque*, but in the place in which they occur not *gratuitous*—

> *" Just as bright day to murky night is changed,*
> *So was his beauteous person, in its full*
> *Down sinking, altered to deformity,*
> *Too hideous. That bright face to cruel snout,*
> *The teeth to fangs sharpened for gnawing steel,*

---

[1] Pattison's " Milton," p. 190.

The feet and hands to fourfold claws, the skin
Of pearly fairness to a dusky hide,
The back, with bristles rough, two dragon wings
Spreads forth.   In short, the Archangel, whom but now
All angels honoured, is transfigured quite,
A medley of seven beasts, each horrible."

—iv. 1950–1962.

Milton had just described Satan thus in fallen glory—

"At last, as from a cloud, his fulgent head
And shape star-bright appeared, or brighter clad
With what permissive glory since his fall
Was left him, or false glitter.   All amazed
At that so sudden blaze, the Stygian throng
Bent their aspect."—*P. L.*, x. 449–454.

Then his transformation thus, we give a few only lines—

"His visage drawn he felt too sharp and spare,
His arms clung to his ribs, his legs entwining
Each other, till, supplanted, down he fell
A monstrous serpent on his belly prone.

.   .   .   .

.   .   .   .   Dreadful was the din
Of hissing through the hall, thick swarming now
With complicated monsters, head and tail,
Scorpion and asp, &c.   .   .   .
.   .   But still greatest he in the midst,
Now dragon grown."

—*P. L.*, x. 511–514, 521–524, 528–529.

We now take leave of Uriel's narrative and the war in heaven, and proceed to the examination of what may be regarded as the sequel to the main action of the drama, in which Gabriel gives the story of the events subsequent to the defeat of Lucifer, issuing in the temptation and fall of man.

This conclusion has been by some critics blamed as unnecessary, and an excrescence which impairs the artistic completeness of the play. However this may be, it has a very important bearing upon the subject of our discussion, for it is not too much to say that here, in about 150 lines of the Dutch drama, are to be found some of the *prima stamina* of the first, second, and ninth books of Paradise Lost. Two somewhat lengthy citations will sufficiently prove that we are not overstating the case—

> " *The contest o'er, he called the scattered host*
> *Together, first his chiefs, each filled with hate,*
> *And placed himself within a hollow cloud*
> *To shun the light of the All-seeing Eye,*
> *A dismal den of fogs, wherein no fire*
> *Save in their glances gleamed ; and 'midst the ring*
> *Of his infernal council seated, he*
> *Rose from his throne in Hell, as God adored.*
> ' *Ye powers, who for our righteous cause so bold*
> *This hurt endured, now is the time to take*
> *For our calamity revenge, with hate*
> *Irreconcilable to persecute,*
> *With guile and force alike, the Heavenly Foe*
> *In His own chosen image.* . . .
>
> . . . .
>
> *My aim is Adam and his race to spoil.*
> *I know through trespass of the primal law*
> *How such a stain indelible on him*
> *To rub, that he with all his progeny,*
> *In soul and body poisoned, never shall*
> *Attain the seat whereout we have been thrust.*
>
> . . . .
>
> *E'en Nature's self shall, by this blow abused,*
> *Well-nigh consume, and seek to nothingness*
> *And chaos to return. I see mankind,*
> *After the image of the Godhead formed,*
> *From God's similitude debased, estranged,*

In will and memory and thought obscured,
Their native light bedimmed and overcast,
And all, on mother's breast, in sorrow born,
A prey to Death's inexorable jaws.
Boldly I mean to play the tyrant's part,
And you, my sons, adored as deities
On altars numberless, on many a shrine
Of towering structure to propitiate
With victims, frankincense, and gold;
Also a throng of men, whose multitude
No tongue can name, all Adam's line to bring
To everlasting ruin, and, in God's despite,
To perpetrate abominable deeds.
My crown and his high feast shall cost him dear."

—v. 1938–1978.

To show how crowded this passage is with Miltonic phrases and turns of thought, and how closely the argument of the first two books of Paradise Lost follows on the lines laid down by Vondel, is no difficult task. Satan likewise calls together his scattered host—

> "He stood and called
> His legions.   .   .   .   .   .
> .   .   .   .   Thick bestrewn
> Abject and lost lay there, covering the flood."
> —*P. L.*, i. 300–310.

Compare the two pictures of the infernal dungeon—

> "Round he throws his baleful eyes,
> That witnessed huge affliction and dismay
> Mixed with obdurate pride and steadfast hate.
> At once, as far as angels ken, he views
> The dismal situation, waste and wild.
> A dungeon horrible, on all sides round
> As one great furnace flamed ; yet from those flames
> No light."—*P. L.*, i. 56–62.

Again—

> " Thus Satan, talking to his nearest mate
> With head uplift above the wave and eyes
> That sparkling blazed."—*P. L.,* i. 192–194.

And in Paradise Regained the Adversary—

> " In mid-air
> To council summons all his mighty peers
> Within thick clouds and dark, tenfold involved,
> A gloomy consistory."—*P. R.,* i. 39–42.

Every point of Vondel's description is brought out in relief. The " hate " which filled the minds of the hellish chiefs, the dismal cave or dungeon, the spectral light, the blazing eyes, the thick veil of clouds.

The second book of Paradise Lost opens with the account of the hellish conclave. Here we find—

> " High on a throne of royal state   .   .   .
> .   .   .   .
> Satan exalted sat."—*P. L.,* ii. 1–5.

And—

> " Towards him they bend
> With awful reverence prone, and as a god
> Extol him equal to the Highest in Heaven."
> —*P. L.,* ii. 477–479.

The contents of Lucifer's address are no less strikingly Miltonic. In Satan's first speech these words occur—

> " We may with more successful hope resolve
> To wage by force or guile eternal war
> Irreconcilable to our Grand Foe."—*P. L.,* i. 120–122.

Again—

> " Let us not slip the occasion.   .   .   .
> .   .   .   .
> Seest thou yon dreary plain, forlorn and wild,

F

> The seat of desolation, void of light ?
> .   .   .   .   Thither let us tend,
> And reassembling our afflicted powers,
> Consult how henceforth we may most offend
> Our Enemy, our own loss how repair,
> How overcome this dire calamity."
> —*P. L.*, i. 178, 180–181, 186–189.

The subtle counsel of Beelzebub, that mankind should be the object to whose destruction or degradation the efforts of Hell should be directed, furnishes our next parallel. The Counsellor points out that, " according to ancient and prophetic fame, another world, the happy seat of some new race called Man, was about this time to be created."

> " Here perhaps
> Some advantageous act may be achieved
> By sudden onset—either with hell-fire
> To waste His whole creation, or possess
> All as our own, and drive, as we are driven,
> The puny inhabitants ; or, if not drive,
> Seduce them to our party, that their God
> May prove their foe, and with repenting hand
> Abolish His own works.   This would surpass
> Common revenge, ...
> .   .   .   .   .   when His darling sons,
> Hurled headlong to partake with us, shall curse
> Their frail original and faded bliss,
> Faded so soon."—*P. L.*, ii. 362–375.

Another passage contains a variation upon the same theme. The Almighty Father thus discloses to the Son the purposes of the Adversary—

> " He wings his way
> Directly towards the new created world
> And man there placed, with purpose to assay
> If him by force he can destroy, or worse,

By some false guile pervert : and shall pervert :
For man will hearken to his glozing lies,
And easily transgress the sole command,
Sole pledge of his obedience ; so will fall
He and his faithless progeny."—*P. L.*, iii. 90–96.

In Satan's soliloquy immediately before entering into the serpent we have the consequences on the universe of man's fall thus depicted—

"Him destroyed
Or won to what may work his utter loss,
For whom all this was made, all this will soon
Follow, as to him linked in weal or woe."
—*P. L.*, ix. 130–134.

In a later book of the Epic Adam thus laments the fate of mankind—

"O miserable mankind! to what fall
Degraded, to what wretched state reserved!
Better end here unborn. .   .
.   .   .   .   .   .   Can thus
The image of God in man, created once
So goodly and erect, though faulty since,
To such unsightly sufferings be debased
Under inhuman pains? Why should not man,
Retaining still Divine similitude
In part, from such deformities be free?"
—*P. L.*, xi. 500–503, 507–513.

Vondel makes Lucifer conclude his speech with the prophecy that his followers would be worshipped in earthly temples as deities, and that the greatest part of mankind, in God's despite, should perpetrate abominations. Here, too, there are passages in Paradise Lost of identical import—

"By falsities and lies the greatest part
Of mankind they corrupted to forsake

God their Creator, and the invisible
Glory of Him that made them to transform
Oft to the image of a brute, adorned
With gay religions, full of pomp and gold,
And devils to adore for deities."—*P. L.,* i. 367-373.

And a few lines farther on—

" The chief were those who from the pit of hell
Roaming to seek their prey on earth, durst fix
Their seats long after next the seat of God,
Their altars by His altar, gods adored
Among the nations round.   .   .   .

    .   .   .   .

    .   .   .   .   . Yea, often placed
Within His sanctuary itself their shrines,
Abominations, and with cursed things
His holy rites and solemn feasts profaned,
And with their darkness durst affront His light."
                              —*P. L.,* i. 381-390.

We now return to that portion of Gabriel's narrative
which is concerned with the temptation of the woman.
The serpent is addressing Eve, and inciting her to eat
the forbidden fruit—

" ' *How glows this fruit with mingled gold and red !*
Seductive feast !   Yea, daughter, nearer step ;
No venom nestles in the immortal leaf.
How tempting is this fruit !   Come, freely pluck :
Knowledge I promise you, and light.   For fear
Of punishment why shrink you then ?   But taste,
And be in wisdom and intelligence
As God Himself.   How much He envies you
This food !   By it distinctions are discerned,
The fashion, cause, and quality of things.'
Forthwith begins the heart of the fair bride
To burn, to kindle.   For the much-praised fruit
She is inflamed.   The fruit allures the eye ;
The eye the mouth, the appetite.   Desire

> *Impels the hand, all quivering, to pluck.*
> *She plucks; she eats.*
>
> .   .   .   .
>
> .   .   .   .
>
> .   .   .   *Heaven mourns with signs of woe.*
> *It thunders, peal on peal.   On every side*
> *Fear, anguish, groans are heard and seen."*
> —v. 2091-2104, 2112-2115.

In the ninth book of Paradise Lost, which contains the parallel narrative, we find traces of almost every line of this quotation from the Lucifer. Not only are ideas and images seized and amplified, but at times the very words reappear. We give three excerpts from the words of the serpent to Eve—

> " I chanced
> A goodly tree far distant to behold,
> Loaden with fruit of fairest colours mixed,
> Ruddy and gold.   I nearer drew to gaze,
> When from the boughs a savoury odour blown.
> Grateful to appetite," &c.—*P. L.*, ix. 575-581.

Again—

> " O sacred, wise, and wisdom-giving plant,
> Mother of Science ! now I feel thy power
> Within me clear, not only to discern
> Things in their causes, but to trace the ways
> Of highest agents."—*P. L.*, ix. 679-683.

> " Ye shall not die.
> How should ye ?   By the fruit ?   It gives you life
> To knowledge."—*P. L.*, ix. 685-687.

> " What are gods, that man may not become
> As they, participating godlike food ?
>
> .   .   .   .
>
> Whoso eat thereof forthwith attain
> Wisdom without their leave.   And wherein lies
> The offence that men should thus attain to know ?
>
> .   .   .   .

> Is it envy ?   And can envy dwell
> In heavenly breasts ?   These, then, and many more
> Causes, import your need of this fair fruit.
> Goddess humane, reach then and freely taste."
> <div align="right">—<i>P. L.</i>, ix. 716–718, 724–727, 728–732.</div>

In this same portion of Paradise Lost a line occurs which seems to retain a verbal reminiscence of the vivid Vondelian lines—

> *" Forthwith begins her heart*
> *To burn, to kindle.   For the much-praised fruit*[1]
> *She is inflamed. . . . The hand, all quivering. . . ."*

Milton compares the snake swiftly rolling in tangles to a wandering fire, compact of unctuous vapour, and then he speaks of this vapour—

> "Kindled through agitation to a flame."
> <div align="right">—<i>P. L.</i>, ix. 637.</div>

The next quotation proceeds continuously with that which ends "reach then and freely taste"—

> "He ended ; and his words, replete with guile,
> Into her heart too easy entrance won.
> Fixed on the fruit she gazed, which to behold
> Might tempt alone." —<i>P. L.</i>, ix. 732–735.

> "Meanwhile the hour of noon drew on and waked
> An eager appetite, raised by the smell
> So savoury of that fruit, which with desire
> Inclinable, now grown to touch and taste,
> Solicited her longing eye."—<i>P. L.</i>, ix. 739–743.

She then soliloquises, after which—

> "Her rash hand in an evil hour ·
> Forth reaching to the fruit, she plucked, she eat.
> Earth felt the wound, and Nature from her seat
> Sighing through all her works, gave signs of woe."
> <div align="right">—<i>P. L.</i>, ix. 780–783.</div>

---

[1] See p. 84, *supra.*

When Adam had likewise sinned—

" Earth trembled from her entrails, as again
In pangs, and Nature gave a second groan ;
Sky loured, and, muttering thunder, some sad drops
Wept."—*P. L.*, ix. 1000–1003.

We here leave the Lucifer, satisfied that at last we
have done some justice to Vondel's merits, and fairly
established what others have hinted at but never proved,
that Milton in the composition of Paradise Lost laid
himself under no slight obligations to this Dutch drama.
We now proceed to examine other poems of Vondel,
which, so far as Miltonic criticism is concerned, offer
to those, who care to accompany us farther, untrodden
fields for discovery and research.

CHAPTER IV.

JOHN THE MESSENGER.

THE ambition of Vondel, as he became conscious of a constant development of his poetical and intellectual powers with increasing years, prompted him, while still in the early prime of life, to devote all his energies to the production of a great Epic poem which should perpetuate his fame. He chose as his subject[1] THE EXPEDITION OF CONSTANTINE THE GREAT TO ROME, and commencing in 1630, gave himself up in earnest for six years to his work. But the poem, although six books out of the twelve were actually completed, was never destined to see the light. The death of the writer's infant child (named Constantine after his hero) in 1633 was followed by that of his wife in 1635. The double blow fell heavily upon Vondel's heart; a gradual distaste began to fill his mind for continuing the literary task which was associated so closely with his great sorrow. He first laid it aside for a time, and then committed the entire MS. to the flames. The CONSTANTINE perished, and with it the project of giving the world another Æneid in the Dutch language.

One Epic poem Vondel did, however, write at a later period of his life; this it is whose title stands at the head of this chapter and with which we are now con-

[1] Brandt's " Leven van Vondel," pp. 46–51 ; Van Lennep, iii. 209, &c.

cerned. The work, which is in six books, deals with the subject of the life and death of John the Baptist, and in smallness of scale, as well as the nature of its contents, bears exactly the same relation to an heroic poem of the grander type, as does " Paradise Regained " to " Paradise Lost."

The "Joannes Boetgezant" (John the Messenger of Repentance) was written in 1662. Milton was at this time, and until 1664, living in Jewin Street, busy with the composition of the first seven books of Paradise Lost.[1] We can imagine him there receiving a copy of Vondel's poem, and can easily conceive that he would be eager to discover how the author of Lucifer, untrammelled any longer by the restrictions of the drama, would avail himself of the wider freedom permitted by the impersonal form of the Epic narrative, and would at once set one of his "readers" to the ungrateful toil of repeating, perhaps many times, in the ears of an exacting taskmaster, several thousand verses in an unknown tongue. These are suppositions, but a series of quotations from the poem will furnish us with solid grounds for accepting them as ascertained facts. We shall show that not only did the Dutch Epic exercise, as its subject would suggest, no slight influence upon certain portions of Paradise Regained, which was chiefly written in 1666,[2] but in a still more striking manner has its language and imagery left traces in Paradise Lost, and that more especially in the earlier books.

At this point we will at once deal with an objection which is certain to occur to many minds as an argu-

[1] Masson's " Life of Milton," vi. pp. 440–444.
[2] Masson's " Poetical Works of John Milton," ii. p. 2.

ment wherewith to rebut our forthcoming evidence. This objection, which at first sight appears somewhat formidable, may be thus formulated. If Milton began to write Paradise Lost in 1658, and the complete MS. was in the hands of the Quaker Elwood in August 1665,[1] how is it possible that a Dutch poem written in 1662 can have affected those earlier books of Paradise Lost, which were probably finished some time before it was published?

The answer is complete.

Milton certainly began his poem in 1658, but scarcely had he done so when the death of Cromwell, and the enormous disturbance of political forces which ensued, speedily diverted his attention from meditative reveries and called him back into the arena of civil and religious strife. He threw himself with all the passionate vehemence of his character into the tumultuous struggle of factions. "A fury of utterance was upon him, and he poured out, during the death-throes of the republic, pamphlet upon pamphlet, as fast as he could get them written to his dictation."[2] He did not believe in the possibility of the Restoration, nor did he fly until the dreaded event actually took place, and his silence became a matter not of choice, but of necessity. He was taken into custody, and not released until December 1660.

After this, and until 1662, he settled down in obscurity in a house in Holborn, near Red Lion Fields,[3] struggling to save what he could of his small fortune, and in daily suspense for his personal security. He was,

[1] Masson's "Life of Milton," vi. p. 496.
[2] Pattison's "Milton," p. 138.
[3] Masson's "Life of Milton," vi. p. 145.

according to a story deemed credible by Mr. Masson,[1] "in perpetual terror of being assassinated, though he had escaped the talons of the law; and so dejected that he would lie awake whole nights." Under these circumstances it is scarcely likely that many additions would be made to the MS. of Paradise Lost,[2] more especially as until his third marriage, February 1663, his domestic worries were scarcely less trying to his mental repose than Royalist persecutions.

But even with regard to that portion of his poem which was in existence prior to the publication of "Joannes Boetgezant," the knowledge we have of Milton's literary method renders the insertion *afterwards* of fresh matter in passages previously written an event by no means abnormal or even uncommon.

"What he thought," says Mr. Masson,[3] "he uttered nobly at first; but then he was always rethinking, and compelling his hand to consequent modifications of what it had already executed. The drafts of his earlier poems, yet extant in his own hand in Trinity College, Cambridge, are a perfect study in this respect. . . . . . . Similarly" (during the composition of Paradise Lost) "we must suppose him—carrying as he doubtless did the whole poem, as far as it was composed, in his memory—not unfrequently going back upon portions of it, and here and there improving expressions, or adding lines and passages for the sake of increased strength or beauty, or indeed making modifications that had become necessary in consequence of some new idea that had struck him farther on as to some part of

---

[1] "Life of Milton," vi. p. 214.
[2] Stern's "Milton und seine Zeit," iv. p. 49.
[3] "Poetical Works of John Milton," Introduction to vol. i. p. 77.

the conduct of the story." Such a statement clears
away all difficulties from our path. We need not pursue the subject farther.

The "Joannes Boetgezant" opens with an autobiographical passage containing an invocation to the
heavenly quires, which is the most important passage
of this character in Vondel's Epic, and naturally in-
vites comparison with the corresponding openings of
the third, seventh, and ninth books of Paradise Lost
and of the first book of Paradise Regained. With each
one of these it will be found to have points of contact.

> " *The Hero who, so great in sight of God*
> *And angels, His pure blood outpoured, it lists*
> *Me now to sing.   .   .   .   .*
>
> *.   .   .   .   .   .*
> *Ye quires of angels, who, in circles ranged,*
> *Worship on high the Lamb, that leads to dance*
> *The maiden chorus, who, with odes renewed*
> *And tones surpassing human song, adore*
> *The faithful Bridegroom of pure souls, my lay*
> *Heroic with celestial strains inspire.*
> *No Mount of Song save that of Paradise*
> *I know, where from God's throne through thousand veins*
> *The living water under rustling leaves*
> *Comes welling up, as crystal pure and bright.*
> *That is my Pegasean spring, my grove*
> *And fountain-head, whereout God's chosen drink.*
> *John's shades and deserts, cell and prison, shall,*
> *If but yon sacred stream refresh my soul,*
> *Change into light and Paradise.   Then speeds*
> *My humble song on desert anchorite,*
> *As loftily as ever songs of old*
> *On conqueror of Troy or Latium.*"—i. 7–8, 24–40.

Paradise Regained thus begins—

> " I who erewhile the happy garden sang
> By one man's disobedience lost, now sing

Recovered Paradise to all mankind,

.   .   .   .   .   .

.   .   .   .   .   .

And Eden raised in the waste wilderness.
Thou Spirit who ledst this glorious Eremite
Into the desert,   .   .   .

.   .   .   .   . inspire,
As Thou art wont, my prompted song, else mute

.   .   .   .

With prosperous wing full summed, to tell of deeds
Above heroic, though in secret done,
And unrecorded left through many an age."

—*P. R.*, i. 7–9, 11–15.

It is impossible not to see that these lines are but a variation upon the sentiments expressed in the concluding portion of the citation from Vondel, and that the very remarkable metaphor contained in the Paradise Regained, i. 7—

"Eden raised in the waste wilderness,"

is but a reproduction of the Dutch—

"Ioannes schaduwen, woestijnen en speloncken
Zullen veranderen in licht en Paradijs." [1]

The Vondelian extract immediately precedes an address by the Father of Grace to Gabriel. In Paradise Regained the Almighty likewise addresses Gabriel, and the argument proceeds—

"So spake the Eternal Father, and all Heaven
Admiring stood a space, then into hymns
Burst forth, and in celestial measures moved,
Circling the throne and singing, while the hand
Sung with the voice."—*P. R.*, i. 168–172.

Surely a close parallel with the Dutch poet's lines (24–28). The third book of "Paradise Lost" furnishes our next—

[1] See also "Joannes Boetgezant," iii. 26–27. This will appear in its place in Appendix.

> " Yet not the more
> Cease I to wander where the Muses haunt,
> Clear spring or shady grove or sunny hill,
> Smit with the love of sacred song ; but chief
> Thee, Sion, and the flowery brooks beneath
> That wash thy hallowed feet, and warbling flow."
>
> —*P. L.*, iii. 25-30.

The invocation to Urania at the commencement of Book vii. contains these lines—

> " Above the Olympian hill I soar
> Above the flight of Pegasean wing."—*P. L.*, vii. 3-4.

In the passage from the ninth book Milton (exactly as Vondel does) compares his heroic poem with the " Iliad " and " Æneid "—

> " Argument
> Not less, but more heroic than the wrath
> Of stern Achilles on his foe pursued,
> Thrice fugitive about Troy wall.
>
> .   .   .   .   .   .
>
> If answerable style I can obtain
> Of my celestial patroness.   .   .
>
> .   .   .   .   .   .
>
> Not that which justly gives heroic name
> To person or to poem ! Me of these
> Nor skilled nor studious, higher argument
> Remains, sufficient of itself to raise
> That name."—*P. L.*, ix. 13-16, 20, 40-45.

Our next quotation, which is of great length, would alone be sufficient to establish the fact of Milton's indebtedness to his contemporary. We break it up for convenience into detachments—

> " *Then spake the gracious Father, inly moved*
> *By human griefs, with unfeigned sympathy :*

'*My Sole-Begotten Heir and Son Elect,*
The Word made Man, in lustre dim, obscure,
And known by few, conceals Himself on earth
These many years. The time is fully come,
When He must openly appear and take
The holy office on His shoulders laid
For the salvation of afflicted man.
Whatever else may vacillate and change,
Our plighted word for aye stands firm. This task
Long purposed let our Messenger begin,
The man, by Heavenly counsel set apart
In mother's womb, for our dear Son the way
And entrance to His kingdom to prepare.'
Thus speaking, He, with ardent glow enflamed,
His promise to assure, long since by oath
Confirmed, and the redemption of mankind
To work out fully, summons Gabriel
Forthwith, who, clad in starry vesture, waits
The high behest, and ever ready stands.
'*Archangel,' saith He, ' who the cousins twain*
Each one her offspring promised.'"—i. 90–111.

We have an exact counterpart to this passage in the address to Gabriel in Paradise Regained, already referred to—

" But contrary unweeting, he (Satan) fulfilled
The purposed council pre-ordained and fix'd
Of the Most High, who, in full frequence bright
Of angels, thus to Gabriel smiling spoke :
Gabriel, this day by proof thou shalt behold,
Thou and all angels conversant on earth
With man and men's affairs, how I begin
To verify that solemn message late
On which I sent thee to the Virgin pure
In Galilee, that she should bear a son."
—*P. R.*, i. 126–135.

The subsequent soliloquy of the Saviour contains several verbal coincidences—

> " My way must lie
> Through many a hardy assay, even to the death,
> Ere I the promised kingdom can attain
> Or work redemption for mankind, whose sins'
> Full weight must be transferred upon my head.
> Yet, neither thus disheartened or dismayed,
> The time prefixed I waited ; when, behold,
> The Baptist (of whose birth I oft had heard,
> Not knew by sight), now come, who was to come
> Before Messiah, and His way prepare.
>
> .   .   .   .
>
> .   .   .   .
>
> And last, the sum of all, my Father's voice,
> Audibly heard from Heaven, pronounced me His,
> Me His beloved Son, in whom alone
> He was well pleased ; by which I knew the time
> Now full, that I no more should live obscure,
> But openly begin as best becomes
> The authority which I derived from Heaven."
>   —*P. R.*, 263-272, 283-289.

With this take—

> " With them came
> From Nazareth the son of Joseph deemed
> To the flood Jordan, came as then obscure,
> Unmarked, unknown."—*P. R.*, i. 24-25.

In the third book of Paradise Lost we have—

> " And in His face
> Divine compassion visibly appeared,
> Love without end, and without measure grace."
>   —*P. L.*, iii. 140-142.

We now reach a series of passages in which Vondel gives full rein to his imaginative powers. The first pictures the descent of Gabriel ; and almost every line of the gorgeously realistic description has left its impress upon Milton's mind. We repeat a few lines of our last quotation for the sake of completeness—

" *He summons Gabriel*
Forthwith, who, clad in starry vesture, waits
The high behest, and ever ready stands."—i. 108-109.

Here follows the address of the Almighty to the Archangel, who is bidden to visit John the Baptist in the desert and urge him to commence his mission and proclaim the advent of the Hero who shall free the world from the dominion of Hell. The poem then proceeds—

" *So spake the Almighty : and in haste prepares*
The Archangel for descent, unfolds his wings,
Splendid as phœnix plumes, with sky-blue tinged,
And gold and purple dyes, amidst the light
Wherein God sits enshrined. The colours change
And mingle, each with each, in varied shades,
Like rainbow tints or peacock's feathered hues
Beneath the sunlight, which beats down direct.
Equipt for flight, he upward springs and strikes
His wings together thrice. The angelic quires
Look round, and with their gaze attend his flight,
While downward prone he speeds, and sweeps
From round to round, and, as he falls, descries
Jerusalem, that heavenward seems to lift
Its crownèd brow enthroned amidst the hills,
By which the royal town is girdled round;
Then wheeled his course beyond great Jordan's stream,
Where the waste desert, bare of herbage, lay.
Here paused the Archangel, hov'ring on his wings
Right o'er the Solitary's cell, just as
An eagle, who at last a spring has spied,
Down-swooping at the babble of the stream,
With the refreshing water slakes his thirst."—i. 126-147.

In the third book of Paradise Lost, when Satan reaches the sun, where—

" Sight no obstacle found here, nor shade,
But all sunshine, as when his beams at noon
Culminate from the equator,"—iii. 615-618,

He—

> "Saw within ken a glorious angel stand,"
>
> —*P. L.*, iii. 622,

>   "And straight was known
> The Archangel Uriel—one of the seven,
> Who in God's presence nearest to His throne
> Stand ready at command."—*P. L.*, iii. 647–650.

Satan himself, assuming the disguise of a stripling cherub—

>   "Wings he wore
> Of many a coloured plume, sprinkled with gold."
>
> —*P. L.*, iii. 641–642.

Here are traces of Vondelian imagery, but a far closer parallel will be found in that passage of the fifth book of Paradise Lost, which tells of the descent of Raphael to Eden. This passage has already been shown to contain many striking coincidences [1] with the language of Belial when, in the opening scene of the Lucifer, he beholds from the brow of heaven the ascent of Apollion. It will now be seen that most of those portions, which do not find their original in Lucifer, are almost verbal reproductions of these lines from " Joannes Boetgezant "—

> "So spake the Eternal Father, and fulfilled
> All justice. Nor delayed the wingèd saint
> After his charge received ; but from among
> Thousand celestial ardours, where he stood
> Veiled with his gorgeous wings, upspringing light,
> Flew through the midst of Heaven. The angelic quires,
> On each hand parting, to his speed gave way.

> . . . .

---

[1] Page 38, *supra.*

From hence   .   .   .   .   .
.   .   .   .   .   . he sees,
Not unconform to other shining globes,
Earth and the Garden of God, with cedars crowned
Above all hills.   .   .   .   .
.   .   . Down thither prone in flight
He speeds, ...
.   .   .   . till, within soar
Of towering eagles, to all the fowls he seems
A phœnix, gazed by all as that sole bird.

.   .   .   .
.   .   . Six wings he wore to shade
His lineaments divine ; the pair that clad
Each shoulder broad came mantling o'er his breast
With regal ornament ; the middle pair
Girt like a starry zone his waist, and round
Skirted his loins and thighs with downy gold
And colours dipt in Heaven ; the third his feet
Shadowed from either heel with feathered mail,
Sky-tinctured grain.   Like Maia's son he stood
And shook his plumes.   .   .   .

.   .   .   .
Him Adam discerned, as in the door he sat
Of his cool bower, where now the mounted sun
Shot down direct his fervid rays."—*P. L.*, v. 246–252,
      258–262, 266–267, 270–272, 277–286, 299–301.

It will be discovered that almost every single thought,
phrase, or image used by Vondel reappears in some portion of the fifty-five Miltonic lines from which the above
excerpts are taken.   The eagles and the phœnix, the
direct rays of the sun, the hasty preparation, the upward spring, the shaking of the plumes, are common to
both passages.   Nay, even

> " *Jerusalem, that heavenward seems to lift*
>   *Its crownèd brows, enthroned amidst the hills,*"

finds its representative in

> " The Garden of God, with cedars crowned
> Above all hills."

' The starry vesture, the wings with sky-blue tinged, and gold and purple dyes," which array with splendour the Archangel Gabriel, find their counterpart in the Miltonic description of " the six wings which shaded the lineaments divine of Raphael." " The regal ornament, the starry zone, the downy gold, the colours dipt in heaven, the sky-tinctured grain," all were suggested by Vondel's lines.

But to make the catalogue complete, we have yet other citations to give from Paradise Lost—one from the eleventh book—

> " He ceased, and the Archangelic Power prepared
> For swift descent ; with him the cohort bright
> Of watchful cherubim.   .   .   .
> .   .   .   .   . All their shape
> Spangled with eyes more numerous than those
> Of Argus."—*P. L.*, xi. 126–131.

The mention of the Argus eyes suggests the description of the peacock in the account of the creation—

> " Whose gay train
> Adorns him, coloured with the florid hue
> Of rainbows and starry eyes."—*P. L.*, vii. 444–446.

The very collocation of images which we find above in " Joannes Boetgezant," i. 131. The third book produces two farther reminiscences of a less pronounced character. Satan, emerging from chaos, has gained the firm opacous globe of this round world. He walks about at large—

> " As when a vulture   .   .   .
> .   .   .   .   .   .
> Dislodging from a region scarce of prey
> To gorge the flesh of lambs or yearling kids

On hills where flocks are fed, flies toward the springs
Of Ganges."—*P. L.,* iii. 431-435.

A little later, Satan, arriving at the foot of the golden
stairs which lead to heaven's gate, looks down with
wonder at the sudden view, and is compared to a scout
who from the brow of some high-climbing hill discovers,
unawares,

" Some renowned metropolis
With glistering spires and pinnacles adorned."
—*P. L.,* iii. 549-550.

The last two similes, of slight importance when isolated,
form added links to a continuous chain of evidence.

We do not pretend to have instituted an exhaustive
examination of Vondel's Epic ; our next piece of translation comes from the beginning of the third book.
The Baptist is described as breaking up and preparing
the ground—

" *That so soon as the All-Blessed One appear,*
Man may, now like to parchèd wilderness
And desert waste, to Eden be transformed,
A heavenly Paradise, where God is praised,
In his first innocence, as he was made,
Ere he so reckless lost his weal and state."
—iii. 25-30.

The idea is a quaint one, but it is the same which is
prominent in the opening lines of Paradise Regained—

" I, who erewhile the Happy Garden sung,
By one man's disobedience lost, now sing
Recovered Paradise to all mankind,

. . . .

And Eden raised in the waste wilderness."
—*P. R.,* i. 3-7.

In this same third book the assembly of heaven is

gathered together, that the Almighty Father may proclaim His counsels and announce the sending of the
Son into the wilderness.   It is thus described—

> *" But high above, (where on the heels of day*
> *No night succeeds, nor dusky clouds nor storms*
> *Obscure the light, which ever shines and streams,*
> *Wherein the realm of spirits draw free breath),*
> *Came the Supreme, (who all the starry rounds*
> *Circling the globe directs and firmly holds,*
> *Bound once for all by laws unchangeable),*
> *And mounted to the topmost seat of Heaven,*
> *By Michael followed and the angelic train,*
> *Who round Him hover both in van and rear.*
> *Some project great He planned that gave to all*
> *Concern, and His imperial heralds quick*
> *Dispatched to the four ends of Heaven to call*
> *The whole assembly forthwith to His court,*
> *Which riseth high, with diamond towers flanked,*
> *In midmost point of Heaven's vast circling orb.*
> *They hasten each their way round the bright ring*
> *Of circuit infinite ; one here beholds*
> *The Dominations, Princedoms, Powers ascend*
> *Through the pure Blue, each in his order ranged.*
> *The trumpet sounds before the praise of God.*
> *In heavenly guise they cast around their limbs* '
> *Robes dyed in rainbow hues, and rich inwrought*
> *With phœnix plumes, beset with pearls and sown*
> *With precious stones.   The sheen of clustering stars,*
> *Amid their fragrant locks, lends to their brow*
> *A gleam and lustre of divinity."*—iii. 175-199.

Any one acquainted with Paradise Lost will at once
turn to the fifth book for the parallel to this.

Raphael thus begins his episodical narrative of the
War in Heaven—

> *" On such day*
> *As Heaven's great year brings forth, the empyreal host*
> *Of angels, by imperial summons called,*

Innumerable before the Almighty's throne
Forthwith from all the ends of Heaven appeared
Under their hierarchs in orders bright.
Ten thousand thousand ensigns high advanced ;
Standards and gonfalons 'twixt van and rear
Stream in the air, and for distinction serve
Of hierarchies, of orders and degrees.

. . . .

. . . Thus when in orbs
Of circuit inexpressible they stood,
Orb within orb, the Father Infinite

. . . . . .

. . . Thus spake :
Hear, all ye angels, progeny of light,
Thrones, dominations, princedoms, virtues, powers."

—P. L., v. 582-591, 594-597, 599-602.

Milton describes the royal seat of Satan—

" High on a hill far blazing, as a mount
Raised on a mount, with pyramids and towers
From diamond quarries hewn."—*P. L.,* v. 757-759.

Compare also a passage which occurs in this same
portion of the fifth book, as much for its differences as
its identities, with the parenthetical lines with which
the extract from Vondel commences—

" Now when ambrosial night, with clouds exhaled
From that high mount of God when light and shade
Spring both, the face of brightest Heaven had changed
To grateful twilight (for night comes not there
In darker veil)."—*P. L.,* v. 642-646.

It is curious that both poets [1] should likewise speak,
in the midst of two descriptive pieces which are closely
akin, of the circling starry rounds in connection with
the angelic movements.

[1] Paradise Lost, v. 620, &c.

In a similar portion of the third book we come across the following—

> " With these (flowers), that never fade, the spirits elect
> Bind their resplendent locks, inwreathed with beams."
>
> —*P. L.*, iii. 361–362.

The sending out of the heralds may be paralleled with—

> "Towards the four winds four speedy cherubim
> Put to their mouths the sounding alchemy
> By herald's voice explained."—*P. L.*, ii. 516–518.

The description of the Eternal Father seating Himself on the throne and His address to the Council of Heaven are too long to be given at length. The first, which appears to have been inspired by the celebrated picture of Van Eyck,[1] is perhaps too minute in its details to be *strictly* Miltonic. The address should be compared with the soliloquy of our Saviour in Paradise Lost, with which it has much in common. At its conclusion occur the following lines—

> "*So spake the Father, and at Nazareth*
> *The Son obeys, and offering up a prayer*
> *To Heaven, as from a golden censer filled*
> *With incense, now, with head uplifted free,*
> *Steps forth to publish, to a world bereft*
> *Of truth and light, His office openly,*
> *And show Himself the Saviour of mankind.*"

At the conclusion of the address of the Eternal Father in Paradise Regained we have a passage of like import—

> "So they in Heaven their odes and vigils tuned.
> ·Meanwhile the Son of God, who yet some days

---

[1] The upper central panel of the great altarpiece in the Cathedral of St. Bavon at Ghent, " The Adoration of the Lamb," represents God the Father seated on His throne.

Lodged in Bethabara, where John baptized,
Musing and much revolving in His breast
How best the mighty work He might begin
Of Saviour to mankind, and which way first
Publish his godlike office, now mature,
One day walked forth alone."—*P. R.*, i. 182-189.

The Saviour's prayer ascending as incense has its analogue in the eleventh book of Paradise Lost. There the Son presents the prayers of our repentant first parents before His Father's throne—

" These sighs
And prayers, which in this golden censer, mixed
With incense, I, thy Priest, before thee bring."
P. L., xi. 23-25.

The rejoicing of Nature at the Saviour's approach is thus told by Vondel—

" *Where'er He placed His feet, His coming seemed*
To bring a blessing down. As after rain
Awaited anxiously, when parched-up fields
For moisture cried, more lovely shines the sun,
The grass bursts forth in verdure and in song,
A vernal wealth of flowers makes gay the hills
And dales. No artist's hand can scene
Or landscape fairer paint, though He
With thousand mingled hues depicts the bow.
Warble the birds. When throat of nightingale
Has ceased to trill, the blithe lark adds her notes.
With freshly murmuring streams the bubbling spring
Waters the herb. The cedar bows her head.
The face of Nature turns to brighter hue
And gladlier smiles. The boisterous storm subsides.
The bee, by scented thyme and bloom enticed,
Sucks honey from the dew. The sheepfolds yield
Their cream. Harts leap with glee. Joy knows no bound."
—iii. 275-290.

Of Eve, it is said, when she went forth among her buds and flowers—

> " They at her coming sprung,
> And, touched by her fair tendance, gladlier grew."
>
> —*P. L.*, viii. 46–47.

In the fourth book of Paradise Regained the Tempter disturbs the rest of the Son of God, sleeping without shelter in the wilderness, by a terrific storm. The narrative proceeds—

> " Thus passed the night so foul, till morning fair
> .   .   . Chased the clouds and laid the winds.
> And now the sun with more effectual beams
> Had cheered the face of earth and dried the wet
> From drooping plant or dropping tree ; the birds,
> Who all things now behold so fresh and green
> After a night of storm so ruinous,
> Cleared up their choicest notes in bush and spray
> To gratulate the sweet return of morn."
>
> —*P. R.*, iv. 432–438.

Again, in the second book of Paradise Lost the same image is found—

> " When from mountain-tops the dusky clouds
> .   .   .   .   .   . o'erspread
> Heaven's cheerful face, the lowring element
> Scowls o'er the darkened landskip snow or shower,
> If chance the radiant sun, with farewell sweet,
> Extend his evening beam, the fields revive,
> The birds their notes renew, and bleating herds
> Attest their joy, that hill and valley rings."
>
> —*P. L.*, ii. 488–495.

Leaving now what may be called the argument of the passage, let us turn to detail. At the opening of the fifth book of Paradise Lost Adam thus addresses his spouse—

> " Awake ! the morning shines, and the fresh field
> Calls us ; we lose the prime to mark how spring
> Our tended plants, ...
>
> .   .   .   .

How Nature paints her colours, how the bee
Sits on the bloom extracting liquid sweet."

P. L., v. 20–22, 25–26.

The delineation of the beauties of Paradise in the fourth book likewise must be placed under contribution, for it too contains lines which may fairly be described as identical both in phraseology and in turn of fancy with lines in the Vondelian extract under consideration. Blossoms and fruit are described as appearing together—

"With gay enamelled colours mixed,
On which the sun more glad impressed his beams
Than in fair evening cloud or humid bow,
When God hath showered the earth ; so lovely seemed
That landskip. And of pure now purer air
Meets his approach, and to the heart inspires
Vernal delight and joy, able to drive
All sadness but despair."—*P. L.*, iv. 149-156.

The succession of images in one portion of the morning hymn of Adam and Eve likewise deserves our notice—

"His praise, ye winds, that from four quarters blow,
Breathe soft or loud ; and wave your tops, ye pines,
With every plant in sign of worship wave.
Fountains, and ye that warble as ye flow
Melodious murmurs, warbling tune His praise,
Join voices, all ye living souls. Ye birds
That, singing, up to Heaven gate ascend,
Bear on your wings and in your notes His praise,
.   .   .   And ye that walk
The earth."—*P. L.*, v. 192-200.

The plot of Paradise Regained is essentially without incident. The poem may be described as one long dialogue in which the principles of Good and Evil, as represented by our Lord and Satan, enter into learned doctrinal arguments, which, though relieved by brilliant passages, are on the whole somewhat sophistical and tedious. The monotony, however, is broken by the introduction of extra-mundane events. Angelic and Infernal Councils are summoned. In the one the Eternal Father calls Gabriel, and announces to him His intention that the Son should be tempted by Satan in the wilderness. Satan, on his part, twice consults his "gloomy consistory" as to the best means by which to oppose the plans of the Almighty and seduce the second Adam, as he had already seduced the first in Eden.

Now we have already shown that the Heavenly Council has its Vondelian counterpart; we shall further find that the same is the case with regard to the only other notable peculiarity in the plan of Paradise Regained. The fourth book of "Joannes Boetgezant" opens with the summoning by Lucifer of a Hellish Council, whose purpose is identical with that of the "gloomy consistory" of the English poem.

The passage in which this is related has not failed to arrest Milton's attention and stimulate his imagination. It runs thus—

> *" At words like these Hell was with wonder seized*
> *And thunderstruck. The abyss with terror quaked.*
> *Its iron gate, on rusty hinges hung,*
> *Began to jar and grate ; the pool of woe*
> *To cast forth from its entrails stench and smoke.*
> *The Prince of Darkness, for his state afraid,*
> *Summons all his infernal counsellors*
> *To court, who thither speed with sinuous path,*
> *Where right in centre of the earth it lies,*
> *As far from Southern as from Northern Pole,*
> *And cuts in equal parts, hanging on chains,*
> *The axis of the world."*—iv. 1–11.

" *To council came god Lucifer, and took*
His seat upon a lofty throne, to which
The outstretched necks of subject monsters gave
Support and stay.   A crown of vipers twined
On his misshapen head he bore, and threw,
Swaying a staff of steel with cloven point,
His glowing glances up.   The lamp, with pitch
And sulphur fed and fat of basilisk,
Cast light around the navel of the waste
Concave, with grime thick overspread.   The Chief,
By all the accursèd band surrounded, sat,
Each ranged in order, still and dumb,
Till he, with voice resounding as a bell,
Began."—iv. 14-24.

We take first the parallel passages from Paradise
Regained.   The Adversary—

" With the voice divine
Nigh thunderstruck, the exalted Man to whom
Such high attest was given a while surveyed
With wonder ; then, with envy fraught and rage,
Flies to his place, nor rests, but in mid-air
To council summons all his mighty peers."
—*P. R.*, i. 35-40.

" He ended, and his words impression left
Of much amazement to the infernal crew,
Distracted and surprised with deep dismay
At these sad tidings."—*P. R.*, i. 106-109.

" He directs
His easy steps, girded with snaky wiles."
—*P. R.*, i. 119-120.

" Satan . . . . with speed was gone
Up to the middle region of thick air,
Where all his potentates in council sat."
—*P. R.*, ii. 116-118.

In the second book of Paradise Lost, Sin unlocks for
Satan the gate of hell.   The effect is thus described.   She

> " Every bolt and bar,
> Of massy iron or solid rock, with ease
> Unfastens.   On a sudden open fly,
> With impetuous recoil and jarring sound,
> The infernal doors, and on their hinges grate
> Harsh thunder, that the lowest bottom shook
> Of Erebus.   .   .   .   .   .
>
> .   .   .   .
>
> So wide they stood, and like a furnace mouth
> Cast forth redounding smoke and ruddy flame."
>   —*P. L.*, ii. 877–883, 887–888.

These lines are only an amplified copy of those[1] of Vondel, whose fallen Lucifer, as depicted in this same extract, doubtless suggested the weird figure of Death, who bars the way of Satan to this same gate of hell—

> " The other shape
> Shook a dreadful dart : what seemed his head
> The likeness of a kingly crown had on."
>   —*P. L.*, ii. 672–673.

In the first book of Paradise Lost, such expressions as—

> " Round he throws his baleful eyes,"—*P. L.*, i. 56 ;

> " A fiery deluge, fed
> With ever-burning sulphur, unconsumed,"
>   —*P. L.*, i. 68–69 ;

> " As far removed from God and light of Heaven
> As from the centre thrice to the utmost pole,"
>   —*P. L.*, i. 73–74 ;

> " With head uplift above the waves, and eyes
> That sparkling blazed,"—*P. L.*, i. 193–194 ;

and this simile, comparing the hellish flames to those of Etna—

---

[1] iv. 3-5.

> " Whose combustible
And fuelled entrails .   .   .   .
.   .   .   .
Leave a singèd bottom all involved
With stench and smoke,"—*P. L.*, i. 233-234, 236-237,

all point to one conclusion, and make it at least probable that their common source is to be found in the
opening of this fourth book of the Dutch Epic. Even
stronger is the corroboration to such a surmise given
by the passage in which Milton follows Vondel in
making the infernal council-chamber to be lighted by
lamps—

> " From the archèd roof
Pendent by subtle magic, many a row
Of starry lamps and blazing cressets, fed
With naphtha and asphaltus, yielded light
As from a sky."—*P. L.*, i. 726-730.

And lastly, not laying weight upon what may appear
a somewhat strained analogy between the figure of
Lucifer seated on his throne supported by the necks of
subject monsters and that of Sin, which " ended foul in
many a scaly fold, a serpent armed with mortal sting,"
the conception of the infernal abode hanging in chains
is reproduced in—

> " Fast by, hanging in a golden chain,
This pendent world."—*P. L.*, ii. 1050-1051.

Likewise the muteness of the hellish assembly appears in—

> " He now prepared
To speak ; whereat their doubled ranks they bend
From wing to wing, and half enclose him round
With all his peers ; attention held them mute."
>
> —*P. L.*, i. 615-619.

The speech of Lucifer next calls for our notice.   We give a portion of it—

> "*Ye trusty Powers, who curse your Doomer's name,*
> *And 'gainst Eternal Light eternal war*
> *Proclaim! to you is known, how we have gained*
> *By eating of an apple power o'er all*
> *The seed of Adam, and these offerings,*
> *To the Lord God of heaven and earth and sea*
> *First hallowed, have enkindled to our praise.*
>
> .   .   .   .
>
> *Ye were permitted after your deep fall*
> *Through the open air to roam.   Now through His name*
> *Driven from the world ye fly.   Now 'tis time to wake.*
> *Both Messenger and Lord our ruin plan.*
> *Then both assail, first John, his Master next.*
> *Let each bestir himself and use his might.*
> *Set forth, Apollion, and work with guile.*
> *If longer we delay, too strong they'll prove.*
> *The growing evil smother in its birth.*"
> *He spoke, and from the iron gate of Hell*
> *Each forced his way above, as with a noise*
> *A flock of ravenous birds comes sweeping down*
> *On carrion, a dead and stinking lure.*
> *So in the land of Jesse's son their chance*
> *They seek, and hurt and damage plan*
> *By covert guile or open violence.*
> *The car of Night had through the starry field*
> *Steep mounted to the top, and, half-way passed,*
> *Hung on the reverse side to slowly glide*
> *Her downward path.   All breathing things lay still,*
> *Asleep at rest.*—iv. 25–31, 47–64.*"

The speech of Satan in Paradise Regained to his associates runs closely parallel to that of Lucifer both in general import and in verbal identities—

> "O ancient powers of air! .   .   .
> .   .   .   .   .   .   Well ye know
> How many ages as the years of men

This universe we have possessed, and ruled
In manner at our will the affairs of earth,
Since Adam and his facile consort Eve
Lost Paradise."—*P. R.*, i. 47–51.

" Ye see our danger on the utmost edge
Of hazard, which admits no long debate,
But must with something sudden be opposed
(Not force, but well-couched hand, well-woven snares),
Ere in the head of nations He appear
Their King, their Leader, and supreme on earth."
—*P. R.*, i. 94–99.

The consequences of the speech are described as follows—

" No time was there
For long indulgence to their fears or grief ;
Unanimous they all commit the care
And management of this main enterprise
To him, their great dictator, whose attempt
At first against mankind so well did thrive
In Adam's overthrow, and led their march
From Hell's deep vaulted den to dwell in light,
Regents and potentates and kings, yea, gods
Of many a pleasant realm and province wide."
—*P. R.*, i. 109–118.

The first address of the Archfiend to the Saviour begins thus—

" 'Tis true I am that spirit unfortunate,
Who, leagued with millions more in rash revolt,
Kept not my happy station, but was driven
With them from bliss to bottomless deep ;
Yet to that hideous place not so confined
By rigour unconniving, but that oft,
Leaving my dolorous prison, I enjoy
Large liberty to round this globe of earth
Or range in air."—*P. R.*, i. 360–366.

The correspondence between these passages and the translated extract in many particulars is sufficiently

obvious. We pass on to point a very curious coincidence between the simile by which Vondel here describes the infernal spirits rushing out from the gates
of hell as a flock of ravenous birds, and that by which
Milton symbolises the issuing from hell gates of the
two strange figures Sin and Death :—

> "As when a flock
> Of ravenous fowl, though many a league remote,
> Against the day of battle to a field
> Where armies lie encamped come flying, lured
> With scent of living carcases."—*P. L.*, x. 273-277.

And when they arrive upon earth—

> "They both betook them several ways,
> Both to destroy or unimmortal make
> All kinds, and for destruction to mature
> Sooner or later."—*P. L.*, x. 610-612.

The images used by Vondel seemed to have none of
them escaped Milton's retentive memory, for that which
closes our translation has its representative in—

> "Now had Night measured with her shadowy cone
> Half-way uphill this vast sublunar vault."
> —*P. L.*, iv. 776-777.

And again, Satan, evading the watchful cherubim—

> "Four times crossed the car of Night."—*P. L.*, ix. 65.

The piece which follows is from the sixth book of
"Joannes Boetgezant," but its subject connects it naturally with our last extract, as it serves at once to
complete the Vondelian picture of hell, and to show
how great are the obligations which the companion passages of Paradise Lost owe to these, their prototype and
exemplar—

" *The lake where Lucifer lay weltering,*
Sunk to his neck, gapes wide with yawning mouth
Set open.   Here a host might freely pass
With horse and chariots in loose array,
O'er stony ground at first, and then through brake
And thicket, rough and wild.   In winding round
The road grows narrower ; not like stairs
Which turn, but as the funnel of a tube.
The fostering light, at first an ingress given,
Pales by degrees, and as oblivious
So deep to press, is changed to twilight dusk
And evening glimmer, like as when the sun,
Beneath the horizon sunk, yet for a time
His streaming lustre leaves upon the waves.
There night still day remains, or day and night
Involved, and light with darkness blent in one.
Here people walk, as when the hosts of Heaven
At night by moonshine march in files to watch,
And pace their rounds by walls of diamond."

—vi. 276-293

Satan is described by Milton as

" Rolling in the fiery gulph,"—*P. L.*, i. 53,

and

" With head uplift above the wave, . . .
    . . . his other parts besides
Prone on the flood, extended long and large."

—*P. L.*, i. 193-195.

The episodes in the second and tenth books of Paradise Lost, in which appear the ghastly personifications of Sin and Death, have already contributed several examples of close agreement with lines from the Dutch Epic.   The simile which we now bring forward was alone wanting to furnish a Vondelian original for the entire passage, which describes the unlocking of the gates of hell by Sin, and the exit of Satan—

> " The gates wide open stood,
> That, with extended wings, a bannered host,
> Under spread ensigns marching, might pass through,
> With horse and chariots ranked in loose array ;
> So wide they stood, and like a furnace-mouth."
> —*P. L.*, ii. 884–888.

We hold that the absolute identity of this simile with that used by Vondel (vi. 277–278), coming, as it does, to reinforce the testimony afforded by the fact that the simile used in the tenth book to describe the exit of Sin and Death from this same hell gate is identical with the Dutch poet's comparison of the issuing forth of the infernal spirits to " ravenous birds in search of carrion," is almost conclusive proof that Milton must have borrowed them directly. It is impossible that such striking coincidences could be the result of chance, or even of unconscious reminiscence.

The entrance to Eden in the fourth book is thus described—

> "A steep wilderness, whose hairy sides
> With thicket overgrown, grotesque and wild,
> Access denied."—*P. L.*, iv. 135–137.

The Fiend, on his journey in search of the new-made universe, finds himself standing at the foot of the stairs which lead up to heaven—

> " Direct against which opened from beneath,
> Just o'er the blissful seat of Paradise,
> A passage down to Earth,—a passage wide.
>
> .   .   .   .
>
> So wide the opening seemed, where bounds were set
> To darkness, such as bound the ocean wave."
> —*P. L.*, iii. 526–528, 538–539.

The same antithesis is here made between the funnel-like opening and the stairs as in Vondel's lines (280–282).

Milton speaks thus in the opening of the third book of Paradise Lost of himself—

> "Escaped the Stygian pool, though long detained
> In that obscure sojourn, while in my flight
> Through utter and through middle darkness borne."
> —*P. L.*, iii. 14-17.

The gradually increasing and weird darkness of the gloomy deep is thus described a little later—

> "But now at last the sacred influence
> Of light appears, and from the walls of Heaven
> Shoots far into the bosom of dim night
> A glimmering dawn."—*P. L.*, iii. 1035-1036.

Satan now

> "Wafts on the calmer wave by dubious light."
> —*P. L.*, iii. 1042.

Hell itself

> "As one great furnace flamed ; yet from those flames
> No light, but rather darkness visible."
> —*P. L.*, i. 62-63.

> "The seat of desolation, void of light,
> Save what the glimmering of those livid flames
> Casts pale and dreadful."—*P. L.*, i. 181-183.

What is this but Vondel's imagery dressed in Miltonic garb ? The simile which is found in the lines—

> "*The light   .   .   .   .   .*
> *.   .   . is changed to twilight dusk*
> *And evening glimmer, like as when the sun,*
> *Beneath the horizon sunk, yet for a time*
> *His streaming lustre leaves upon the waves,*"

has been seized, modified, and applied to the appearance of the fallen Archangel as he proudly surveyed the serried ranks of his infernal host—

> " His form had yet not lost
> All her original brightness, nor appeared
> Less than Archangel, ruined and the excess
> Of glory obscured ; as when the sun, new-risen,
> Looks through the horizontal misty air
> Shorn of his beams."—*P. L.*, i. 591–594.

In the closing lines of our extract we are reminded of Gabriel and his angelic guards keeping watch o'er Paradise. The place of the watch is thus described—

> "Where Heaven
> With earth and ocean meets, the setting sun
> Slowly descended, and with right aspect
> Against the eastern gate of Paradise
> Levelled his evening rays. It was a rock
> Of alabaster."—*P. L.*, iv. 539–544.

Here we have the level evening rays once more, and an alabaster rock in place of diamond walls. Adam speaks of hearing—

> "Celestial voices to the midnight air
> Singing their great Creator ! oft in bands
> While they keep watch or nightly rounding walk."
> —*P. L.*, iv. 684–685.

And the direct narrative tells us that—

> "The Cherubim
> Forth issuing at the accustomed hour, stood armed
> To their night-watches in warlike parade."

And a few lines farther on—

> " He (Gabriel) led his radiant files,
> Dazzling the moon."—*P. L.*, iv. 780–798.

We now choose a passage of a different character ; it

is an excerpt from that portion of Vondel's fifth book which describes Herod's birthday feast.

Herod's sin in loving Herodias is compared to that of Eve in lusting after the forbidden fruit—

> *" Such was the brief delight which charmed the soul*
> *Of Eve, a taste of apple-juice."*—v. 46-47.

The splendour of the feast is thus related—

> *" The marble floor was strewn with flowery rain,*
> *The walls with curtains draped, and balmy gales*
> *From Araby their blissful odours waft.*
>
> *A crowd of maids and youths move to and fro,*
> *Alike in age and symmetry of form,*
> *And served the coolèd wine.*
>
>   *All that the table offered was*
> *Surpassing of its kind.*
>
> *It seemed, as if both field and wood in chase*
> *Had yielded all their game. From branches hang*
> *Lemons, pomegranates, oranges of gold,*
> *Like showers dropping on each fair dame's lips.*
> *An air of Paradise, tempered and pure,*
> *Refreshed the hearts of all, who sat at meat.*
> *The splendour and luxurious excess*
> *Most amply gratified each several taste.*
> *Material costliness here yields to art,*
> *So fine the work on gold and silver chased,*
> *The jewelry and festal robes.*
>
> *The joyous monarch bade his Ganymede*
> *With luscious nectar fill a royal cup,*
> *Whereout his father Herod used to drink.*
>
> *The palace wide re-echoed with the sound*
> *Of heavenly harmony, while on their heads*
> *The chamberlain a festal garland placed,*
> *'Mid mingled tones of song and pipe and string."*
>
> —v. 297-300, 310-314, 321-330, 372-375, 388-391.

We will compare these lines, in the first place, with that interlude,' amid the almost continuous dialogue, of Paradise Regained, wherein an account is given of the dainties set before our Lord by the Tempter after His fast—

> " A table richly spread in regal mode,
> With dishes piled, and meat of noblest sort
> And savour—beasts of chase or fowl of game.
>
> .   .   .   .   .   .
>
> Alas ! how simple to these cates compared
> Was that crude apple that diverted Eve !
> And at a stately sideboard, by the wine
> That fragrant smell diffused, in order stood
> Tall stripling youths rich clad, of fairer hue
> Than Ganymede or Hylas ; distant more,
> Under the trees now tripped, now solemn stood,
> Nymphs of Diana's train.   .   .   .
>
> .   .   .   .   .   .
>
> And all the while harmonious airs were heard
> Of chiming strings or charming pipes, and
> Winds of gentlest gale Arabian odours fanned
> From their soft wings, and Flora's earliest smells.
> Such was the splendour."
> —*P. R.*, ii. 340–343, 349–355, 361–365.

We submit that these two sets of excerpts cannot have been penned independently.   A passage in the fourth book of the same poem appears as if a continuation of the above.   The Tempter had exhibited to the Saviour the splendour and luxury of Rome—

> " Thou may'st behold,
> Outside and inside both, pillars and roofs,
> Carved work, the hand of famed artificers
> In cedar, marble, ivory, or gold."
>
> .   .   .   .   .   .

To whom the Son of God unmoved replied—

" Nor doth this grandeur and majestic show
   Of luxury, though called magnificence,
   More than of arms before allure mine eye,
   Much less my mind ; though thou shouldst add to tell
   Their sumptuous gluttonies and gorgeous feasts
   On citron tables, ...
      .   .   . How they quaff in gold,
   Crystal, and myrrhine cups, embossed with gems
   And studs of pearl."
                  —*P. R.*, iv. 57–60, 110–115, 118-120.

The last lines of the Vondelian excerpt, taken with
the first line,

   " *The marble floor was strewn with flowery rain,*"

afford a curious parallel with—

" Now in loose garlands thick thrown off, the bright
   Pavement, that like a sea of jasper shone,
   Impurpled with celestial roses smiled.
   Then, crowned again, their golden harps they took,
   .   .   .   .
      .   .   . And, with preamble sweet
   Of charming symphony, they introduce
   Their sacred song and waken raptures high."
              —*P. L.*, iii. 362–365, 367–369.

And in the next book of Paradise Lost—

                  "Of pure, now purer air
   Meets his approach, and to the heart inspires
   Vernal delight and joy, able to drive
   All sadness but despair. Now gentle gales
   Fanning their odoriferous wings dispense
   Native perfumes, and whisper whence
   They stole their balmy spoils,   .
      .   .   .   .   .
   Sabean odours from the spicy shore
   Of Araby the blest."—*P. L.*, iv. 153–159, 162-163.

" Groves where rich trees wept odorous gums and balm,
Others whose fruit, burnished with golden rind,
Hung amiable."—*P. L.*, iv. 248–250.

                  " To their supper fruits they fell,
Nectarine fruits which the compliant boughs
Yielded them, sidelong as they sat recline
On the soft downy bank damasked with flowers."
                  —*P. L.*, iv. 331–334.

We have not space to discuss the " Joannes Boetgezant" at greater length. We have given citations
enough to show that Milton was thoroughly familiar
with it, and did not scruple to take hints and sugges-
tions from its language and imagery.

There would be no difficulty in very largely increasing by quotations the number of single similes common
to the two poets, such as the following, both from the
third book of " Joannes Boetgezant."

Vondel is speaking of the Divine justice, and represents the Father of Mercy before He executes judgment
as showing—

        " *To His children first His rod,*
  A comet with a tail, as fiery red
  As blood, the token of God's wrath."—iii. 117–118.

The same conception appears in—

            " High in front advanced,
The brandished sword of God before them blazed,
Fierce as a comet."—*P. L.*, xii. 632–634.

Or, again, take this simile—

    " *Whene'er on summer day a breeze springs up*
  And gently blows upon a sea of corn,
  Then on its stalk the heavy ear bends low
  Its head,"—iii. 143–145,

with—

> " As when a field
> Of Ceres ripe for harvest waving bends
> Her bearded grove of ears, which way the wind
> Sways them."—*P. L.*, iv. 979-982.

We will only mention farther that the Dutch Epic concludes with the journey of John's spirit through the infernal regions under the conduct of Raphael, in the course of which he encounters and addresses the patriarchs and prophets of the Old Dispensation. This passage, like the vision of Adam upon the " Spectacular Mount" in the eleventh and twelfth books of " Paradise," is an imitation of the similar episode in the sixth " Æneid." Knowing, then, from the evidence adduced, that Milton must have read this Dutch "Hellereis," it is at least a plausible supposition that from hence he first conceived the idea of concluding his own Epic by a passage of like character based upon the same original.

CHAPTER V.

REFLECTIONS ON GOD AND RELIGION.

In the year preceding that in which he wrote "Joannes Boetgezant," Vondel, among other productions of his prolific pen, gave to the world a didactic poem, "Reflections on God and Religion." This poem, which is of great length,[1] is divided into five books, whose contents are indicated by their headings—(1.) Of God; (2.) Of God's Attributes; (3.) Of God's Works; (4.) Of Religion; (5.) Of Private Religion.

Written upon the Lucretian model, this treatise in verse is very discursive, and touches upon an infinity of religious, scholastic, metaphysical, and scientific questions. With the manner in which Vondel has dealt with these generally we have no concern, except in so far as they have a bearing upon certain portions of the conversations which take place in Paradise Lost between Adam and the Archangel Raphael. "It is," says Mr. Masson,[2] "in these conversations that there occur poetical summaries of Milton's physics, physiology, and metaphysics. Especially curious is that long passage (viii. 15-178) in which the relative merits of the Ptolemaic theory of the cosmos and the Copernican theory are made the subject of an express discussion

---

[1] 7400 lines.

[2] "Life of Milton," vi. p. 551.

between Adam and the Archangel." The passages
have attracted the special attention of all commentators upon the Paradise Lost, and Mr. Masson, in particular, has discussed the views and opinions of Milton
in a very full and exhaustive manner. Mr. Pattison
remarks,[1] "The vastness of the scheme of ' Paradise Lost '
becomes more apparent to us if we remark that within
its embrace there seem to be equal place for both the
systems of physical astronomy which were current in
the seventeenth century. . . . Sharp as is the contrast
between the two systems, the one being the direct
contradictory of the other, they are lodged together,
not harmonised, within the vast circuit of the poet's
imagination."[2] Now the passages containing these
Miltonic theories, which have attracted so much attention, were written probably in the spring of 1664. We
propose now to compare them with some extracts from
Vondel's treatise, which was published somewhat more
than two years before.

> " *The motions that are seen fear no dispute,*
> *Whether Copernicus or Ptolemy*
> *Declare the earth around the sun to turn*
> *Or sun around the earth.   The movement lies*
> *In one or other, twist them as they may.*
> *If the first heavenly round draw with itself*
> *The lower spheres, and above the topmost*
> *No reasoning can another reach which drives*
> *The others and itself stands still, then men*
> *Climb up into the fixed realm, His Throne,*
> *To shake, yet not disturb, who moveth all*
> *And maketh all beneath Himself rotate*

---

[1] Masson's "Life of Milton," vi. 523-536; "Poetical Works of
John Milton," Intr., 89-99.
[2] Pattison's "Milton," p. 180.

According to His laws.   This to surmount,
Free-thinkers fancy that a principle
Indwelling and of mighty force in each
Celestial sphere impels the starry rounds."

—i. 416-428.

In Raphael's discourse occur the following lines—

"This to attain, whether Heaven move or earth,
Imports not, if thou reckon right ; the rest
From man or angel the Great Architect
Did wisely to conceal and not divulge
His secrets, to be scanned by them who ought
Rather admire ; or, if they list to try
Conjecture, He His fabric of the Heavens
Hath left to their disputes."—*P. L.,* viii. 70-77.

"What if the sun
Be centre to the world, and other stars,
By his attractive virtue and their own
Incited, dance about him various rounds ?
.   .   .   .
Or save the sun his labour, and that swift
Nocturnal and diurnal rhomb supposed
Invisible else above all stars, the wheel
Of day and night."—*P. L.,* viii. 122-125, 133-136.

These paragraphs, which contain that acknowledgment of doubt as to the truth of the rival Ptolemaic
and Copernican theories, on which Milton's biographers
dwell with such marked emphasis, whether or no they
were suggested by that portion of Vondel's poem from
which the translated extract has been taken, at least
express the same opinions in terms strikingly analogous.
The citation which follows will make this similarity
even more apparent. Its argument dwells upon the
smallness of the earth compared to the infinite expanse
of the universe.

" *So wide is this our world, no traveller*
  Hath seen or visited its whole extent,
  And yet its earthly bulk, with heavenly to compare,
  A single speck to the star-gazer's eye;
  For when earth stands amidst the stars in light,
  Her globe indents the sky, as if a speck.
  Is every star as great as this our world,
  Or greater, as astronomers assert?
  And shine they just as bright, however far
  Apart, and tiny in our sight? Who can
  From here below with mind of man embrace
  The heavenly round, where stars in thousands gleam
  Like diamonds on this translucent ring,
  Fit to adorn the immeasurable hand
  Of God, which holds in span both east and west?
  But be the earth so great as measures say,
  How great is then the vault of Heaven beyond?
  Or gauge the height of Heaven, if so you can,
  To this world's navel or Hell's middle point,
  Hath space like this an end and certain bounds,
  Who then can God's infinity conceive?
  What is this universe, if viewed by God
  In bulk, but as a drop of morning dew!"

—iii. 232–235, 241–260.

In Paradise Lost Adam thus speaks—

" When I behold this goodly frame, this world
  Of heaven and earth consisting, and compute
  Their magnitudes,—this earth a spot, a grain,
  An atom, with the firmament compared,
  And all her numbered stars that seem to roll
  Spaces incomprehensible (for such
  Their distance argues, and their swift return
  Diurnal), merely to officiate light
  Round this spacious earth, this punctual spot."

—*P. L.*, viii. 15–23.

Thus Raphael in reply—

> " For Heaven's wide circuit, let it speak
>   The Maker's high magnificence, who built
>   So spacious, and His line stretched out so far,
>   That man may know he dwells not in his own—
>   An edifice too large for him to fill,
>   Lodged in a small partition, and the rest
>   Ordained for uses to his Lord best known."
>
> *—P. L.*, viii. 100-106.

The last two lines of the extract from Vondel—

> " *What is this universe, if viewed by God*
>   *In bulk, but as a drop of morning dew !* "—

contain an idea which Milton has put into shape.
When Satan has emerged from chaos, he beholds
" far off the empyreal heaven," and "fast by, hanging
in a golden chain "—

> " This pendent world, in bigness as a star
>   Of smallest magnitude, close by the moon."
>
> *—P. L.*, ii. 1053-1054.

The world, being not the earth, but the entire universe, "hung drop-like"[1] from heaven, the abode of
God. On this Satan, at length "alighted, walks "—

> " A globe far off
> It seemed ; now seems a boundless continent."
>
> *—P. L.*, iii. 422-423.

These lines in their turn are but another form of the
comparison set forth in the beginning of the Vondelian
passage. ·

Lastly, from the triumphal song of creation—

> " Great are Thy works, Jehovah ! infinite

---

[1] Masson, " Poetical Works," vol. i. p. 89.

Thy power ! what thought can measure Thee or tongue
Relate Thee ! .   .   .   .   .

.   .   .   .

Witness this new-made world, another Heaven,
Of amplitude almost immense, with stars
Numerous, and every star perhaps a world
Of destined habitation."—*P. L.*, vii. 602–604, 618–623.

We give another quotation from this third book of
the " Reflections," which treats of " God's Works." It
is impossible to do more than select from so extensive
a poem a few salient examples of a specially Miltonic
character. This treats of the same subject as its pre-
decessors—

> " *How marvellous that Heaven exactly knows*
> *Each day upon its axis just to turn,*
> *To pass in muster all the Heavenly host*
> *Before the eyes of man from east to west !*
> *What bow or field-piece can its ball or shaft,*
> *What lightning shoot so swift through air or cloud ?*
> *What water down a rock so quickly fall ?*
> *Thus keeps the wandering star her lines and course*
> *From west to east, now quicker, now more slow,*
> *To that abode wherein the Seven find,*
> *Or high or low, the quarter for their watch*
> *Set many hundred thousand miles apart.*"
>
> —iii. 987–997.

A few lines before we find a comment on lunar astronomy—

> " *Here must Hevelius*[1] *lend no telescope*
> *To search upon the aspect of the moon*
> *For spot and stain and light with prying glass,*
> *And land and water place on lunar chart.*"
>
> —iii. 968–971.

---

[1] A well-known Dantzic astronomer.

I

Turning to Raphael's disquisition, we have—

> " The swiftness of those circles attribute,
> Though numberless, to His omnipotence
> That to corporeal substances could add
> Speed almost spiritual."—*P. L.*, viii. 107–110.

> "What if the sun
> Be centre to the world, and other stars,
> By his attractive virtue and their own
> Incited, dance around him various rounds ?
> Their wandering course, now high, now low, then hid,
> Progressive, retrograde, or standing still,
> In six thou seest ; and what if, seventh to them,
> The planet earth, so steadfast though she seem,
> Insensibly three different motions move ? "
> —*P. L.*, viii. 122–130.

Adam declares his wonder at the apparent motion of the firmament—

> " Reasoning, I oft admire
> How Nature, wise and frugal, could . . .
> .   .   On their orbs impose
> Such restless revolution day by day,
>
> .   .   .   .   .   .
> Speed to describe whose swiftness number fails."
> —*P. L.*, viii. 25, 30–32, 38.

Raphael suggests the possibility of an interchange of light between the earth and moon—

> " Reciprocal, if land be there,
> Fields and inhabitants.   Her spots thou seest
> As clouds."—*P. L.*, viii. 144–146.

This allusion to the moon and her surface adds to the many points of contact between this and the astronomical lesson given in answer to the inquiry of Adam. There is, however, a closer parallel to the actual words in the first book of Paradise Lost—

> "The moon, whose orb
> Through optic glass the Tuscan artist views
> At evening, . . . to descry new lands,
> Rivers or mountains, in her spotty globe."
> —*P. L.*, i. 287–291.

There are many passages in the "Reflections" dealing with such subjects as the Wisdom and Foreknowledge of God, the Free Will of Man, the relations between Body and Spirit; merely descriptive pieces, as of storms, landscapes, and natural objects ; others, such as the one we now bring forward, on more general themes, which might be compared with portions of Milton's works of like import. The citations we have already made all have a close relationship to that portion of the dialogue between Adam and his Heavenly Guest which occurs in the first half of the eighth book of Paradise Lost, and which treats solely of the celestial movements. The one which follows, discusses a widely different topic, the same which furnishes the subject-matter for the second half of the eighth book of Paradise Lost, the beauty of woman and her relations to man. It is well known that Milton's views on this latter point were peculiar and strongly pronounced. The sentiments of Vondel thus find expression.

> " *The loveliness of woman, which on earth*
> *All else surpasseth, nor heart nor eye*
> *E'er fills with surfeit, which kindles to flame*
> *The very lions, here its living charms*
> *Unveils, fair as becomes God's handiwork,*
> *That man might taste the exuberant delights*
> *Of sensuous passion, which, of growth eterne,*
> *In contemplation of the Deity,*
> *Had, until now, its sole fruition found.*
> *The aspect and delight, rich source of bliss,*

Of female loveliness, hath thousands plunged
Headlong in woe, and shipwreck of their state,
Health, life, and weal.   The wisest, strongest men
Are drawn along and fettered, like her slaves,
By shackles of bright flowing hair.   No beast
Thus raves, bewitched by elfish sprite,
Like man misguided, blind, his every wish
And lust indulges, God and name and fame
And honour throws aside, that he with love
In some false charmer's amorous flames may melt,
Like ice or waxen bust in heat of fire.
To this may lead the dissolute misuse
Of Beauty, and thus dearly purchases
A foolish man this fleeting bliss, the which
But scarce enjoyed, remorse in secret comes,
And follows each abuse of Heavenly gifts
Close on the heels.   Unhappy was he then
Who fell into her snares, caught, overcome,
For one glance of her eyes ; as in a dream,
The joy, like mist, is gone.   What purpose then
Doth Beauty fill, and what the end and aim
Of God in forming thus this image fair,
Which lures souls to their hurt ?   Doth God design
To bind man's heart by wedded vows, and teach
Him in this fair to find a fairer still,
A yearning, which the soul in God alone
Can satisfy, in Plenitude Divine
Of beauty and delight ?   This song of ours
Should WOMAN *with still lovelier attributes*
Invest, but that we fear her siren charms
Would even saints seduce, if winning grace,
Virtue, discernment, softness, should descend
From Heaven and hover round her comely form
Of faultless symmetry." —iii. 419–452.

In Paradise Lost Adam pleads with the Almighty
for a companion who should be his equal; for the
brute—

> "Cannot be human consort. They rejoice
> Each with their kind, lion with lioness."
>
> —*P. L.*, viii. 391-392.

And just as Vondel declares that before woman came man did not taste of the joys of sensuous passion—

> " *Which, of growth eterne,*
> *In contemplation of the Deity,*
> *Had, until now, its sole fruition found,*"

so the reply of the Almighty to Adam is couched in these terms—

> " A nice and subtle happiness I see
> Thou to thyself proposest in the choice
> Of thy associates, Adam, and wilt taste
> No pleasure, though in pleasure solitary.
> What think'st thou, then, of me and this my state?
> Seem I to thee sufficiently possessed
> Of happiness or not, who am alone
> From all eternity?"—*P. L.*, viii. 399-406.

Adam tells of the creation of Eve—

> " So lovely fair,
> That what seemed fair in all the world seemed now
> Mean, or in her summed up, in her contained
> And in her looks, which from that time infused
> Sweetness into my heart unfelt before,
> And into all things from her air inspired
> The spirit of love and amorous delight."
>
> —*P. L.*, viii. 471-477.

He thanks God for granting his prayer, and speaks of Him as—

> " Giver of all things fair—but fairest this
> Of all Thy gifts."—*P. L.*, viii. 493-494.

In his subsequent narrative occur the following lines—

" Here passion first I felt,
Commotion strange ; in all enjoyments else
Superior and unmoved ; here only weak
Against the charm of beauty's powerful glance."
—*P. L.*, viii. 530–533.

" When I approach
Her loveliness, so absolute she seems
And in herself complete, so well to know
Her own, that what she wills to do or say
Seems wisest, virtuosest, discreetest, best."
—*P. L.*, viii. 546–550.

" To consummate all,
Greatness of mind and nobleness their seat
Build in her loveliest, and create an awe
About her as a guard angelic placed."
—*P. L.*, viii. 556–559.

At the Hellish Council in "Paradise Regained,"
Belial counsels Satan to tempt our Lord by sensual
delights—

" Set women in His eye and in His walk,
Among the daughters of men fairest found,

.   .   .   .   .   .

Skilled to retire, and in retiring draw
Hearts after them, tangled in amorous nets.
Such object hath the power to soften and tame
Severest temper, smooth the rugged'st brow,
Enerve and into voluptuous hope dissolve,
Draw out into credulous desire, and lead
At will the manliest, resolutest breast."
—*P. R.*, ii. 161–167.

" Samson Agonistes " furnishes also at least one striking parallel passage—

" Whate'er it be, to wisest men and best
Seeming at first all heavenly, under virgin veil,
Soft, modest, meek, demure,

Once joined, the contrary she proves—a thorn
Intestine, ...
.   .   .   .   Or by her charms
Draws him awry, enslaved,
Into dotage, and, his sense depraved,
To folly and shameful deeds, which ruin ends.
What pilot so expert but needs must wreck
Embarked with such a steersmate at the helm ?"

—S. A., 1034–1045.

It will be noted that the first quotation comes from the first book of the "Reflections;" the other three from the third book, which treats of God's works. It is in these same two books that the other passages of Miltonic character, to which we have alluded, will be chiefly found.

CHAPTER VI.

ADAM IN BANISHMENT.

THE play whose title stands at the head of this chapter was written by Vondel when in his seventy-third year, as a sequel to his "Lucifer." The poet has in his dedicatory preface stated his purpose to be "the representation upon the stage, learnedly and without offence, of Adam's banishment, the tragedy of all tragedies," [1] herein following the example of Hugo Grotius, whose Latin poem the "Adamus Exul," upon the same subject, was well known in Holland. Vondel, while diverging widely from his predecessor in the language, and notably in the lyrical character of large portions of his play, has avowedly built upon the same lines. He has taken Grotius for his model, but at the same time was so careful not to be a slavish imitator, that he has even departed from the Biblical record, and made his Tempter not to assume the form of a serpent, but of a winged dragon [2] (een geschubden Draak).

The poem was published early in 1664. The following considerations, in fact, render it probable that it appeared in the month of March of that year at the latest. We have already mentioned that Vondel's

---

[1] "Het treurspel aller treurspelen."
[2] An exhaustive comparison of the two poems will be found in Van Lennep's "Vondel," x. 422–456.

" Gysbrecht van Amstel " was written for the dedication of the new theatre at Amsterdam, which was built at the cost and for the benefit of the governors of the Wees-en-Oudemannenhuis in the year 1637.[1] This theatre was, a quarter of a century later, either rebuilt or at least enlarged and restored, and there can be but little doubt that the aged Vondel wrote his " Adam in Banishment," which is dedicated " Aan de Kunstbeminnende Heeren Vaders van het Oudemannenhuis en Weeshuis," in the hope that it would be selected by them for representation at the opening of the restored theatre.[2] These governors of the Orphanage, as we have said, had the supreme direction over the affairs of the theatre, but the actual manager was a certain Jan Vos, who was a personal enemy of Vondel, and systematically tried to injure the great poet's reputation by mounting his pieces in an inferior manner and by placing his best rôles in the hands of incapable actors.[3] Through the influence of this man, " the tragedy of all tragedies " was put on one side, and a composition by Marie Vos, his own daughter, was chosen and recited at the opening ceremony, which took place on March 24, 1664.

This date, then, gives us, as a superior limit for the time of publication of the " Adam in Banishment," the early part of the month of March ; nor is corroborative evidence wanting to establish its accuracy. Two poems were written criticising adversely Vondel's play, one of them of considerable length, and these were both in print in the summer of 1664.[4]

[1] Brandt's " Leven van J. Vondel," p. 53.
[2] Van Lennep, x. 350.
[3] Brandt's " Leven," p. 89 ; Stilleman's " J. Vondel," p. 53.
[4] For details see Van Lennep.

This being the case, it is by no means an improbable supposition that a copy may have found its way into Milton's hands in the autumn or winter of this same year, at the very time when he was engaged upon that portion of "Paradise Lost" which treats of the Fall of Man. The winter, we are told by his nephew, was the time when Milton composed the greater portion of his poem. "His vein never happily flowed but from the autumnal equinoctial to the vernal, and whatever he attempted [in the other part of the year] was never to his satisfaction, though he courted his fancy ne'er so much."[1]   As we know that a complete copy of the Epic was in Elwood's hands in the month of August or September 1665, we may, therefore, reasonably assign the composition of the last four books to the winter and spring (1664–65). We should, therefore, naturally expect that if the "Adam in Banishment" exerted any influence upon the language of "Paradise Lost," it would be upon the tenth, and possibly upon portions of the ninth book. We shall show that this is precisely what the evidence we shall adduce proves to have been the case. It is almost possible to mark the exact point at which the Dutch play began to affect the language and ideas of Milton. That part of the ninth book which tells of the temptation and sin of Adam and Eve contains Vondelisms, but they are derived from "Lucifer," and not from "Adam." Immediately afterwards, in the scenes of remorse and penitence, we meet with traces of the latter play, which become more abundant as we proceed.

One exception must be made to this statement. The "Adam" opens with a long soliloquy of Lucifer. This

[1] Masson's "Life of Milton," vi. 464.

has so much in common with the soliloquy of Satan at the opening of the ninth book, that we may conjecture that this was not composed, at least in its present form, at the time when Milton first dictated that portion of his poem in which it appears, but was interpolated or recast a few months afterwards.

Apart from any question as to the obligations of Milton to Vondel, it is surely a wonderful coincidence, and one that points to a curious affinity between the two poets, that at the very time when the Englishman was, after long years of musing and preparation, slowly girding himself to the task, which he had set before him from his youth, of writing a great poem upon the subject of the Fall of Man, his Dutch contemporary should produce a drama,[1] the finest, in many respects, of all his works, which covers the same ground, and that, again, immediately before Milton had reached that portion of his Epic, which dwells upon the actual Fall and its consequences, Vondel should likewise have chosen this precise episode as the subject for dramatic treatment. The fact of the appearance of the two plays at the exact moment when, as a historical fact, they did appear, is far more remarkable than the subsequent fact, which we are establishing, that they were perused, and to some extent utilised, by Milton.

This part of our task, however, claims our attention, and we shall commence with an examination of that passage to which reference has already been made, the soliloquy of Lucifer with which the play opens. It will be necessary to give it almost *in extenso*—

" I, once excelling in the realms of Light,
And now from Light eterne exiled in gloom,

---

[1] The Lucifer.

Come thundering up from out the sulphurous lake
Below, and, not overstepping thus the bounds
Of my confinement, haunt the regions here
Above; for though the Foe did make my form
Abhorred and hideous, yet was I allowed,
With you, my Hellish mates, here met in flight,
To stretch our sway o'er sea and earth and air.
The Prince of this World finds it suits his state
To shun the day.   His splendour grows by dusk,
Wherefore he chooses night for this attempt.
Though darkness now begins to leave the fields,
Still may the foe of light in shadow plunge,
By cave, hedge, covert, thicket, brake and wood.
Where am I here?   The clear-toned nightingale
Is herald to the sun and radiant dawn.
I hear with morning-coolness life revive
And joyous chirping midst the leaves and trees.
The rippling of four streams strikes on the ear,
Which, from one hillside source, spread far and wide.
This tells sufficiently what Earth we tread.
Here flows Euphrates' stream ; here Eden blooms,
The realm, the charge of Adam and his spouse.
Here with my follower I needs must hide
Among the trees, in park or myrtle walk,
Then spy before, behind, on either side,
And scheme how best to hatch some evil plot.
For, alien from good, this cursed doom
I hate, and in His creatures seek to spoil
And ravish Him whose essence nought can hurt.
To this end did I found my Hellish realm,
Which shall endure for aye.   No plan too bold
For me, who shrank not from the assault of Heaven,
So Vengeance seize the world within her teeth
And drag the Universe from its fixed seat,
That once more by my might Heaven's axis crash.
I wish henceforth to give Him constant work,
And, though His bolts have driven me from my throne,
To let Him see what I can do, though fall'n.

What if our force should fail to reach above ?
The upper Powers must see that force enough
Remains to cross His will in all His works.
The name Almighty is a title, and no more,
An impotent, vainglorious boast. Did He know how
To utterly destroy one being that exists,
'Twere o'er with me ! I should cease to be,
Or cease at least to rule these realms below.
His might's too weak, when mine to leeward lies.
It cannot reach the ship that keeps the wind.
We shall with canvas spread sail round the cape,
And enter the rich port whereto we steer."—i. 1-52.

At this point we break off, as the rest of the soliloquy
admits of separate consideration. It cannot fail to
strike even a careless reader of the above that its
tone and statements are exactly those of the Miltonic
Satan. The opening lines have an exact counterpart
in Paradise Regained—

> " 'Tis true I am that spirit unfortunate,
>   Who, leagued with millions more in vast revolt,
>   Kept not my happy station, but was driven
>   With them from bliss to the bottomless deep.
>   Yet to that hideous place not so confined
>   By rigour unconniving, but that oft,
>   Leaving my dolorous prison, I enjoy
>   Large liberty to round this globe of earth
>   Or range in air."—*P. R.*, i. 358-366.

Again—

> " O ancient Powers of air and this wide world
>   (For much more willingly I mention air,
>   This our old conquest, than remember Hell,
>   Our hated habitation)."—*P. R.*, i. 44-47.

And

> " Demonian spirits, now, from the element
> Each of his reigu allotted, rightlier called
> Powers of fire, air, water, and earth beneath."
>
> —*P. R.*, ii. 122–125.

Turning to the ninth book of Paradise Lost, we find—

> " Satan, who late fled before the threats
> Of Gabriel out of Eden, now improved
> In meditated fraud and malice, bent
> On man's destruction, maugre what mishap
> Of heavier on himself, fearless returned
> From compassing the earth, cautious of day."
>
> —*P. L.*, ix. 53–58.

> 　　　　　　　" There was a place
> Where Tigris, at the foot of Paradise,
> Into a gulph shot underground, till past
> Rose up a fountain by the Tree of Life.
> In with the river sunk, and with it rose
> Satan, involved in rising mist, then sought
> Where to lie hid."—*P. L.*, ix. 71–77.

> " If I could joy in aught—sweet interchange
> Of hill and valley, rivers, woods, and plains,
> New land, new sea, and shores with forest crowned,
> Rocks, dens, and caves !　But I in none of these
> Find place or refuge.　　　.　　　.　　　:　　　.
> 　　.　　　.　　　.　　　All good to me becomes
> Bane, and in Heaven much worse would be my state.
> But neither here seek I, no, nor in Heaven
> To dwell, unless by mastering Heaven's Supreme.
>
> 　.　　　.　　　.　　　.　　　.　　　.　　　.　　　.
>
> For only in destroying I find ease
> To my relentless thoughts ; and him destroyed,
> Or won to what may work his utter loss,
> For whom all this was made, all this will soon
> Follow, as to him linked in weal and woe :

In woe then, that destruction wide may range !
To me shall be the glory sole among
The Infernal Powers, in one day to have marred
What He, Almighty styled, six days and nights
Continued making."
—*P. L.*, ix. 115–119, 122–125, 129–138.

The resemblance between these extracts and the Vondelian passage is very strong both in general character and individual expressions. This simile, which occurs in the passage descriptive of the approach of the Serpent to Eve, coming as it does in this same portion of Paradise Lost, affords a sufficiently close parallel to that which closes our quotation—

"Sidelong he works his way,
As when a ship by skilful steersman wrought,
In Niger river's mouth or foreland, where the wind
Veers oft, as oft so steers and shifts her sail."
—*P. L.*, ix. 510–513.

Another parallel is given below.

The following lines from Moloch's speech in the Hellish Council, though taken from the second book, show so remarkable an affinity with a portion of our extract from the "Adam," that we may fairly conjecture that here also revision or interpolation may have taken place—

"More destroyed than thus,
We should be quite abolished and expire.
What fear we then ? What, doubt we to incense
His utmost ire ? which, to the height enraged,
Will either quite consume us, and reduce
To nothing this essential—happier far
Than miserable to have eternal being !
Or, if our substance be indeed divine,
And cannot cease to be, we are at worst
On this side nothing ; and by proof we feel

> Our power sufficient to disturb His Heaven
> And with perpetual inroads to alarm,
> Though inaccessible, His fatal throne :
> Which, if not victory, is yet revenge."
>
>   *—P. L.*, ii. 92–106.

And again at the end of the same book appears the nautical simile referred to above—

> " Satan with less toil and now with ease
> Wafts on the calmer wave with dubious light,
> And, like a weather-beaten vessel, holds
> Gladly the port, though shrouds and tackle torn."
>
>   *—P. L.*, ii. 1041–1044.

We translate a further passage from Lucifer's soliloquy—

> *" He from suspicion here a heavenly watch,*
> *To curb the realm of darkness, set,*
> *Who should protect this spot and share*
> *Man's danger : thus we stoop to work*
> *By stealth ere they be rousèd to resist."*—i. 56–60.

Satan, in similar language, complains that God—

> " Subjected to his (man's) service angel wings
> And flaming ministers, to watch and tend
> Their earthly charge. Of these the vigilance
> I dread, and to elude, thus wrapt in mist
> Of midnight vapour, glide obscure."
>
>   *—P. L.*, ix. 155–159.

Lucifer proceeds—

> *" Yet 'tis too soon. One must the second spring*
> *Not make at hazard, since the first hath failed.*
> *Tread then more softly and occasion seek*
> *Most opportune, from whence and how one best*
> *By daylight the Creator may assail*
> *In some one of His creatures, great or small.*
> *All damage tends to gain. One must begin*

By gradual steps, and from below ascend
And mount on high.   Who steadily ascends
At last his object strikes and thence recoils.
Push on a ripe resolve ; that wins a stroke.
Let's see what hap the opening day will bring.
The rising sun will fill this pleasant seat
With life and colour.   Adam and his wife
Will through this garden, rich with varied bloom,
Walk hand in hand, scarce less than angels blest,
Their every need from God's full bosom poured.
One must their mutual converse note from far,
And spy what means best serve us to assail
And hurt these creatures.   In some corner hid,
Attend what is forbidden, what enjoined,
On pain of life or death ; for the Supreme
Is friend to none but those who serve to swell
His love for glory and renown.   One cause
Why you, my Heavenly comrades, down to Hell
Were thrust as rebels."—i. 71-93.

The ninth book of Paradise Lost contains the following—

> " Thus the orb he roamed,
> With narrow search and with inspection deep
> Considered every creature, which of all
> Most opportune might serve his wiles."
>
> —*P. L.*, ix. 82-85.

Satan, in lines already quoted, tells how, to elude the
vigilance of the cherubic watch, he must, wrapt in mist
of midnight vapour, glide obscure—

> " Pry
> In every bush and brake, where hap may find
> The serpent sleeping, in whose mazy folds
> To hide me and the dark intent I bring.
>
> .   .   .   .
>
> But what will not ambition and revenge
> Descend to ?   Who aspires must down as low

K

As high he soared, obnoxious, first or last,
To basest things. Revenge, at first though sweet,
Bitter ere long, back on itself recoils.
Let it ; I reck not, so it light well aimed,
Since higher I fall short, on him who next
Provokes my envy, this new favourite
Of Heaven, this man of clay."
—*P. L.*, ix. 159–162, 168–176.

We hold that this passage openly proclaims its Vondelian origin ; its language simply re-echoes that of the first part of our quotation. Proceeding, we next find Satan, like Lucifer—

" Waiting close the approach of morn."
—*P. L.*, ix. 191.

The description of morning in Paradise follows—

" Now whenas sacred light began to dawn
In Eden on the humid flowers, . . .
. . . . Forth came the human pair,
And joined their vocal worship to the quire
Of creatures wanting voice."
—*P. L.*, x. 192–195, 197–199.

With this we must take—

" O earth ! how like to Heaven, if not preferred
More justly, seat worthier of gods."
—*P. L.*, ix. 99–100.

In the tenth book we find Satan acting just as Lucifer said he would act—

" He, after Eve seduced, unminded slunk
Into the wood fast by, and changing shape
To observe the sequel, saw his guileful act
By Eve, though all unweeting, seconded
Upon her husband."—*P. L.*, x. 332–336.

And flying from the Son of God—

" Returned
By night, and listening where the hapless pair
Sat in their sad discourse and various plaint,
Thence gathered his own doom."—*P. L.*, x. 341-344.

The scornful words with which our extract concludes
are but a compendious form of one of Satan's answers
to our Saviour in Paradise Regained—

" He seeks glory,
And for His glory all things made, all things
Orders and governs ; nor content in Heaven
By all His angels glorified, requires
Glory from men—from all men, good or bad ;

.   .   .   .

From us, His foes pronounced, glory He exacts."
—*P. R.*, iii. 110-114, 120.

It will be noted that almost the entire soliloquy of
Satan from the ninth book has been here placed under
contribution, and, with its immediate context, is, in fact,
a kind of revised version of (what may be styled) the
prologue to the Dutch play.

It is otherwise with the rest of the first act, and with
the second, third, and first part of the fourth acts of
Adam in Banishment. These have little or nothing in
common with the corresponding portion of Paradise Lost.
The material which either poet has used is necessarily
Biblical, but here the resemblance ceases. The language,
the play of fancy, the turns of thought, are diverse and
independent.

The latter portion of the drama, on the contrary, is
once more rich in coincidences with the end of the
ninth and greater part of the tenth books of Paradise
Lost.

This result, apparently so anomalous, is not far to

seek.   Milton had already completed to his satisfaction
the story of the Temptation and Fall of man before
Vondel's play came into his hands.   The effect of
acquaintance with it would doubtless be shown, precisely as it is shown, by a marked change in the
relationship of the two poems to each other.   We pass
suddenly from a portion of Paradise Lost, which
bears no traces of "borrowings" from the corresponding portion of the "Adam," to another which has an
exactly opposite character.   Knowing, as we do ap-
proximately, the date of the publication of the Dutch
play, and that the ninth book of Paradise Lost was
in all probability composed some six or seven months
afterwards, we find that all the facts dovetail one into
another, and satisfy all the requirements and tests alike
of external and internal evidence.

In the first extract we give from the fourth act of the
"Adam," Eve tempts her husband to share in her act of
trespass—

> "*Am I your flesh and bone ?*
> *Then bear you as a man, and let us live*
> *Joined in one lot.   I offer gifts divine.*
> *Your knowledge thus shall to the stars ascend,*
> *And you become in wisdom like to God.*
> *Make use of your free-will, and show we now*
> *The first-fruits of your love, and grant my prayer.*
> *Deny me not.   Compliance getteth peace.*"

—iv. 1322–1329.

Thus Eve to Adam in Paradise Lost—

> "This tree is   .   .   . of divine effect
> To open eyes, and make them gods who taste.
>
> .   .   .   .
>
> Thou, therefore, also taste, that equal lot
> May join us, equal joy as equal love."

P. L., ix. 865–866, 881–882

And again—

> "One heart, one soul in both ; whereof good proof
> This day affords, declaring thee resolved
>
> .   .   .   .
>
> To undergo with me one guilt, one crime,
> If any be, of tasting this fair fruit,
> Whose virtue .   .   . hath presented
> This happy trial of thy love."
> —*P. L.*, ix. 967–968, 971–975.

Eve's words of reproach at a later time are a comment on the last lines of the extract—

> "Too facile then, thou didst not much gainsay ;
> Nay, didst permit, approve, and fair dismiss."
> —*P. L.*, ix. 1158–1159.

The next quotation represents Adam in doubt—

> *"Oh, what a strife! Here woman stands ; there God.*
> *Here prayers besiege ; there stern forbiddance lowers.*
> *Shall I the love of my fond wife forego,*
> *Or Heavenly favour to disfavour change ?*
> *A tempest rages fierce within my soul."*—iv. 1338-1342.

The effects of Adam's yielding are thus represented in Paradise Lost—

> "She embraced him, and for joy
> Tenderly wept, much won that he his love
> Had so ennobled as of choice to incur
> Divine displeasure for her sake."—*P. L.*, ix. 990–994.

The following line describes Adam as—

> "In a troubled sea of passion tost."—*P. L.*, x. 717.

And again—

> "High winds worse within
> Began to rise, . . . and shook sore
> Their inward state of mind."—*P. L.*, ix. 1122-1125.

The Vondelian Eve reproaches her husband—

> *" Another rib lies nearer to your heart,*
> *That God may fashion you another wife,*
> *Such as you like."*—iv. 1383-1385.

The Miltonic Adam answers the reproach—

> " Should God create another Eve, and I
> Another rib afford, yet loss of thee
> Would never from my heart."—*P. L.*, ix. 911-914.

The fifth act of the " Adam " opens with a dialogue between Lucifer and his follower, Asmode, who describes to his chief the effects of the Fall, of which he had been an eye-witness. He tells how the demons drove the guilty pair to hide their shame and nakedness in the thorns and thickets, and then proceeds—

> *" We tore*
> *The white robe of their pristine innocence.*
> *There lie the fugitives besmeared with mire*
> *And stained with drops of blood. They weep and cry.*
> *We heard them, each the other for this crime*
> *With curses blaming. Eden loud resounds*
> *With piteous lamentations. Adam tears*
> *His face in his despair, and from his head*
> *Uproots the hair, and wakes the echoes round,*
> *Thus crying loud : How have I fallen ! how !*
> *It was my Enemy, and not my bride,*
> *To whom I lent mine ear. My flesh hath played*
> *Me traitor. I have followed evil paths.*
> *Vile appetite hath wounded with its sting*
> *My wife and me in turn. Alas ! this comes*
> *From love of woman. My own rib and flesh*
> *Hath me betrayed : such love costs far too dear."*
>
>   —v. 1485-1499.

Milton likewise recounts the effects of the Fall upon our first parents—

" Innocence, that as a veil
Had shadowed them from knowing ill, was gone."
            —*P. L.*, ix. 1054-1055.

" If this be to know
Which leaves us naked thus, of honour void,
Of innocence, of faith and purity,
Our wonted ornaments now soiled and stained,
And in our faces evident the signs
Of foul concupiscence."—*P. L.*, ix. 1073-1078.

" Not at rest or ease of mind,
They sat them down to weep. Nor only tears
Rained at their eyes, but high winds worse within
Began to rise, high passions—anger, hate,
Mistrust, suspicion, discord."—*P. L.*, ix. 1122-1126.

" Thus Adam to himself lamented loud.

. . . .

. . . .   On the ground
Outstretched he lay, on the cold ground, and oft
Cursed his creation."—*P. L.*, x. 845, 850-852.

" O woods, O fountains, hillocks, dales, and bowers !
With other echo late I taught your shades
To answer and resound far other song."
            —*P. L.*, x. 860-862.

The latter portion of the extract, in which Adam
accuses his wife and denounces female love, has its
counterpart in the passage which follows—

" Out of my sight, thou serpent ! That name best
Befits thee, with him leagued, thyself as false
And hateful. . . . . .

. . . . . .

Fooled and beguiled—by him thou, I by thee,
To trust thee from my side, imagined wise,
Constant, mature, proof against all assaults,
And understood not all was but a show
Rather than solid virtue, all but a rib
Crooked by nature, . . . from me drawn.

  .   .   .   Oh, why did God,
Creator wise, that peopled high Heaven
With spirits masculine, create at last
This novelty on earth, this fair defect
Of nature ?"—*P. L.*, x. 867–869, 880–892.

The next quotation is a continuation of Adam's lament—

"*Ambition hath destroyed and lured me on.*
Demons of Hell rise up to seize their own.
I feel e'en now my limbs by war disturbed ;
The flesh strives with the spirit.   Reason, will,
And understanding, shaken unawares,
Fell all too late with crushing terror struck.
Woes from without I feel and woes within."

         —v. 1502–1508.

With this compare—

"To Satan only like, both crime and doom.
O conscience ! into what abyss of fears
And horrors hast thou driven me !"

       —*P. L.*, x. 841–843.

The continuation of a passage which has already been brought forward has a particularly close verbal similarity to the lines of Vondel—

"Began to rise high passions—anger, hate,
Mistrust, suspicion, discord, and shook sore
Their inward state of mind, calm region once
And full of peace, now tost and turbulent :
For understanding ruled not, and the will
Heard not her love, both in subject now
To sensual appetite, who from beneath,
Usurping over sovran reason, claimed
Superior sway."—*P. L.*, ix. 1123–1131.

And again—

> " These were from without
> The growing miseries, which Adam saw
> Already in part, though hid in gloomiest shade,
> To sorrow abandoned, but worse felt within."
>
> —*P. L.,* x. 714-717.

The next quotation contains the bitter interchange of taunt and reproach between Adam and his wife—

> " *Eve. Shift then your guilt upon my neck alone.*
> *Ad. Cause of my fall and of mishaps so great*
> *Thereout to spring! this comes of wedded bonds.*
> *Our marriage was not sealed on terms like these.*
>
> .   .   .   .
>
> *Eve. Man should in piety his wife excel.*
> *Ad. Let this accursed tree its witness bear*
> *Who first, decoyed by the forbidden fruit,*
> *Durst bring a stain on Eden's purity.*
> *Eve. The weaker sex to sudden passion yields.*
> *Ad. Your fatal passion hath destroyed my peace.*
> *Eve. Man, as the head, should exercise restraint,*
> *And firmly stand when womankind gives way.*"
>
> —v. 1566-1578.

The similar dispute at the end of the ninth book of Paradise Lost runs on lines identical with the above—

> " *Ad.* Would thou hadst hearkened to my words, and stayed
> With me, as I besought thee, when that strange
> Desire of wandering, this unhappy morn,
> I know not whence possessed thee. We had then
> Remained still happy."—*P. L.,* ix. 1134-1138.

> " *Eve.* Imput'st thou that to my default, or will
> Of wandering, as thou call'st it ?   .   .
>
> .   .   .   .
>
> Being as I am, why didst not thou, the head,
> Command me absolutely not to go,
> Going into such danger as thou saidst ?
>
> .   .   .   .

Hadst thou been firm and fixed in thy dissent,
Neither had I transgressed, nor thou with me."
          —*P. L.*, ix. 1145–1146, 1155–1157, 1160–1161.

" *Ad.*   Thus it shall befall
Him who to worth in women overtrusting,
Lets her will rule : restraint she will not brook."
                    —*P. L.*, ix. 1182–1185.

And again, in the next book, Adam laments the creation of woman—

" This mischief had not then befallen,
And more that shall befall—innumerable
Disturbances on earth through female snares."
                    —*P. L.*, x. 895–897.

He describes himself as—

" Linked and wedlock bound
To a fell adversary, his hate or shame :
Which infinite calamity shall cause
To human life, and household peace confound."
                    —*P. L.*, x. 905–908.

Adam is the speaker in the next extract. His words recall at once the soliloquy of Milton's Adam in the tenth book of Paradise Lost—

" *So drags the instant pleasure of an hour*
Behind it a long chain of griefs and woes.
Life offers me no satisfaction more.
My fancy pictures to me dreadful Death,
Who hideous scowls where'er I go or stay.
Oh, open wide your lap ! receive me, Earth,
For all my pleasure now is past and gone !
Receive me once again !   From you I came ;
To you the body comes.   The spirit takes its flight
And seeks some secret dwelling-place, to which
A doom of justice bears it for misuse
Of blessings from above.   Why tarries Death ?

Life is repellent to me; the dismal night
Far dearer than the day; so open is
My shame. If it may be my lot to die,
Avert it not, since Death is cause for joy."

—v. 1587–1600.

The parallel passage furnishes the following citation—

" O fleeting joys
Of Paradise, dear bought with lasting woes !

.   .   .   .

.   .   .   . His doom is fair,
That dust I am, and shall to dust return.
O welcome hour whenever ! Why delays
His hand to execute what His decree
Fixed on this day ? Why do I overlive ?
Why am I mocked with death and lengthened out
To deathless pain ? How gladly would I meet
Mortality, my sentence, and be earth
Insensible ! how glad would lay me down
As in my mother's lap ! There I should rest.

.   .   .   . Yet one doubt
Pursues me still—lest all I cannot die ;
Lest that pure breath of life, the spirit of man,
Which God inspired, cannot together perish
With this corporeal clod. Then in the grave,
Or in some other dismal place, who knows
But I shall die a living death !"

—*P. L.*, x. 741–742, 769–779, 782–788.

We give, as the last excerpt from the "Adam," the
lines in which Eve begs for pardon from her husband—

" *Eve. The snake seduced me with his subtil tricks.*
Ad. Thou art the subtil snake who cause my death.
Eve. .   .   .   .

If these my tears and prayers submissive fail
To move you, then permit me, on my plaint,
That I with you and at your side may die,

Because to me there is no charm in life
Without your fellowship.   My share in fault
I seek not to disown.   My appetite
Incited you to this unhappy fate.
Then let us, linked together in one lot,
Pay our due penalty for such a crime."

—v. 1621–1633.

With the first two lines may be compared—

"Out of my sight, thou serpent!   That name best
Befits thee, with him leagued, thyself as false
And hateful,"—*P. L.,* x. 867–869,

with the supplication of Eve—

"Eve
Not so repulsed, with tears that ceased not flowing
And tresses all disordered, at his feet
Fell humble, and, embracing them, besought
His peace, and thus proceeded in her plaint :
Forsake me not thus, Adam ! witness Heaven
What love sincere and reverence in my heart
I bear thee, and unweeting have offended,
Unhappily deceived ! Thy suppliant,
I beg and clasp thy knees ; bereave me not,
Whereon I live, thy gentle looks, thy aid,
My only strength and stay.   Forlorn of thee,
Whither shall I betake me, where subsist ? "

—*P. L.,* x. 909–921.

A few lines from Eve's soliloquy after partaking of
the fruit complete our list of coincidences—

"Confirmed, then, I resolve
Adam shall share with me in bliss or woe.
So dear I love him, that with him all deaths
I could endure, without him live no life."

—*P. L.,* ix. 830–834.

These selected quotations from Adam in Banishment prove that a more than chance agreement sub-

sists, both in character and phraseology, between the soliloquy with which the play opens and the analogous soliloquy of Satan in the ninth book of Paradise Lost, and between that part of the play and that part of the Epic which deals with the disputes between Adam and his wife consequent on their act of sin. The influence which it exerted on Milton's mind has left marked traces behind it, but to a much less extent than in the case of the Lucifer, or even of Joannes Boetgezant. The "Adam," in truth, came into the English poet's hands too late, and was in itself, despite its lyrical beauties, not of sufficiently intrinsic merit to leave that same strong impress upon the pages of Paradise Lost, as that splendid work of imagination to which, in his advanced old age, its author designed it as a sequel.

CHAPTER VII.

SAMSON.

THE entire originality of the "Samson Agonistes" has never been seriously questioned. Todd, who discusses so elaborately the history of the controversy as to the origin of " Paradise Lost," devotes but a single page (of his Appendix to the " Samson ") to showing how slight are the grounds for supposing that certain obscure poems upon the subject, whose titles he gives, had ever been read by Milton;[1] nor in any later commentator, English or Dutch, upon Milton or upon Vondel, have we ever seen the suggestion made that in the composition of his drama upon " Samson " the English writer might possibly be under obligations to any Dutch work.

Yet there is a Vondelian drama entitled " Samson," which was published in the year 1660, that is to say, eleven years before " Samson Agonistes " issued from the press, and *at least* five before its composition was commenced.

We have already established the fact of Milton's knowledge of the Dutch language and intimate acquaintance with several of Vondel's works, and have proved that throughout " Paradise Lost," and in many parts of " Paradise Regained," the subtle influence of the

[1] Todd's " Milton," vol. iv. p. 498.

writings of the Dutch poet upon the mind of his great
contemporary is to be traced, now in the main plot,
now in some episode, now in metaphors, in imagery,
in mere verbal reminiscences. The mere fact, then,
that a Vondelian drama upon the story of Samson
had been published six or seven years before the writing of the "Samson Agonistes" would appear to be a
striking and suggestive coincidence, and one to stimulate
critical inquiry ; and the coincidence seems still more
striking when upon examination we perceive'that each
play is framed on the same antique Greek model, and
that each deals solely with the events of the last day
of Samson's life. A *prima facie* case is made out,
which demands further and more detailed investigation.

The merits and demerits of the "Samson Agonistes"
have been very variously assessed by different critics.
With the question, however, of its excellence from the
purely literary standpoint we have here no concern.
It suffices us to note the two special characteristics,
which give to this poem a remarkable interest. These
are—(1.) the personal element, which is inwoven into
and runs throughout the whole drama ; (2.) its form,
which aims at reproducing a tragedy modelled upon
those of Ancient Greece. Let us consider each of these
points separately, and discuss their bearing upon the
connection which we seek to establish between Milton's
work and that of Vondel upon the same subject. "In
one point of view," to quote the words of Mr. Hayley,[1]
"the 'Samson Agonistes' is the most singularly affect-
ing composition that was ever produced by sensibility
of heart or vigour of imagination. To give it this parti-

[1] Todd's "Milton," vol. iv. p. 495.

cular effect, we must remember that the lot of Milton
had a marvellous coincidence with that of his hero in
three remarkable points: first, he had been tormented
by a beautiful but disobedient and disaffectionate wife;
secondly, he had been the great champion of his
country, and as such the idol of public admiration;
lastly, he had fallen from that height of unrivalled
glory, and had experienced the most humiliating
reverse of fortune. In delineating the greater part of
Samson's sensations under calamity he had only to describe his own," &c. And Mr. Masson,[1] who treats the
subject at great length, thus concludes his argument:
" Nothing put forth by Milton in verse in his whole
life is so vehement an exhibition of his personality,
such a proclamation of his own thoughts about himself, as his ' Samson Agonistes.' The Hebrew Samson
among the Philistines, and the English Milton among
the Londoners of the reign of Charles II., were, to all
poetic intents, one and the same person."

It is, in fact, needless to multiply authorities or to
furnish independent proofs from the drama itself of the
existence of this strong personal element, since upon
this question there is no difference of opinion among
Miltonic commentators.

In the list of subjects which Milton had drawn up
in 1641 as containing possible materials for tragedies
we find the following :—

" No. 17. Samson Marrying, or in Ramath-Lechi."
" No. 18. Samson Pursophorus, or Hybristes, or Dagmalia."

A quarter of a century later the poet selected the last

---

[1] Masson's " Life of Milton," vol. vi. p. 670.

of these, dealing with the story of the last day of Samson's life, because he discerned in the Jewish hero,

"Blind, disheartened, shamed, dishonoured, quelled,"

the counterpart of himself in his humiliation, poverty, and want of sight. The drama was the outpouring of the anguish of his soul, bruised and dejected by the events of the Restoration and the sorrows of his own life.

But while we have no hesitation in saying that Milton chose the "Dagmalia" for dramatic treatment from a feeling that in it he had the materials wherewith to frame a fictive representation of his own personal griefs, we none the less venture confidently to assert that it was Vondel's poem which first suggested to him the fitness of the theme. For, curiously enough, when we turn from the "Samson Agonistes" to the Dutch drama, we find the personal element, which can be traced throughout, to be the key to the full understanding of the work.

Vondel, indeed, was not blind, but in every other respect his position, at the time when he composed this drama, bore a closer analogy to the mournful lot of Samson than did that of the English poet during his residence at Artillery Walk, Bunhill.

Born in 1587, a veteran in years, but still in full possession of his great intellectual faculties, the illustrious Vondel in 1658 was, as we have already described him,[1] the acknowledged head, the pride and glory, of the most brilliant age of Dutch literature. He had shown himself to be a master in every species of poetical writing, dramatic, lyrical, religious, didactic, satirical. *Nihil tetigit, quod non ornavit.* But, above all things,

---

[1] *Supra*, c. ii. p. 21.

L

he was a supreme singer, one of the most gifted lyrical
poets of his own, perhaps of any, age.[1] Had the
literary language which he created, and whose re-
sources he wielded with such consummate ease and
prodigal power, retained to our own times its short-
lived inspiration, there can be but little doubt the
name of Vondel would now have not a provincial, but
a world-wide reputation.

In his personal character the poet was chiefly remarkable for his unostentatious disposition and his
regular habits and domestic attachments. He had
very deep religious convictions, and became in later
years a devoted adherent of Roman Catholicism. He
had passed his life in ceaseless literary toil, but, despite
his high merits and the patronage of princes and nobles,
who, as is so frequently the case, gave but few tangible
proofs of their favours, he had not in his old age
succeeded in securing for himself more than a modest
competency. After his wife's death in 1635, he continued to live at Amsterdam with his two surviving
children, a son called after his own name, and a
daughter named Anna. This son was from his child-
hood a source of trouble to his father, and, as he grew
up, he showed himself to be both dissolute and stupid.
The story is told of him, that once when Vondel's
tragedy upon Joseph in Dothan was being discussed in
his presence, he inquired " whether Joseph were a
Catholic ? " [2]

He[3] married young, and had two children, but, un-

---

[1] On this see especially " De Reizangen in Vondel's Treurspelen door
Nicholas Beets."

[2] Brandt's " Leven van J. V.," pp. 80-83.

[3] Joost the younger.

fortunately, his wife died. He thereupon took to himself in second wedlock a woman of profligate habits, a very Delilah, who played upon her husband's weaknesses, and incited him to the greatest irregularities.[1] His father, who about this time had made a metrical version of the Psalms of David, was so afflicted by his son's extravagance and disgraceful conduct, that he was heard to say, "that were it not for the consolation which he derived from the Psalms, he would have died from wretchedness."

But the worst was not yet come. The prodigal became immersed in debt. He squandered all his own substance, and also large sums which he borrowed from others. He found himself utterly ruined and compelled to fly the country. At this point his father came forward to lend him a helping hand, and to give him a chance of reformation by paying his debts and sending him as an emigrant to the East Indies. The graceless young man departed, and died upon the voyage. His father sacrificed at least 40,000 florins, the whole of his modest savings, in satisfying the creditors, and, at the age of seventy-one, found himself penniless.

Too proud to make application for assistance to his many powerful patrons, none of whom now came forward to give him help in this sore time of unmerited distress, Vondel obtained through some connections of his wife the humble post of book-keeper at the city pawnbroking bank, at a salary of 680 florins a year.[2]

In this servile position had the noble old man to

[1] Her name was Baertgen Hooft. For a more favourable view of her character see "Vondel's Portretten" door A. Thijm, pp. 89-120.

[2] See "Een dichter aan de bank van leening." Tooneelspel, 1867, door J. van Lennep.

spend ten long weary years, sitting at his desk from
morning till night in discharge of his task of mechanical
drudgery. But even now, oppressed by the weight of
years and calamity, he did not neglect the service of
the Muses. The pen which in the daytime entered
pledges in the ledger, at night was employed in trans-
cribing the "Jephtha," the "Samson," and the other
dramas and poems which were composed during this
trying time.[1]

The "Samson" was written when Vondel had now
been toiling for about two years at his humiliating
occupation. It is scarcely possible to doubt but that
the choice of subject was dictated by the poet's sense
of the analogy between his own fallen condition and
that of the Jewish hero, a captive among the Philistines
and condemned to labour at the public mill. But we
are not left to mere conjecture. The following passage,
which occurs in the dedicatory preface to the play, places
the matter in the clearest light :—"The hero, Samson,
endowed by the Almighty with such invincible might
and strength, was at last disarmed through the wanton
charms of a profligate woman, to warn reckless youth
to be on their guard against the seductive attractions
of fickle beauties, whereby so many worthy men have
fallen low. I judge it not unserviceable to represent
Samson in his humiliation, in order to keep back
wanton spirits from irregularities, and to teach them
to use the gifts which spring from God to His honour."

Who can fail here to read between the lines the
unmistakable references to the history of his unfortu-

[1] This period of ten years was the most prolific of Vondel's life.
Between his seventieth and eightieth year he published about 35,000
lines of poetry, including the finest half of his lyrical compositions.
Thijm's "Portretten," p. 168.

nate son, and the grievous consequences which in his own case had followed "from reckless youth being seduced by the charms of a profligate woman"?

But we must not dwell any longer upon this point, however interesting. We shall in the sequel point out several passages in the play which bear out our contention. As we are not writing a biography of Vondel, we here confine ourselves strictly to our thesis.

> " Qui farem punto, come buon fattone,
> Che, com 'egli ha del panna, fa la gonna." [1]

We proceed to the consideration of that which has always been held to be the distinguishing characteristic of "Samson Agonistes," its dramatic form.[2] Milton himself in his preface, entitled "Of that sort of Dramatic Poem called Tragedy," thought it necessary to give an explanation of the method he has adopted.

He begins by defending himself against the Puritan dislike to stage-plays by "vindicating tragedy from the small esteem, or rather infamy, which in the account of many it undergoes at this day, with other common interludes," and then dwells upon the fact that "in the modelling of this poem, with good reason, the ancients and Italians are followed, as of much more authority and fame," and concludes by asserting that "of the style and uniformity and that commonly called the plot . . . they only will best judge who are not unacquainted with Æschylus, Sophocles, and Euripides, the three tragic poets unequalled yet by any, and the best rule to all who endeavour to write tragedy." Upon

---

[1] Dante, "Paradiso," cant. xxxii. 139.

[2] See the Essays from Johnson's "Rambler" and Cumberland's "Observer" which are given in Todd's "Milton," vol. iv. pp. 344-357.

this Mr. Masson makes the following comment:[1]—
"'Samson Agonistes,' therefore, was offered to the world
as a tragedy of a different order from that which had
been established in England. It was a tragedy of the
severe classic order, according to that noble Greek
model, which had been kept up by none of the modern
nations, unless it might be the Italians."

Now we have already stated that one of our *prima
facie* grounds for investigating the possible connection
between the "Samson Agonistes" and Vondel's drama
upon the same subject lay in the fact that both plays
were composed after the rules and regulations of the
ancient Greek tragedy. Yet such a statement about a
Dutch work appears to be considerably at variance
with the language of Milton's preface and of Mr.
Masson's Introduction. The one implies, the other
asserts, that "tragedy of the severe classic order according to the noble Greek model had been kept up by
none of the modern nations, unless it might be the
Italians." In the face, then, of so positive an assertion,
we feel that, before we venture to base any argument
upon our statement as to Vondel's method, we must be
prepared to verify our facts and array our evidence.
We proceed to do so.

Born of humble parentage, Vondel's early education
had been somewhat neglected, but he supplied his
deficiencies in later life by an application and persever-
ance which were prodigious. He acquired a familiar
acquaintance with the French, German, and Italian
languages, and then, at the age of twenty-six, under the
able guidance of his accomplished friend Hugo Grotius,
the indefatigable student turned his attention to Latin;

[1] "Milton's Poetical Works," vol. ii. p. 93.

and yet four years later he commenced the task of learning Greek. And he was not satisfied with a merely superficial knowledge of these tongues. He made himself thoroughly at home with the masterpieces of classical literature. He rendered the whole of Virgil into Dutch verse, and some portions as many as three times; and afterwards translated in a similar manner the greater part of Horace, of Ovid, and other Latin poets; and at intervals during his long life he occupied his leisure-time in giving Dutch metrical versions of a number of Greek plays.[1] His last literary efforts were his translation of the "Phœnissæ" and "Trachiniæ," at the age of eighty-two, and a paraphrase of the "Metamorphoses" of Ovid two years later.[2]

Now his primary object in undertaking these tasks was not so much to make known the Greek and Latin authors to his countrymen, but to familiarise himself with their thoughts, their style, and their diction, and, in the case of the dramatists, with their form.[3] Commencing his literary life at a time when religious mysteries and moralities (Spelen van Zinne) represented the highest dramatic art and were the only public spectacles, Vondel deliberately set himself to the task of reforming the popular tastes and restoring to the drama something of the elevation and dignity, both in matter and manner, of the classic tragedy.

All his earlier plays, and notably the "Palamedes" and the "Gysbrecht van Amstel," were avowedly imi-

---

[1] "Electra" of Sophocles, 1639; "Œdipus Rex," 1660; "Iphigenia in Tauris," 1666; "Phœnissæ" and "Trachiniæ," 1669.

[2] Brandt's "Leven," p. 67.

[3] Vondel, unfortunately for his style, became acquainted with the so-called plays of Seneca before those of the Greek dramatists. He translated "Hecuba," 1625; "Hippolytus," 1628.

tations of the best Greek examples,[1] and are modelled in accordance with the rules of Aristotle and Horace. One of the chief features of the Vondelian drama is the large use made of the chorus.[2] The poet, feeling that in the choral odes he could give free play to his lyrical genius, has here freely indulged his natural bent; and in so doing, he alone, of all the modern writers of so-called classical tragedy, has grasped the fact that the Hellenic drama had its origin in rhythmic song, and that the choral ode is not an excrescence, but should gather round it the action and movement of the play. And so Vondel's chorus are not only singers, but, as in the classic drama, they act as interpreters of the action, mediators and moralists, and not unfrequently take part in the dialogue.[3]

How entirely original and self-evolved was this attempt of the Dutch poet to revive the best traditions of the Hellenic tragedy may be judged from the fact that Vondel was fifty years of age at the time of the appearance of Corneille's " Le Cid." [4] But Vondel was not satisfied with these his earlier efforts. He determined to write a play which should conform in all its minutest details to the Aristotelian requirements. The subject he selected was the story of the death of Jephtha's daughter, and the play appeared in 1659, the very year after his misfortunes, and the year before the publication of the "Samson."

---

[1] See " Commentatio de Græcæ Tragediæ ratione et Nobillissima Vondellii fabula Gysbrecht van Amstel ad eam exacta." Auctore P. Huët, 1821, p. 89, &c.

[2] " J. Vondel, Etude Historique et Litteraire," par l'Abbé A. Stillemans, pp. 16, 17.

[3] See at length N. Beet's " Reizangen van Vondel."

[4] " Dichter, J. Vondel," Du Bois, p. 39.

To this play, the " Jephtha," he contributes a somewhat lengthy preface (which may be compared to
Milton's preface to the " Samson Agonistes "), in which
he subjects his own tragedy to a close and critical
review, in order to show that in every respect it con-
forms to the required regulations; and he further
assures his readers that he has spared no pains to gain
the fullest information upon the subject. We quote
his own words. " In order," he says, " that we might
in no way fall short of our exemplar, we refreshed our
memory by reading over and re-reading the poetics of
Aristotle and of Horace, and the commentators upon
their works, such as Robertellus, Madius, Lombardus,
Scaliger, Heinsius, Hugo Grotius, Vossius," &c. He
concludes with the following quaint sentence :—" We
judge it not unserviceable to analyse this tragedy
in its details, that students tossed upon the waves of
dramatic authorship may use it as a stage-compass, so
as to avoid all the rocks and shoals of error, and shipwreck from unlawful constructions, and at length,
fully equipped, may sail into the wished-for haven of
the perfection of the dramatic art." A learned writer,
Jerome de Bosch, invokes this play in support of his
thesis that " great writers remain at their ease even
when tied down by the strictest rules." [1]

Vondel was accustomed at times, before commencing
a new work, to translate a Greek play, as if for the
purpose of perfecting and refining his art by close
study of the old masters. He thus translated the
" Electra " of Sophocles immediately before he wrote
his tragedy " De Maeghden," founded upon the history
of Saint Ursula; and after publishing (what may be

[1] Du Bois, p. 61.

called) his specimen play after the Greek model, the
" Jephtha," as if still not satisfied with the result, he
translated " Œdipus Rex " as a prelude to the composition of the " Samson."   It is just possible that the
fate of Œdipus may have suggested to Vondel's mind
the dramatic capabilities of the story of the blind
Jewish hero.   Certain it is that the influence of Sophocles can be traced in the second and third acts of the
" Samson."   The interview, in particular, between the
High Priest of Dagon and the Prophetess of Akkeron,
in which the former makes light of the portents and
the dubious reply of the oracle, recalls forcibly the
arrogant levity of Jocasta, and there are in this portion
of the play some passages of στιχομυθία which have a
peculiarly Sophoclean ring.

But we need not pursue the subject farther.   We have
now shown that the two most noticeable characteristics
of the " Samson Agonistes," the personal element which
runs through it and its dramatic form, modelled upon that
of the ancient Greek tragedy, are even more markedly
the special features of the " Samson " of Vondel.   We
know, further, that the Dutch play preceded the English
one by at least five years.   It only remains for us to
show from internal evidence that Milton was acquainted
with the language of Vondel's play in order to complete
the chain of evidence, and make it more than probable
that the one is the direct descendant of the other.

The first act of the earlier tragedy bears a considerable resemblance to what may be called the first act [1]
of the " Samson Agonistes."   Each commences with
a Euripidean prologue.   The speaker in the one case

[1] The " Samson Agonistes " naturally divides itself into parts, which
correspond to the five acts of the legitimate drama.

is Dagon, in the other, Samson, but, with an appropriate difference of tone, the matter of either soliloquy is the same. Dagon triumphs over his fallen foe and recites his great deeds in order to gloat over his present humiliation. Samson likewise dwells upon the glories of his past career, but in a spirit of self-reproach and utter despondency.

Vondel then begins the real action of his play by a short dialogue between Samson and his keeper, who guides the blind hero to a seat in a hollow oak, where he leaves him to breathe the air and enjoy the sun-light, while he proceeds to ask instructions from his superior at the court, where all the lords are gathered for Dagon's festival. "Samson Agonistes," as the following quotation will show, opens in an analogous manner—

SAMSON (*Attendant leading him*).

"A little onward lend thy guiding hand
To these dark steps, a little farther on ;
For yonder bank hath choice of sun or shade.
There am I wont to sit when any chance
Relieves me from my task of servile toil.
  .   .   .   Here I feel amends
The breath of heaven fresh blowing, pure, and sweet,
With day spring-born ; here leave me to respire.
This day a solemn feast the people hold
To Dagon, their sea-idol, and forbid
Laborious works ; unwillingly this rest
Their superstition leaves me."—1-5, 9-15.

A Chorus [1] in either case closes the act by moralisings over the triumph of idolaters and the fall of God's champion.

Again, in both the Dutch and English plays the opening of the second act discloses the Chorus finding

[1] Vondel's Chorus consists of Jewish maidens, Milton's of Danites.

Samson as he sits solitary in his blindness. Colloquies take place, certain passages of which contain close verbal similarities.

The Vondelian Chorus do not at first recognise the hero; they ask—

> "*What man sits in this oak in solitude*
> *Alone? He seems, to utter beggary*
> *Reduced, to beg of us an alms.*"—ii. 184.

Samson discovers himself and declares his miserable state; upon which the Chorus—

> "*God help us all! O what a sight for us!*
> *How can we fix our thoughts or credit it?*"—ii. 196-197.

Compare with these Milton's lines—

> "This, this is he; softly a while;
> Let us not break in upon him.
> O change beyond report, thought, or belief!
>
> .   .   .   .   .
>
> In slavish habits, ill-fitted weeds,
> O'erworn and soiled,
> Or do my eyes misrepresent?"—115-118, 121-124.

Samson's words—

> "*I have for many months, in fetters yoked,*
> *In the mill-prison here my sad time spent,*
> *Thus blind, as you may see, ill-used and aged,*"[1]
> —ii. 204-206,

recall these—

> "My task of servile toil
> Daily in the common prison else enjoined me,
> Where I, a prisoner chained, .   .
> Grind in brazen fetters under task,
>
> .   .   .   .   .   .

---

[1] These and other citations surely contain bitter personal allusions to the condition of the aged and destitute poet, condemned to unworthy drudgery in the pawnbroking office.

Blind among enemies. O worse than chains,
Dungeon, or beggary, or decrepit age,"—5-7, 35, 69-70,

taken from the opening soliloquy of " Samson Agonistes."

Samson (Vondel's) asks for a draught of water, which
is given him. The Chorus then inform him (exactly
as Milton's Chorus do under the same circumstances)
that they have come from his native land to offer consolation. The whole passage is so important in its
bearing upon the Miltonic question, that we translate
it at length.

Samson has just allayed his thirst and expresses his
gratitude—

" *Sam. When through God's power a fountain sprang*
From out the ass's jaw, I, parched in fight,
Refreshed my soul and drank. The wondrous fount
My anguish thus allayed. Upon you all
May Heaven's blessing rest for kindness done.
Chorus. Samson, our valorous prince, what pain is ours
To find you thus in miserable plight!
We, Jewish maidens, to this festival
Are come from East and West, to seek for you
And offer consolation, as the time,
And not our wish, give opportunity.
No brute's so shameless as a thankless man.
We owe, defender of our land, to thee
Help, service, honour; that we know.
O bear your sorrow patiently, till God
Dispose. What heart-ache! what sore agony!
Though sun refuse his light, God can your soul
Illumine with an inward flame more bright
Than sheen of thousand suns. Who can confine
The Might Supreme? He, who endowed your frame
With wondrous strength, concealed in your hair,
Is mighty, should He please, in you to work,
To arm and strengthen you, though shorn of locks."
—ii. 211-230.

At this point, for convenience we pause, and turn our attention to Milton's drama.

We first quote the words of Manoah to his son, which should be compared with the beginning and end of the extract—

> "God, who caused a fountain at thy prayer
> From the dry ground to spring, thy thirst t' allay
> After the brunt of battle, can as easy
> Cause light again within thine eyes to spring,
> Wherewith to serve Him better than thou hast ;
> And I persuade me so.   Why else this strength ·
> Miraculous yet remaining in those locks ?
> His might continues in thee not for nought,
> Nor shall His wondrous gifts be frustrate thus."
>   —580–589.

With this must be taken the following lines, which contain an image parallel with one of Vondel's—

> " But he, though blind of sight,
>   With inward eyes illuminated,
>   His fiery virtue roused
>   From under ashes into sudden flame."[1]
>   —1686–1689.

We now revert to the commencing lines spoken by the Chorus, and compare them with the words with which the corresponding Miltonic Chorus commence their address to Samson—

> " He speaks : let us draw nigh.   Matchless in might,
> The glory late of Israel, now the grief !
> We come, thy friends and neighbours not unknown,
> From Eshtaol and Zora's fruitful vale
> To visit or bewail thee ; or, if better,
> Counsel or consolation we may bring,
> Salve to thy sores."—178–184.

---

[1] See " Paradise Lost," iii. 50–54.

The answers of Samson contain two passages which are paraphrases on the Vondelian line which condemns ingratitude—

> " How counterfeit a coin are they who ' friends '
> Bear in their superscription (of the most
> I would be understood). In prosperous days
> They swarm, but in adverse withdraw their head."
>
> —190–193.

And again—

> " Whom God hath of His special favour raised
> As their deliverer ? If he aught begin,
> How frequent to desert him, and at last
> To heap ingratitude on worthiest deeds."—273–276.

We draw special attention to this, because we have here not only similarity of expression, but the same chain of thought. For Milton's Chorus proceed thus—

> " Tax not divine Disposal,"—210,

and moralise upon the theme—

> " Just are the ways of God,
>   And justifiable to men,"—293–294,

making use therein of Vondel's words in the line—

> " As if they would confine the Interminable."—307.

We conclude our analysis of this extract with the production of one more parallel passage—

> " God, when He gave me strength, to show withal
> How slight the gift was, hung it in my hair.
> But peace ! I must not quarrel with the will
> Of Highest Dispensation."—57–62.

The next quotation, which tells the story of Samson's hapless love, is almost continuous with the previous translation—

"*Sam.   O would I had from Philistine*[1] *women kept*
Aloof, by nature treacherous and false.
Well may I rue the day when I at length
In Sorec with Dalilah fell in love,
Light, wanton, full of greed.   To drift at will
On favour or disfavour of a wench
Is on a tranquil sea at time of need
To tarry long and venture recklessly.
She, who on promised offers turned her eyes,
By hostile gold seduced, both night and day
Pressed me with importunity to tell
The secret of my strength, all in her height
And glow of love ; a storming of their heart
Seldom by men withstood.   Had then, alas!
My mind as strong in native power and force,
Been as my body, I had firm remained ;
This must I needs confess.   Yet knew I well
How to delude her thrice and play her false."

—ii. 237-250.

The circumstances of the poet when he penned these lines, and the miserable ending of his prodigal son through the snares of a wanton woman, give to this excerpt an autobiographical interest and pathos.

We do not look in vain to that same dialogue between the Chorus and the Miltonic Samson, from which we have already quoted, and which corresponds in its position to this opening scene of Vondel's second act, for parallel passages—

" *Sam.*   The next I took to wife
(O that I never had ! fond wish too late)
Was in the Vale of Sorec, Dalilah,
That specious monster, my accomplished snare."

—227-230.

---

[1] Compare the scanning of this line with " Samson Agonistes," 577.

And immediately before—

> " Who, like a foolish pilot, have shipwrecked
> My vessel, trusted to me from above,
> Gloriously rigged, and for a word, a tear,
> Fool ! have divulged the secret gift of God
> To a deceitful woman. . . .
> Immeasurable strength they might behold
> In me ; of wisdom nothing more than mean.
> This with the other should at least have paired."
> —198-202, 206-209.

The regret at yielding to a deceitful woman, the comparison to a vessel endangered at sea, and of bodily with mental strength, are to be found in both writers. Once more a succession of ideas in common. Such co-incidences thus recurring can scarcely be due to chance.

There is, however, another and longer narrative in " Samson Agonistes " which tells of the treachery of Delilah. From this we now quote. The language will be seen to bear a close similarity to that of our translation—

> " In this other was there found
> More faith, who also in her prime of love,
> Spousal embraces, vitiated with gold,
> Though offered only, by the scent conceived
> Her spurious first-born, Treason against me !
> Thrice she essayed, with flattering prayers and sighs
> And amorous reproaches, to win from me
> My capital secret, in what part my strength
> Lay stored, in what part summed, that she might know ;
> Thrice I deluded her, and turned to sport
> Her importunity. .   .   .   .
> .   .   . She surceased not day nor night
> To storm me."—387-397, 404-405.

If there be one portion of " Samson Agonistes " which has been more quoted than another, it is that latter

M

portion of the hero's soliloquy in which he mourns the loss of his sight. This is the passage in which, more intensely than elsewhere, Milton seems to be giving utterance to the sorrows of his own heart, to his grief at the calamity which had befallen him. Yet, strangely enough, we discover some of the most characteristic expressions in this lament of Milton in the work of his predecessor in the same field, as will be seen in the two citations we now make, the one from the second, the other from the third act of Vondel's play. In the former, the Chorus (here playing the part of Manoah in the "Agonistes") are supplicating the Prince of Gaza on behalf of Samson, and, to excite his pity, dwell upon the greatness of the misfortunes which have brought the Jewish champion to such a miserable state. They acknowledge that the injuries he has done to the Philistines are beyond pardon—

> " *But the relentless fate which fell on him,*
> *The light extinct, in night of darkness sunk,*
> *What else is this than half his life to lose ?*
> *Half death he suffers, since, bereft of strength,*
> *The foeman bored out both his eyes.*"—ii. 484–488.

In the latter, it is Samson who declares that for him all favours are now in vain—

> " *No man, no prince can give me back mine eyes.*
> *I mourn my sight ; 'tis more than half the life.*
> *My daylight once for all hath set ; no more*
> *I hope for dawn ; eternal night is mine,*
> *Yet in the night all other creatures sleep*
> *And rest. Such rest shall Samson never see.*"
> 　　　　　　　　　　　　　　　—iii. 871–876.

The parallel passage of Milton is so familiar to all educated Englishmen that it appears almost superfluous to quote the well-known lines. We select only those which are necessary to establish the close resemblance between the language of the two poets—

> " But chief of all,
> O loss of sight, of thee I most complain !
> . . . .
> Sight, the prime work of God, to me is extinct.
> . . . .
> Inferior to the vilest now become
> Of man or worm, the vilest here excel me.
> . . . .
> Scarce half I seem to live, dead more than half.
> O dark, dark, dark,[1] amid the blaze of noon
> Irrecoverably dark, total eclipse,
> Without all hope of day.
> . . . .
> Then had I not been thus exiled from light,
> As in the land of darkness, yet in light,
> To live a life half dead, a living death."
>   —66–69, 73–74, 79–83, 97–100.

There is one other place where Milton's Samson utters a cry of despair, and here, too, there seems to be a reminiscence of the latter of the two extracts from Vondel—

> " Sleep hath forsook and given me o'er ;
> . . . . . .
> Thence faintings, swoonings of despair,
> And sense of Heaven's desertion
> . . . . . .
> Left me all helpless, with the irreparable loss
> Of sight. . . . .
> Nor am I in the list of them that hope ;
> Hopeless are all my evils, all remediless."
>   —629, 631–632, 644–645, 647–648.

The Chorus, in the course of their supplicatory inter-

---

[1] This seems a reminiscence of Vondel's " een nacht van duisternissen " —a night of darknesses.

view with the Prince above referred to, speak of
Samson as—

> *" This hapless man, ensnared, surprisèd, seized,*
> *Bereaved of heavenly light, with chains oppressed,*
> *To labour doomed, at stern taskmaster's will."*
>
> —ii. 569–571.

Compare the words of Manoah—

> " Ensnared, assaulted, overcome, led bound,
> Thy foes' derision, captive, poor, and blind,
> Into a dungeon thrust, to work with slaves."—365–368.

In the third act (Vondel) a dialogue takes place between the Princess of Gaza and the High Priest of
Dagon, the latter of whom, after some demur, agrees to
the wish of the Philistine lords that the Hebrew
prisoner should play before them at the festival—

> *" Princess. Through force of prayer the gods delivered him*
> *Into our hands.   Now all the lords desire*
> *That Samson at this solemn feast of joy,*
> *The enemy so late endowed with strength*
> *Invincible, on a triumphal stage*
> *Might in the temple play to Dagon's praise,*
> *And the delight of all.   .   .   .*
>
> .   .   .   .
>
> *Priest. Let Samson don fresh clothes.   Wide open set*
> *The place for public show.   We bless the play*
> *In honour of our god, great Dagon's name."*
>
> —iii. 756–761, 774–775.

Take with this the lines in which the officer in " Samson
Agonistes" commands the appearance of Samson at the
feast—

> " Samson, to thee our lords thus bid me say :
> This day to Dagon is a solemn feast,
> With sacrifices, triumph, pomp, and games ;
> Thy strength they know surpassing human rate,

And now some public proof thereof require
To honour this great feast and high assembly.
Rise, therefore, with all speed and come along,
Where I will see thee heartened and fresh clad."

—1310–1317.

And also the following words of Manoah—

" This day the Philistines a popular feast
Here celebrate in Gaza, and proclaim
Great pomp and sacrifice, and praises loud
To Dagon as their god, who hath delivered
Thee, Samson, bound and blind, into their hand :
So Dagon shall be magnified."—436–441.

Out of a number of such-like coincidences in language
and metaphor, which might be given from this portion
of the drama, we think it necessary to present but one
more, which is taken from a lyrical soliloquy which
Samson utters immediately before following his keeper
to the festival—

" *The angel of my birth descending,*
My drooping courage once more stayed,
As on my knees for strength I prayed,
Through all my limbs fresh vigour sending.
God's Spirit, which from mother's womb
Hath led me on to high achievement,
Bids me now calmly bear bereavement,
Prepares for me a glorious tomb."—iv. 1077–1084.

There are two passages of Milton to compare with
this, both lyrical. The farewell words of the Chorus
to Samson as he follows the officer run thus—

" Send thee the angel of thy birth to stand
Fast by thy side ;   .   .   .   .
     .   .   . That Spirit that first rushed on thee
In the camp of Dan,
Be efficacious in thee now at need,

> For never was from Heaven imparted
> Measure of strength so great to mortal seed
> As in thy wondrous action hath been seen."
>
> —1431–1432, 1435–1440.

The other comes from Samson's reverie, and the Chorus which follows, at the close of what may be styled Milton's second act—

> " I was his nursling once and choice delight,
>   His destined from the womb,
> Promised by Heavenly message twice descending.
>
> .   .   .   .
>
>   He led me on to mightiest deeds
>   Above the nerve of mortal arm.
>
> .   .   .   .
>
>   This one prayer yet remains, might I be heard,
>   No long petition—speedy death,
>   The close of all my miseries and the balm."

The Chorus moralise upon this, and state that though—

> " Many are the sayings of the wise
> Extolling patience as the truest fortitude,"

yet that such advice is of little avail to the sufferer—

> " Unless he feel within
> Some source of consolation from above,
> Secret refreshings that repair his strength
> And fainting spirits uphold."
>
> —633–636, 638–639, 649–654, 663–666.

And now, before we proceed to examine the fifth act of Vondel's drama, which has a stronger affinity to "Samson Agonistes" than any other portion of the play, except perhaps that which treats of the treachery of Delilah, we shall endeavour to render into their original metres two lyrical odes assigned to the High Priest of Dagon and the Choral Singers, whom he is addressing. They are interesting not merely from having numerous points of contact with Milton's poem, but as specimens, though far below the level of his best efforts, of Vondel's lyrical art.

The High Priest is the speaker, his audience the singers who are to take part in the sacred procession at Dagon's festival—

> " *Solemn pageantry along,*
>   *Graced of yore by play and song,*
> *To great Dagon's name redounding,*
> *For our mortal foe confounding.*
>   *Let the archers on the route*
>   *First advance with drum and flute,*
> *Festal horn and soft recorder.*
> *Then God's ministers in order,*
>   *Pair by pair, their stately ranks*
>   *Muster for this rite of thanks,*
> *And with oaken garlands crownèd,*
> *Duly keep this feast renownèd.*
>   *Let the quires their notes of praise*
>   *Blent with pipe and viol raise,*
> *In their wake blind Samson bringing,*
> *Torches flashing, censers swinging,*
>   *Followed by a gallant train.*
>   *Throned aloft on sacred wain,*
> *Dagon next, our shrine and treasure;*
> *We, submiss to do his pleasure,*
>   *March behind, and all the great*
>   *Chiefs and princes of the state,*
> *While lords and ladies, bright in hue,*
> *Form a long courtly retinue.*
>   *Sacred singers, forward press*
>   *On the path your god doth bless.*"
>
>   —iv. 1379–1404.

With these directions compare the account given by the Messenger in " Samson Agonistes " of this same festival—

> " As the gates I entered with sunrise,

The morning trumpets festival proclaimed
Through each high street.   .   .   .
    .   .   .   .   Immediately
Was Samson as a public servant brought,
In their state livery clad ; before him pipes
And timbrels ; on each side went armed guards ;
Both horse and foot before him and behind,
Archers and slingers, cataphracts and spears.
At sight of him the people with a shout
Rifted the air, clamouring their god with praise."
                    —1598-1600, 1614-1621.

The following is the hymn of praise in which the
Singers reply to the High Priest's injunctions—

" *Great is Dagon, Chief of Powers,*
    Who God's foeman unawares
    Hath encompassed in our snares,
At whose might each giant cowers.
    Who alone inspired dismay,
Swordless, all their arms disdaining,
Like a princely host campaigning,
    Marshalled in its deep array.

Great is Dagon, Chief of Powers,
    Who God's foeman led in bands
    And betrayed to hostile hands,
Shamed and blind, in harlot's bowers.
    See the champion sunk low,
Who Philistine armies scattered
And their pride in battle shattered ;
    See how Gaza triumphs now.

Great is Dagon, Chief of Powers,
    Who God's foeman, once for all,
    Brought to such a direful fall.
Quail not, friends, when Samson lowers ;
    At the hour of sacrifice,
On this temple stage inveighing,
Ye shall see him grimly playing
    His sad part in tragic guise."—iv. 1405-1428.

Now the text of this hymn, the refrain with which each verse begins, is precisely contained in the lines of Milton—

> " This day the Philistines a popular feast
> Here celebrate in Gaza, and proclaim
> Great pomp and sacrifice and praises loud
> To Dagon, as their god, who hath delivered
> Thee, Samson, bound and blind, into their hands,
> Them out of thine, who slew'st them many a slain."
> —433-438.

The speaker was Manoah, who shortly before had apostrophised his son—

> " O miserable change !   Is this the man,
> That invincible Samson, far renowned,
> The dread of Israel's foes, who with a strength
> Equivalent to angels walked their streets,
> None offering fight ; who single combatant
> Duelled their armies ranked in proud array,
> Himself an army ?"—340-346.

Even more nearly does the language of the first of the Miltonic choral odes recall that of Vondel—

> " Can this be he,
> That heroic, that renowned,
> Irresistible Sampson ? whom unarmed
> No strength of man . . . . could withstand ;
> Who   .   .   .   .   .   .
> Ran on embattled armies clad in iron,
> And, weaponless himself,
> Made arms ridiculous,
>
> .   .   .   .   .   .
> In scorn of their proud arms and warlike tools,
> Spurned them to death by troops."
> —123-127, 129-131, 137-138.

Even the line—

> " *At whose might each giant cowers* "—
> .

has its representative in the episode of Harpatha, of
whom the Chorus say—

"His giantship has gone somewhat crestfallen."—1244.

We now pass on to the consideration of the fifth act
of Vondel's play, which contains the account of the
revenge of Samson and the destruction of the Philistines. The narrative bears the most striking analogy
to that of the " Samson Agonistes," both as to the action
and the diction. In both poems (for the unity of place
is in both strictly maintained) the Chorus are represented as standing at some distance from the scene of
the catastrophe, and the tidings are brought by an
escaped spectator who is flying from the scene of destruction. Where the two writers differ in subordinate
details, it is generally through a stricter adherence on
the part of the Dutch writer to the facts of the Biblical
narrative.

In Vondel's account we are to imagine the Chorus
standing, as before, by the hollow oak and near to
Dagon's temple. They hear a terrible crash and up-
roar, which fills them with bewilderment and panic.

" *Chorus. O mercy ! mercy ! Help us now, O God !*
Relieve us in this need ; we cry from earth
To Thy high throne ! What is this sudden shock ?
O where, where do we stand ?   This hideous shout
Deafens our ears.   This dust obscures our sight.
A cloud of ruin rises in the air.

The town is full of shrieks and groans ; the noise,
The cry, the wailing spreads throughout the streets.

We dare not venture out for further news ;
But stay awhile beneath this temple fence.
Here cometh one, amazed, perplexed, cast down ;

> *Let us inquire of him the state of things.*
> *A moment stand, so please you, friend, and tell*
> *To us the accident and how it chanced.*
> *Mess. O Hebrew maidens, Gaza's all undone,*
> *The whole Philistine land in deepest woe.*
> *Chorus. How fared Samson? Is he alive or dead?*
> *Mess. All dead and cold, but timely met his death,*
> *No longer blind and fastened to a chain.*
>
> . . . . . .
>
> *Maltreated, harassed, buffeted, provoked,*
> *He hath in his revenge himself destroyed.*
> *Chorus. We then have lost our judge, for ever lost;*
> *'Tis terrible! but further in detail*
> *Relate to us all that you saw and heard."*
> —v. 1460-1468, 1471-1487.

In the Miltonic narrative the Chorus and Manoah
(in a place nigh to Gaza but somewhat retired) are
discussing of the old man's mission to ransom his son,
when suddenly Manoah breaks off his discourse with
the startled exclamation—

> " O what noise !
> Mercy of Heaven ! what hideous noise was that ?
> Horribly loud, unlike the former shout.
> *Chorus.* Noise call you it, or universal groan,
> As if the whole inhabitation perished ?
>
> . . . .
>
> Blood, death, and deathful deeds are in that noise,
> Ruin and destruction at the utmost point.
> Of ruin indeed methought I heard the noise.
> *Man.* . . . .
> Some dismal accident it needs must be.
> What shall we do ?—stay here or run and see ?
> *Chorus.* Best keep together here, lest, running thither,
> We unawares run into danger's mouth.
>
> . . . .
>
> *Man.* . . . . . .
> A little stay will bring some notice hither.

Chorus.   .   .   .   .   .   .
> To our wish I see one hither speeding,
> An Ebrew, as I guess, and of our tribe.

Mess. O whither shall I run, or which way fly
> The sight of this so horrid spectacle,
> Which erst mine eyes beheld, and still behold ?

.   .   .   .

Man. The accident was loud, and here before thee
> With rueful cry ; yet what it was we hear not.
> No preface needs ; thou seest we long to know.

.   .   .   .

Mess. Gaza yet stands, but all her sons are fallen,
> All in a moment overwhelmed and fallen.

.   .   .   .

Man. Suspense in news is torture ; speak them out.
Mess. Then take the worst in brief : Samson is dead.

.   .   .   .

.   .   .   .

> At once both to destroy and be destroyed,
> The edifice where all were met to see him
> Upon their heads and on his own he pulled.

Man. A dreadful way thou took'st to thy revenge :
> More than enough we know ; but, while things yet
> Are in confusion, give us, if thou canst,
> Eye-witness of what first or last was done,
> Relation more particular and distinct."
> —1508–1515, 1519–1522, 1536, 1539–1543, 1552–1555,
>   1558–1559, 1569–1570, 1587–1596.

We have made these extracts as brief as we could,
and have contented ourselves with bringing forward
the most salient points in these dialogues between the
Chorus and Messenger in the one case, and between the
Chorus, Manoah, and Messenger in the other. Our next
task is to compare the two narratives of the catastrophe.
The following is a portion of the description as given
by the Dutch poet—

" *Samson we saw, first in procession led,*
Before the shrine step up, with strings and pipes,
With songs of triumph and with shouts of joy.
He patient bore the people's taunts and jeers,
And, quiet as a lamb, refrained his wrath,
But meanwhile vengeance in his mind revolved.
The sacrificial feast with pomp began
More splendid than is wont, from stress of joy
That now the land her greatest enemy
A captive in her hands in thraldom keeps.

. . . . . .

. . . *A din of voices rose,*
Which grew with wine as the great cup went round
To Dagon's honour and his fellow-gods.

. . . . . .

They, as the feast drew on, to sport inclined,
Made ready. When blind Samson to his guide :
Pray, lead me, keeper, where the theatre
On two main pillars leans, which the vast weight
Of all the building hold, that we, by play
And dance o'ertired, may rest awhile, and then
With unabated force begin once more."

—v. 1492–1502, 1525–1533.

Here we pause. For purposes of analysis and comparison our quotations already err on the side of excessive length. We now give the Miltonic parallel—

" The feast and noon grew high, and sacrifice
Had filled their hearts with mirth, high cheer, and wine,
When to their sports they turned. Immediately
Was Samson as a public servant brought.

. . . . . .

At sight of him the people with a shout
Rifted the air, clamouring their god with praise,
Who had made their dreadful enemy their thrall.
He, patient but undaunted, where they led him
Came to the place. . . . .
. . . He his guide requested,

> As overtired, to let him lean awhile
> With both his arms on those two massy pillars
> That to the arched roof gave main support."
>   —1612–1615, 1620–1624, 1630–1634.

Compare also with Vondel's description of the sacrificial feast—

> " While their hearts were jocund and sublime,
>   Drunk with idolatry, drunk with wine,
>   Chaunting their idol."—1669–1671.

These passages, taken from the concluding portions of the plays, are so full of minute coincidences, that, even if taken by themselves, and apart from other testimony, it would be scarcely possible to hold that they were entirely unrelated to each other. But when we consider them not in isolation, but as merely a portion of the internal evidence we have accumulated, and so hardly more important than that which we have adduced from other parts of the plays ; and when, further, this strong internal evidence in favour of our thesis, that Milton was much indebted to the language of Vondel's " Samson," is supported by external evidence equally convincing that he likewise borrowed from the same poem the dramatic form he has adopted and his particular treatment of the subject, we feel that all reasonable doubt has been removed. In such matters we cannot, of course, attain to *absolute* certainty, but our argument is practically unassailable.

A few words in conclusion.

It will be admitted, we think, after making every possible deduction from the long array of parallel passages set forth in the preceding pages for resemblances which are accidental, for material derived from common sources, for comparisons that are strained, that we are justified in describing this disclosure of the obligations of Milton to Vondel as A CURIOSITY OF LITERATURE. We have already plainly stated, but again repeat, that depreciation of Milton's supreme poetical merits lies as much beyond our power as it is outside our purpose. A closer acquaintance with his works tends not to diminish, but to increase the homage due to the great Puritan Poet, the wonder felt at the rich stores of his erudition, at the gigantic sweep of his imagination. Milton had no need to borrow from Vondel or any other poet, however eminent, and the stern uprightness of his character forbids us to place an evil construction upon his tendency to "plagiarise." He undoubtedly interpreted in the widest manner the liberty accorded to every great writer of building in for the embellishment of his work the materials provided to his hand from well-known and recognised sources, and, conscious of pre-eminence, never scrupled to extend to his own appropriations from others the qualification contained in his own definition—"To borrow, and better in the borrowing, is no plagiarie."

But borrowing is a sin which grows by the using. And the very large use which Milton has made, without acknowledgment, of the ideas and language of a distinguished contemporary, from works but recently published, and written in a tongue unknown to the vast majority of English readers, cannot be altogether excused or defended.

At the same time, it must be conceded that the seventeenth century permitted much greater license in these matters than would be countenanced by the stricter literary morality of our own days. The following excerpt from an extremely interesting essay by Vondel[1] is evidence on this point, and shows that the Dutch poet himself was no purist. " Knowledge of foreign tongues," he writes, " is no slight advantage, and the translating of celebrated poets helps the coming poet, just as the copying of masterpieces of art the student of painting. One thus observes the art of the best masters, and learns, *dexterously stealing*, to make another's one's own. In this manner has Virgil, himself the prince of poets, borrowed from Homer and others, and imported from the Greek language with such judgment that he has won imperishable renown."

He then adds a few words of warning to the reader, which are, in their bearing upon the subject of this work, curiously apposite—

" If, then, you wish to pluck some flowers upon the Dutch Helicon, so manage it that country-folk (de boeren) do not notice it, and that it do not too palpably attract the attention of the learned."

[1] "Aanleidinge ter Nederduitsche Dichtkunst " van Vloten, vol. ii. p. 54.

APPENDIX.

BATAVIAN ANTHOLOGY. By John Bowring. P. 143.

(Portion of Chorus from Vondel's " Palamedes.")

P. 26.   O sweetly-welcome break of morn !
Thou dost with happiness adorn
The heart of him who cheerily—
Contentedly, unweariedly—
Surveys whatever Nature gives,
What beauty in her presence lives,
And wanders oft the banks along
Of some sweet stream with murmuring song.
Oh ! more than regal is his lot,
Who, in some blest secluded spot,
Remote from crowded cares and fears,
His loved, his cherished dwelling rears !
For empty praises never pining,
His wishes to his cot confining,
And listening to each cheerful bird
Whose animating song is heard :
When morning dews, which zephyr's sigh
Has wafted, on the roses lie,
Whose leaves beneath the pearl drops bend ;
When thousand rich perfumes ascend,
And thousand hues adorn the bowers,
And from a rainbow of sweet flowers,
Or bridal robe for Iris made
From every bud in sun and shade,

N

Contented there to plant or set,
Or snare the birds with crafty net ;
To grasp his bending rod and wander
Beside the banks, where waves meander,
And thence their fluttering tenants take ;
Or, rising ere the sun's awake,
Prepare his steed, and scour the grounds,
And chase the hare with swift-paced hounds ;
Or ride beneath the noon-tide rays
Through peaceful glens and silent ways,
Which wind like Cretan labyrinth :
Or where the purple hyacinth
Is glowing in its bed ; or where
The meads red-speckled daisies bear,
While maidens milk the grazing cow,
And peasants toil behind the plough,
Or reap the crops beneath their feet,
Or sow luxuriant flax or wheat.
Here flourishes the waving corn,
Encircled by the wounding thorn ;
There glides a bark by meadows green,
And there the village smoke is seen ;
And there a castle meets the view
Half fading in the distance blue.

   .   .   .   .   .

   .   .   .   .   .

All the following extracts from Vondel's Works are taken from Van Vloten's complete edition. Schiedam : H. A. M. ROELANTS. MDCCCLXIV.

LUCIFER.

P. 37.   Heer Belzebub ! gij Raad van's Hemels Stedehouder,
Hij steigert steil, van kreits in kreits, op ons gezicht.
Hij streeft den wind voorbij, en laat een spoor van licht
En glansen achter zich, waar zijn gezwinde wiecken
De wolken breken.   Hij begint ons lucht te riecken,
In eenen andren dag en schooner zonneschijn,

Daar 't licht zich spiegelt in het blaauwe kristalijn.
De hemelkloten zien met hun gezicht, van onder,
Terwijl hij rijst, hem na, een ieder in't bijzonder,
Verwonderd om dien vaart en goddelijken zwier,
Die hun geen Engel schijnt, maar eer een vliegend vier,
Geen star verschiet zoo snel.   —i. 10, &c.

P. 39.   Verwittigd uit den hoogen
Door's Hemels afgezant, die neder quam gevlogen
Nog sneller, dan een star, die door de lucht verschiet.
                        —v. 1739, &c.

P. 40.   Ik zie de goude bladen,
Met perlen van de lucht, den zilvren dauw geladen.

.   .   .   .

'T Gezicht bekoort den mond. Wie zou niet watertanden
Naar aardsche lekkernij ? hij walgt van onzen dag,
En hemelsch mann', die 't ooft der aarde plukken mag.
                        —i. 29, &c.

P. 41. 'K Verzwijg mijn henevaart, om niet te reppen, hoe
Gezwind ik nedersteeg, en zonk door negen bogen,
Die sneller dan een pijl, rontom hun mid punt vlogen.
Het rad der zinnen kan zoo snel niet ommeslaan,
In ons gedachten, als ik, lager dan de maan
En wolken, afgegleên bleef hangen op mijn pennen
Om 't oostersche gewest en landschap t'onderkennen.
                        —i. 44, &c.

P. 42. Van verre zag men hier een hoogen berg verschieten,
Waaruit een waterval, de wortel van vier vlieten,
Ten dale neder bruist. Wij streken steil en schuin
Voorover neet ons hooft, en rustten op de kruin
Des bergs, van waar men vlak de zalige landouwen
Der onderwelt en haar weelde kon aanschouwen.
                        —i. 53, &c.

P. 44. In 't midden rijst de berg, waaruit de hooftbron klatert,
Die zich in vieren deelt en al het land bewatert,
Geboomte en beemden laaft, en levert beeken uit,

Zoo klaar gelijk kristal, daar geen gezicht op stuit
De stroomen geven slib en koesteren de gronden.

.   .   .   .

Hier zaaide Vrou Natuur in steenen een gestarnt,
Dat onze starren dooft.   Hier blinkt het goud in d'adren
Hier wôu Natuur haar schat in eenen schoot vergadren.

—i. 61, &c.

P. 45.   Dan zwelt de boezem der landouw van kruid en kleur
En knop en telg en bloem en allerhanden geur,
De dauw ververscht ze's nachts.   —i. 74, &c.

P. 45.   De bergleeuw kwispelde hem aan met zijnen staart,
En loech den meester toe.   De tijger lêi zijn aard
Voor's Koning's voeten af.   De landstier boog zijn
          horen
En d'olifant zijn snuit.   De beer vergat zijn toren.

—i. 91, &c.

P. 46.   Geen schepsel heeft om hoog mijne oogen zoo behaagd
Als deze twee om laag.   Wie kon zoo geestig strenglen
Het lichaam en de ziel, en scheppen dubble Englen
Uit kleinaarde en uit been !   Het lichaam schoon van
          leest,
Getuigt des Scheppers Kunst, die blinkt in 't aanschijn
          meest,
Den spiegel van 't gemoed.   Wat lid mij kon verbazen,
Ik zag het beeld der ziele in 't aan gezicht geblazen
Bezit het lijf iet schoons, dat vindt man hier bij een.
Een Godheid geeft haar glans door's menschen oogen heen
De redelijke ziel komt uit zijn tronie zwieren.
Hij heft, terwijl de stomme en redenlooze dieren
Naar hunne voeten zien, alleen en trotsch het hooft
Ten hemel op naar God, zijn Schepper, hoog geloofd.

—i. 104, &c.

P. 47.   De man en vrou zijn bêi volschapen, even schoon,
Van top tot teen.   Met recht spant Adam wel de kroon,
Door kloekheid van gedaante en majesteit van 't wezen,
Als een ter heerschappij des aardrijks uitgelesen ;
Maar al wat Eva heeft vernoegt haar bruigom's eisch :

Der leden tederheit, een zachter vel en vleisch,
Een vriendelijker verf, aanminnigheit der oogen.
—i. 150, &c.

P. 47. Nu blinkt geen Serafijn, in 't hemelsch Heiligdom
Als deze in 't hangend haar, een goude nis van stralen,
Die schoon gewaterd, van den hoofde nederdalen
En vloeyen om den rug. —i. 168, &c.

P. 50. Al schijnt het Geestendom alle andre t'overtreffen,
God sloot van eeuwigheid het menschdom te verheffen,
Ook boven 't Engelsdom, en op te voeren tot
Een klaarheid en een licht, dat niet verschilt van God
Gij zult het eeuwig Woord, bekleed met been en âren,
Gezalft tot Heer en Hooft en Rechter, al de scharen
Der Geesten, Engelen en menschen te gelijk,
Zien rechten, uit zijn troon en onbeschaduwd Rijk.
—i. 217, &c.

P. 51. Zou God een jonger zoon, geteeld uit Adams lenden,
Verheffen boven hem? —ii. 418, &c.

P. 53. Gij vat het recht : het past rechtschape Heerschappijen
Geensins, haar wettigheid zoo los te laten glijen ;
Want d'oppermacht is d'eerste aan haare wet verplicht ;
Verandren voeght haar minst: Ben ik een zoon van licht,
Een heerscher over 't licht, ik zal mijn recht bewaren:
Ik zwicht voor geen geweld, noch aartsgeweldenaren.
Laat zwichten al wat wil ; Ik wijk niet eenen voet.
Hier is mijn Vaderland. Noch ramp, noch tegenspoed,
Noch vloeken zullen ons verwaren, noch betoomen :
Wij zullen sneven, of dien hoek te boven komen.
Is 't noodlot dat ik vall', van eere en staat beroofd,
Laat vallen, als ik vall' met deze krone op 't hoofd,
Dien schepter in de vuist, dien eersliep van vertrouwden,
En zooviel duizenden als onze zijde houden.
Dat vallen strekt tot eer en onverwelkbren lof ;
En liever d'eerste vorst in einig lager hof,
Dan in 't gezaligd licht de tweede, of nog een minder ;
Zoo troost ik mij de kans, en vrees nu leed noch hinder.
—ii. 427.

P. 57.   Zooveel 't geoorlofd zij te melden uit God's bladen ;
      Veel weten kan altijd niet vordren, somtijds schaden.
      De Hoogste ontdekt ons slechts wat hij geraden vindt.
      Het al te sterke licht schijnt serafijnen blind.
      De zuivre Wijsheid woû ten deel haar wil bezeglen
      Ten deele ontsluiten.   Zich te schikken en te regeln
      Naar heur gestelde wet, dat voegt den onderzaat,
      Die aan zijn meesters last en wil gebonden staat.
                                —ii. 483, &c.

P. 58.   Genoeg u met uw lot
      En staat en waardigheid, u toegelêid van God
      Hij hief u in den top van alle Hierarchijen ;
      Doch niet om jemand's glans en opgang te benijen.

      . . . .

      Zoo buig ze ook voor 't besluit der Godheid, die het al
      Wat wegen heeft uit niet, of namaals wezen zal,
      Bestiert tot zeker eind.   —ii. 501, &c.

P. 59.   Nu leeren wij allengs God's wijsheit tegen stappen
      Erbiedig en beschroomt.   Zie openbaart bij trappen
      Het licht der wetenschappe en kennisse en begeert,
      Dat ieder, op zijn wacht, zich onder haar verneêrt.
                              —ii. 555, &c.

P. 59.
  Ap.   Geleende macht te wegen
      In eene zelve schaal met d'Almacht ! haar gewicht
      Weegt over. Wacht uw kroon ; wij vallen veel te licht.
  Bel. Zoo licht niet, of de kans zal eerst in twijfel hangen.
                          —ii. 612, &c.

P. 60.   De wacht is hem betrouwd.   Hij houdt op alle Hoven
      Getrouw een wakende oog.   .   .   .   .
      ..   .   .   .   Wat tuig, wat stormgevaert
      Kan tegens hem bestaan, en d'opperbenden slopen ?
      Al zette's Hemels slot zijn diamant poort open
      Het vreesde list, noch laag, noch overrompeling.
                   —ii. 632–633, 638–641.

P. 61.   Zijn tronie glad vernist van veinzen en bedriegen,
      In 't mommen niemand kent, die haar voorbij kan
      vliegen.   —ii. 663.

P. 61.   Het lust ons   .   .   .   .   .
Op een gewichtig stuk, dat zal me niet mislukken :
Het wit is Michäel de slagveêr uit te rukken.—ii. 590.

P. 62.   Gij ziet, hoe 't Hemelsch heer, geharrenast in 't goud
En in 't gelid gesteld, zijn beurt en schildwacht houdt ;
Hoe deze star gedaald ; en gene in top daar boven,
De klaarste en minder klaar in luister kan verdooven ;
Hoe d'eene een kleine ronde, en d'andre een grooter
     schrijft ;
De laagste Hemel snelst, de hoogste langsaam drijft ;
En evenwel verneemt ge, in deze oneffenheden
Van ampten, licht, en kreits en stand en trand en treden,
Geen tweedract, nijd, noch strijd ; des Albestierders stem
Geleidt dit maatgezang, dat luistert scherp naar Hem.
                                        —iii. 971.

P. 62.   Is't geene helf, gij sleept een staart van 't derde deel
Der Geesten mede ?   —iii. 1244.

Des Hemels derde deel heeft reede zijnen standert
Die valsche Morgenstar gezworen.   —iv. 1336.

P. 63.   Ik zag Gods blijdschap zich met een wolk van rouw
Beschaduwen ; in 't end de wraak een vlam ontsteken
In d'oogen van het licht.   —iv. 1362.

P. 63.   Zie had haar zegel en gelijkenis gedrukt
Op uw geheiligd hoofd en voorhooft, overgoten
Met schoonheit, wijsheit, gunst, en wat er komt gevloten,
En stroomen, zonder maat, uit aller schatten bron,
Gij blonkt in 't Paradijs, voor 't aanschijn van de zon
Der Godheit, uit een wolk van dauw en versche rozen.
Uw feestgewand stond stijf van perlen en turkosen
Smaragden, diamant, robijn en louter goud.—iv. 1470.

P. 65.   Och, Stedehouder ! wat verbloemt gij uw gepeinzen
Voor 't alziende oog ? gij kunt uw oogmerk niet ont-
     veinzen.   —iv. 1541.

Ik handhaaf 't heilig Recht, door hoogen nood geperst.
                                        —iv. 1536.

P. 66. *Luc.* Wat baat het, schoon men zich op 't uiterste berâ ?
Heir is geen hoop van peis.   *Raph.* 'K verzeker u genâ.
—iv. 1631, &c.

P. 66. De gansche Hemel, van den grond op tot de kruin
Der aartspaleizen, juicht op Michäels bazuin
En zwaayende banier.   De veldslag is gewonnen.
Ons schilden schitteren, en scheppen nieuwe zonnen
Uit elke schildzon straalt een triomfanten dag.
Daar komt Uriel zelf, de Schildknaap, uit den slag
En zwaait het vlammend zwaard, dat, scherp van weder-
    zijden
Gewet van 's Hemels wraak en gramschap, onder 't
    strijden
Door schild en harrenas, en helm van diamant,
Gevaagt heeft, slinks en rechts.   —v. 1717–1726.

P. 67. De Veldheer Michäel, verwittigd uit den hoogen
Door 's Hemels afgezant, die neder kwam gevlogen,
Noch sneller dan een star, die door de lucht verschiet,
Hoe Lucifer zoo trotsch zich tegens 't hoog Gebied
Had opentlijk gekant, gereed hem aan te voeren
Die hem bewierookten, zijn starre en standert zwoeren ;
Schoot voort, op 't aanstaan van den trouwen Gabriel,
Het schubbig panser aan en gaf terstont bevel
Aan al zijn oversten en hoofden en cornellen,
De heeren, in God's naam, in hun geleên te stellen,
Om met gemeene macht en kracht, op 't luchtich ruim
Van 't zuivre hemels blaauw, al dit meineedig schuim
Te vagen, al dit spook in duisternis te domplen,
Eer zij op 't ongezienste ons mochten overromplen.
—v. 1739, &c.

P. 69. Het groeide snel, en wies gelijk éen halve maan ;
Het wet zijn punten, zet twee horens op ons aan.
—v. 1769, &c.

P. 70. De trotsche standert, daar de dag scheen op te klaren
Uit zijne Morgenstar, werd van Apollion
Gehandhaaft, achter hem, zoo moedig als hij kon.
—v. 1780, &c.

P. 70. Omringd van zijn staffiers en groene livereyen,
Hij, wrevlig aangevoerd van onverzoenbren wrok,
In 't gouden panser, dat, op zijn wapenrok
Van gloeyend purper blonk en uitscheen, steeg te wagen
Met goude wielen, van robijnen dicht geslagen.
De Leeuw en felle Draak, ter vlucht gereed en vlug,
Met starren overal bezaaid op hunnen rug
In 't parele gareel, gespannen voor de wielen
Verlangden naar den strijd, en vlamden op vernielen
De heerbijl in de vuist, de scheemrende rondas,
Waarin de morgenstar met kunst gedreven was,
Hing aan den slinken arm, gereed de kans te wagen.
                                    —v. 1788, &c.

P. 72. O Lucifer! gij zult dien hoogmoed u beklagen.
Gij, fenix onder al wat God daar boven looft !
Hoe steekt gij, onder 't heer, zoo fier met hals en hooft,
En helm en schoudren uit ! Hoe heerlijk past u 't
        wapen
Als waar't natuurelijk uw wezen aangeschapen !
O hooft der Engelen, niet hooger ! Keer weêrom.
                                    —v. 1800, &c.

P. 73. Zoo stonden zij gekant en slagreê, drom bij drom,
Een ieder op zijn lucht en hoefslag, en bij rijen
Gesnoerd aan hun gezag, om 't schoonst van wederzijen,
Wanneer de dolle trom en klinkende trompet
Zich mengen, het geluid geweer en handen wet,
En steigert in den trans van 't heilig licht der lichten ;
Een klank, waarop terstond een zwangre wolk van
        schichten
Geborsten, slag op slag, een gloênden hagel baart
Een storm en onwêer, dat de Hemelen verwaart,
De hofpijlaren schudt : de kreitsen en de sterren
Verbijsterd in hun ronde en ommeloop, verwarren
Op zwijmen op de wacht, en weten niet waar heen
Te drijven.   —v. 1806, &c.

P. 75. De dolle Lucifer hervat den strijd drie reizen,
En stut de flaauwte van zijn regement zoo trotsch

Gelijk het zeegedruisch al schuimende op een rots
Gestuit wordt, reis op reis, en meer niet uit kan rechten.
                                    —v. 1836, &c.

P. 75. De heerbijl in zijn vuist, aan d'eene en d'andre zijde,
        Den toescheut stuit en sloopt, of schut ze op zijn rondas,
        Tot dat hem Michäel, in 't schitterend harrenas,
        Verschijnt, gelijk een God, uit eenen kring van zonnen :
        "Zit af, O Lucifer ! en geef het God gewonnen
        Geef over uw geweer, en standert ; strijk voor God !
        Voer af dit heillos heer, dees goddelooze rot,
        Of anders wacht uw hoofd "Zoo roept hij uit den
            hoogen
        D'Aartsvijand van God's naam, hardnekkig, onbewogen,
        En trotscher op dat woord, hervat in aller ijl
        Den slag, tot driewerf toe, om met zijn oorlogs bijl
        Den diamanten schild, met een God's naam, te kloven ;
        Maar wie den Hemel tergt gevoelt de wraak van boven.
        De heerbijl klinkt en springt op 't heilig diamant
        Aan stukken."   —v. 1908, &c.

P. 77. Gelijk de klare dag in naaren nacht verkeert,
        Wanneer de zon verzinkt, vergeet met goud te brallen,
        Zoo wordt zijn schoonheit ook, in't zinken, onder 't
            vallen,
        In een wanschapenheid veranderd, al te vuil ;
        Dat helder aangezicht in eenen wreeden muil ;
        De tanden in gebit, gewet om staal te knaauwen ;
        De voeten en de hand in vierderhande klaauwen ;
        Dat glistrend parlemoer in eene zwarte huid
        De rug, vol borstlen spreidt twee Drakevleugels uit.
        In kort, d'Aartsengel, wien noch flus alle Englen vieren,
        Verwisselt zijn gedaante en mengelt zeven dieren
        Afgrijslijk onder een.   —v. 1950, &c.

P. 79. Hij rukte, na den slag, 't verstrooide heer bijeen
        Doch eerst zijne Oversten, die voor elkandre gruwen,
        En zette zich, om't licht van't alziende oog te schuwen,
        In eene holle wolk, een duistre moortspelonk
        Van nevlen, daar geen vier dan uit hun blikken blonk ;

En, midden in den ring des Helschen Raads gezeten,
Hief uit zijn zetel aan, te Helsch op God gebeten :
"Gij machten, die zoo trotsch voor ons gerechte zaak
Dien afbreuk hebt geleên ! nu is het tijd om wraak
Te nemen van ons leed, en listig en verbolgen,
Met onverzoenbren wrok den Hemel te vervolgen
In zijn verkoren beeld, en 't menschelijk geslacht
Te smoren in zijn wieg en op gang, eer het macht
In zijne zenuw krijge en aanwinne in zijne erven.
Mijn wit is Adam en zijn afkomst te bederven
Ik weet, door 't overtreên der eerstgestelde wet,
Hem aan te wrijven zulk een onuitwischbre smet,
Dat hij, naar lijf en ziel, met zijn nakomelingen
Vergiftigt, nimmer zal ten zetel innedringen,
Waaruit men ons verstiet ;   .   .   .
.   .   .   .
Natuur zal van dien slag geteisterd, schier verteren,
En wenschen in een Niet of Mengelklomp te keeren
Ik zie den Mensch, die naar het beeld der Godheit zweemt,
Van Gods gelijkenis verbasterd en vervreemd,
In wil, geheugenis, en zijn verstand ontluisterd.
Het ingeschapen licht beneveld en verduisterd ;
En wat den dag beschreit, in's moeders bangen schoot,
Gevallen in den muil der onvermijbre Dood.
Ik wil de tiranny verheffen, altijt stouter,
En u, mijn zoons ! gewijd tot godheên, op het outer,
In kerken, zonder taal, tot aan de lucht gebouwd,
Vereeren offervee, en wierook geur, en goud,
Ook zoo veel menschen, als geen tong vermag te noemen,
En al wat Adam teelt in eenwigheid verdoemen,
Door gruwelstuk op stuk, God's naam ten trots begaan.
Zoo dier wil hem mijn kroon, en zijn triomffest staan.

—v. 2038-2078.

P. 84.   Hoe gloeit dit ooft van goud en karmozijn te gader !
Hoe noodt u dit banket ! ei, dochter ! treê wat nader ;
Hier nestelt geen venijn in dit onsterflijk loof.
Hoe lokt dees vrucht ! ei pluk, ei pluk vrij ! Ik beloof
U wetenschap en licht. Wat deist ge, bang voor schennis ?

Tast toe, en wordt God zelf, in wijsheid, en in kennis,
En wetenschap gelijk, en eere en majesteit,
Hoe zeer Hij 't u benij. Zoo vat men 't onderscheid,
Het wezen, en den aard, en d'eigenschap der zaken.
Terstond begint het hart der schoone bruid te blaken,
T'ontvonken, en zij vlamt op d'aangepreze vrucht.
De vrucht bekoort het oog, het oog den mond, die zucht.
De lust beweegt de hand al bevende te plukken
Zoo plukt ze, en proeft en eet.   —v. 2091, &c.

.   .   .   .

De Hemel treurt in rouw   .   .   .

.   .   .   .   .   .

Het weêrlicht veis op reis, het dondert slag op slag
Al wat men hoort en ziet is schrik en angst en zuchten.
                    —v. 2112, 2114-2115.

JOANNES BOETGEZANT.

P. 92. Het lust me, van den held te zingen, die, zoo groot
        Voor Gode en Engelen, zijn zuiver bloed vergoot

.   .   .   .

Gij, Englekooren, die omhoog, van trans in trans,
Het Lam eert, dat den rei der maagden leidt ten dans,
Die, door het nieuwe lied en onnazingbre toonen,
Den trowen Bruidegom der zuivre zielen kronen ;
Gelêi met uw gezang mijn Hemel-heldenwijs !
Ik ken geen Zangberg dan het hemelsch Paradijs,
Daar, uit den troon van God en 't Lam, door duizend
      aders
Het levend water, op geruisch van pallembladers,
Komt op gesprongen, klaar 'en louter, als kristal.
Dat is mijn paardebron, mijn bosch en waterval
Waaruit de Koningen en Gods gezalfden dronken
Ioannes 'schaduwen, woestijnen, en spelonken
En kerker zullen, zoo uw Hemelbron mij laaft
Veranderen in licht en Paradijs. Dan draaft
Mijn laag woestijn-gedicht op een woestijn-beminner
Zoo trotsch, als d'ouden ooit op eenen overwinner
Van Troje of Latium.   —i. 7, 24, &c.

P. 94. Toen sprak de Vader der Genade, in'hart bewogen
Met's menschen jammeren, uit louter mededoogen
"Mijn eenig Erfgenaam en uitgekoren Zoon,
De glorie van mijn rijk en eeuwig rijke kroon,
Het menschgeworden Woord schuilt, flaauw van glans
en luister,
Bij weinigen gekend, om laag noch stil en duister,
Een rij van jaren. Het word tijd en meer dan tijd,
Dat Hij te voorschijn kome, en eens zich zelven kwijt
In 't heilzame ampt, tot heil der droeve sterfelijken
Hem op den hals gelegd. Laat al wat wil bezwijken
En wanklen in zijn trouwe, ons woord houde eeuwig
stand.
'T Beeoogde heil vange aan van's Hemel's afgezant
In moeders lichaam, door den Hemelraad bescheiden
Om onzen lieven Zoon den intreê te bereiden
Ter poorte van het rijk, dat Hij bezitten moet.
Zoo sprekende, en ontvonkt van onuitbluschbren gloed,
Om zijn beloften, lang met een eed gestaaft, te sterken,
En's menschdoms eeuwig heil volkomen uit te werken,
Verdaagt fluks Gabriel, die, in het starlicht, kleed,
Zich, op het hoog gebod, gedurig houdt gereed.
"Aartsengel!" zegt Hij "die voor hene bêi de nichten
Elk hare vrucht beloofde, en nooit in uwe plichten
Den last verzuimde, u van den Hemel op gelegd."
—i. 50, &c.

P. 97. Zoo sprak d'Almachtige, en d'Aartsengel, om te rennen,
Bereidt zich, en ontvouwt, zoo schoon als fenixpennen,
Zijn vleugels, geschakeerd van hemelsch blauw en goud
En purper, in het licht, daar zich de Godheid houdt.
Men ziet de verwen zich verandren en schakeeren,
Gelijk de regenboog of schoone pauweveêren,
In 't licht der zonne, die recht tegens over staat
Reisvaardig in zijn vlucht verheft hij zich, en slaat
De pennen tegens een wel driewerf, dat de reyen
Der Englen ommezien, en zijne vlucht geleyen
Met hun gezicht; terwijl de vlieger nederstijgt,
En zwaait van ronde in ronde, en onder 't dalen krijgt

Jeruzalem in 't oog, dat zijn gekroonde kruinen
Ten hemel opwaart heft uit d'omgelege duinen,
Waarvan de koningsstad in 't ronde omcingeld scheen.
Toen volgde hij de streek, die naar den rijksstroom heen
Hem 't woest quarante wees, niet rijk van groente en
    lover.
Hier hing d'Aartsengel op zijn pennen, streek voorover
Op's woestijniers spelonk ; gelijk een adelaar,
Die uit de hoogte in 't ende een springbron wordt
    gewaar,
En nederzwevende den dorst lescht, op 't geklater
Des verschen watervals, aan 't hartverkwikkend water.
                                        —i. 126, &c.

P. 101.   Op dat, zoodra hierop d'Alzegenaar verschijn,
          De mensch, geleken een verwilderde woestijn
          En dorre wildernis, verandere in een Eden
          Een hemelsch Paradijs, daar God wordt aangebeden,
          In d'eerste oprechtheid, recht als hem de Schepper
              schiep,
          Eer hij te reukeloos zijn heil en staat verliep.
                                        —iii. 25, &c.

P. 102.   Maar boven (daar geen nacht den dag volgt op de
              hielen,
          Nooit donkre nevels noch slagredens nedervielen,
          Die 't licht verduisteren, dat eeuwig schijnt en straalt,
          Waarin het geestendom den vrijen adem haalt)
          Kwam d'opperste (die al de starrelichte ronden
          Rondom den aardkloot drijft, en eeuwig houdt gebonden
          Aan hunne noodwet, eens voor eeuwig vastgesteld,
          Gestegen in den top der hemelen, verzeld   .
          Met veldheer Michäel en eenen stoet staffieren,
          Die rondom hem en voor en achter henezwieren
          Hij overlêi wat groots, dat ieder nadacht gaf
          En vaardigte terstond de rijksher outen af,
          Om al den hemelraad terstond uit vier gewesten
          Ten hoof te dagen, dat, met diamanten vesten
          Gesterkt, in 't midpunt rijst van's hemelsch ronden kring
          Zij strijven elk hun weegs, rondom den heldren ring

Der eeuwigheit. Men ziet hier op de heerschappijen,
De vorstendommen, en de machten opwaarts glijen
Door 't zuiver hemelsch blauw, en ieder uit zijn hof.
De veldbazuin vooruit bazuint zijn konings lof.
Gewaden slingren om hun leên, als hemeldrachten
Vol regenbogen, rijk gewrocht van fenix-schachten,
Bezet met perlen, en bezaaid met puik gesteent ;
Het blinkende gestarnte, in 't geurig haar, verleent
Het voorhooft eenen glans en goddelijken luister.

—iii. 175, &c.

P. 104. Zoo sprak de vader, en de zoon te Nazareth
Gehoorzaamt dit besluit, en, offrende een gebed
Den Hemel op, gelijk een goude schaal, vol geuren.
Stapt hene, om nu het hoofd vrijmoedig op te beuren
En aan de wereld, schuw van 't lang beloofde licht
Der waarheid, openbaar t' ontvouwen zijnen plicht,
Te toonen, dat hij is de Heiland der geslachten.

—iii. 265, &c.

P. 105. Waar hij de voeten zette en aankwam, scheen de zegen
Te vallen uit de lucht ; gelijk na eenen regen,
Verwacht met smarte en daar de dorre beemd om riep,
De zon veel schooner schijnt, het gras groeit, dat het
          piep.
Een lent van bloemen verft de heuvels en de dalen.
Geen schilder kan landouw en landschap schooner
     malen,
Als hij een regenboog van duizend verwen mengt.
'T gevogelt kwinkeleert. De blijde leeuwrik brengt
Zijn tonen bij, en volgt de keel der nachtegalen.
De bronaar laaft het groen met versche waterstralen.
De ceder neigt zijn kroon. Natuur zet heur gelaat
Naar blijschap, en verkeert in eenen andren staat.
De winterbuyen, laang aan 't buldren, waayen over.
De bie, verlekkerd op den tijm en bloem en lover,
Zuigt honig uit den dauw. De schaapskooi levert
     room.
De harten huppelen. De blijschap kent geen toom.

—iii. 275, &c.

P. 108.   Dc Hel ontzette zich voor zulk een donderwoord ;
          Al d'Afgrond daverde.   De roestige ijzerpoort
          Begon op haar gebit te knarsen en te kraken,
          De jammerpoel een stank en rook en smook te braken
          Ten balge uit, dat het licht verduisterde aan de lucht.
          De grootvorst van den nacht, voor zijnen staat beducht,
          Verdaagde datelijk alle onderaardsche raden,
          Die spoedden zich ten hoof door slangbochtige paden,
          Daar, recht in 't middelpunt des aardrijks, even wijd
          Van Zuid-en Noord-as, 't hof op ketens hangt en snijdt
          De spil der wereld juist in twee gelijke deelen.
          Wat gruwzaam is, vloeit hier door duizend zwarte kelen
          Naar toe, op 't schor getoet der nare hofklaroen.
          God Lucifer verscheen te rade, en zette toen
          Zich op den hoogen stoel, wien d' onderdane nekken
          Van ongedierte en draak ten stut en steunsel strekken,
          Hij spande een addrekroon om zijn wanschapen hoofd,
          En zwaayende den staf van staal, aan 't punt gekloofd,
          Sloeg gloênde blikken op.   De lamp, vol pek en zwavel
          En basiliscusvet, verlichtte in 't rond den navel
          Van 't woeste raadshol, dik en vet begroeit van roet.
          'T Gestoelte werd bekleed van dit gevloekt gebroed,
          Een ieder naar zijn staat.   Zij zaten stil, als stommen,
          En hij begon aldus, gelijk een klok, te brommen :
          Getrouwe machten, die 's Verdoemers naam verzwoert,
          En tegens 't eeuwig licht een eeuwig oorlog voert,
          U is bekend, hoe wij door 't eenig appel-bijten
          Macht kregen over al het zaad der Adamijten ;
          En d'offeranden, eerst geheiligd aan den Heer
          Van hemel, aard eu zee, ontstaken tot onze eer.
                                          —iv. 1, &c.

P. 112.   Men gunde u, na uw val, door d'ope lucht te zweven,
          Nu vlucht ge, door zijn naam ter wereld uitgedreven.
          Het is nu wakens tijd.   'T zij afgezant of heer,
          Zij zwoeren ons bederf ; men ga hun bei te keer.
          Ioannes moet er eerst, en dan de meester kleven ;
          Een ieder reppe zich.   U wordt de macht gegeven.
          Apollion trêe voor en stell' zijn list te werk ;

Want zoo men langer draal', zij vallen ons te sterk.
Men smore 't wassend kwaad bij tijds in zijn geboorte.
Zoo sprak hij, en elk stoof zijns weegs uit d'ijzerpoorte
Omhoog. Gelijk een vlucht roofvogels met geraas
Komt vallen op een kreng, een dood en stinkende aas.
Zoo zoeken ze op den grond van Jesses rijk en erven
Hun kans, en leggen toe op schenden en bederven,
Door heimelijk bedrog op openbaar geweld.
De slede van den nacht was door het starlicht veld
Nu steil in top gevoerd, en hing van wederzijden
Gereed ten halven wege, om langzaam neêr te glijden.
Wat ademt lag en sliep gerust.   —iv. 53, &c.

P. 115. De poel, daar Lucifer ten halze in kwam te smoren,
Gaapt wijd, en spalkt den mond wijd open tot aan de
ooren.
Men vaart er in ruimschoots, met paarden en karos,
Eerst over keizelsteen en dan door kreupelbosch
En heggen, wild en woest. De weg in 't ommezwaayen
Loopt enger, anders dan de wenteltrappen draayen,
Of als kinkhorens, de neêrrollen op een punt
Het koestrend licht, in 't eerst den ingang nog gegund,
Verflauwt allengs, en als vergeet zoo diep te dringen,
Genaakt men twijfellicht en avondschemeringen ;
Gelijk wanneer de zon, beneên de kim gedaald,
Nog schijnsel nalaat, dat een poos ter zee uitstraalt,
Dan is het nacht noch dag, of dag en nacht gemengeld,
En teffens duisternis en licht, dooren gestrengeld
Men wandelt hier, gelijk in maneschijn bij nacht,
Wanneer het hemelsch heer in orden trekt te wacht,
En op zijn ronde past, langs diamante wallen.
                                        —vi. 276, &c.

P. 119. Zoo stond een korte lust, die Eva zich verbeelde
Een mond vol appelsaps.   —v. 46-47.

De marmervloer bestrooid met een gebloemden regen ;
De wanden met tapijt behangen, en een zegen
Uit Arabye zwaait hun wyrookgeuren toe.
                                        —v. 297, &c.

O

Het woelt er hene en weer van maagden en van knechten,
Alle even jeugdig, en alle even schoon van leest.
Men schenkt den koelen wijn, die teffens lijf en geest
En God verheught.   Al wat der tafel aanzat muntte
In pracht voor andren uit.   —v. 310, &c.

Nu schenen veld en bosch van wildbraad leêg gevangen
Limoen, olijf, granaat, en goude oranje hangen
Aan takken druipende de joffer in den mond.
Een paradijslucht, pas gematigd en gezond
Verkwikte 't hart van al die hier te gader zaten.
De weelde en overdaad, nu teffens uit gelaten,
Bejegenden elkandre uit onderlinge gunst
Der stoffen dierbaarheid most wijken voor de kunst
En arbeid, aan het goud en zilverwerk gehangen
Kleenoodje en feest gewand.   —v. 321, &c.

De koning vrolijk liet een koninklijke schaal
Vol lekkren nectar van zijn Gauymedes schinken
          —v. 372–337.

De hemelsche musiek doorgalmde 't groot paleis
De rijkhofmeester brocht de beide sluyerkronen,
En spande ze om hun hooft, op 't mengelen der tonen
Van zang en fluit en snaar.   —v. 388, &c.

P. 122.   Dan toont de Vader zacht van aard
Zijn kindren eerst de roede, een star met eenen staart,
Zoo vierig rood als bloed, den voorboô van God's tooren.
          —iii. 117.

P. 122. Wanneer bij zomerdag een Koelte komt gevaren
En lieflijk blayen in een zee van korenaren,
Dan buigt de zwangere aar het hooft op haren halm.
          —iii. 143.

BESPIEGELINGEN VAN GOD EN GODSDIENST.

P. 125. Hij kan 't bewegen, dat gezien wordt, niet ontschre-
          euwen,
     Hetzij Copernicus of d'eer der Ptolomeewen
     Het aardrijk om de zon om 't aardrijk draai',
     De roering hangt in 't een of 't ander hoe men 't zwaai'.

Zoo d'eerste hemelring met zich trekt lager bogen,
En boven d'opperste geen reden kan beoogen
Een ander, die hen drijft en stil staat te gelijk,
Dan stijgt men klimmende in het onbewogen rijk,
Des Albewegers stoel, te schokken, noch verzetten,
Terwijl hij 't ouder zich al omdraait naar zijn wetten.
Om dit t' ontworstelen verciert het los gezin,
Dat een inwonende en een krachtig grondbegin
In enkel hemelkreits de starren draait en ronden.
—i. 416, &c.

P. 127. Het aardrijk is zoo groot dat niemand, hoe bevaren,
In vijftig eeuwen en nog drie paar honderd jaren,
Den ganschen aardkloot heeft doorwandeld en bezocht ;

. . . .

En nog in 't aardsch gevaart, bij 't hemelsch te gelijken,
Een enkel punt in 't oog, verlieft op starrekijken ;
Want wanneer d'aardkloot recht de starren staat in 't
licht
Dan snijdt die kloot geen punt uit 's hemels aangezicht.
Is elke star zoo groot als d'aardkloot in haar rijzen,
Of grooter, naar 't besluit van alle starrewijzen,
En schijnen ze evenwel, hoe wijd zij staan van een,
Dus klein op ons gezicht ; wie kan van hier beneën,
Met zijn gedachtenis, het hemelsch rond bepalen,
Daar zoo veel duizenden van diamanten pralen
Aan dien doorluchten ring, gepast als aan de hand
Van Gods onmeetbaarheid, die Oost en West bespant ?
Is d'aardkloot nu zoo groot, gelijk de meters sluiten,
Hoe groot is dan 't gewelf der hemelen van buiten !
Nu peilt de hoogte van den hemel, zoo gij kunt,
Tot 's aardrijks navel toe of 's afgronds middelpunt :
Heeft deze grootheid nog haar eind en zekre palen,
Wie kan d' oneindigheid van God dan achterhalen ?
En wat is dit heelal, in dien men God beschouw,
In grootheid meerder dan een druppel morgendouw !
—iii. 240, &c.

P. 131. De schoonheid van de vrouw, die 't al te boven gaat
Op aarde, en nimmermeer het hart en oog verzaadt,

Ontvonkt de leeuwen zelfs, ontdekt zich hier in 't leven,
Zoo schoon als God haar schiep, om aan den mensch te
   geven
En proef van weelde en lust, die, eeuwig uitgestort,
In God's bespiegeling alleen genoten wordt.
Het aanzien en genot der schoonheid van de vrouwe,
Een zaligheid geschat heeft duizenden in rouwe
En schipbreuk van hun staat, gezondheid, lijf en ziel,
Gedompeld over 't hoofd. De wijsste en sterkste hiel
En boeide ze, gelijk haar slaven, aan de keten
Van 't blond en hangend haar zoo raast geen dier, bezeten,
Betooverd van het spook, als d'overdwaalsche mensch,
Die blindling, op dit aas der schoonheid, ieder wensch
En wellust aanbijt, God en naam en faam en stammen
Ter zijde zet, om zich in 's vleisters minnevlammen
Te smilten, als het ijs of wassen beeld in 't vier.
Dat kan een wulpsch misbruik der schoonheid, en zoo dier,
Zoo dier bekoopt een dwaas dit schijngoed, 'twelk genoten
Nog nauwlijks, of berouw komt, schichtig toegeschoten,
En treedt het misbruik van Gods schepsel op de hiel !
Elendig was hij dan, die in haar strikken viel,
Gevangen en gesmoord, om eenen blik der oogen,
Een vreugd, in eenen droom, gelijk een damp, vervlogen.
Wat eischt dees schoonheid dan ? wat was Gods wit en end,
In 't scheppen van dit beeld, dat macht van zielen
   schendt ?
Hij wil het hart des mans aan hare trouw verbinden,
En leeren in dit schoon een grooter schoonheid vinden,
Een wellust, die de ziel in God genieten zal,
Die d'opperschoonheid is en weelde en 't éenig Al.
Gij zoudt in dit gezang de vrouw nog schooner hooren,
Maar 'k vrees door dees meermin een Heilig te bekoren,
Indien bevalligheid en deugd en gunst en geest
Van boven vall' en zwier' in 't lichaam, schoon van
   leest.   —iii. 419, &c.

P. 129.   Wat is 't een wonder, dat de hemel weet te passen
        Elk etmaal juist rontom te drijven op zijne assen,
        Te monstren 't hemelsch heer, in aller menschen oog,

Van Osten naar het West ! wat veldkortouw, wat boog
Kan kogel ofte pijl, wat bliksemstralen schieten
Zoo snel door lucht en zwerk ? Wat watervallen vlieten
Zoo snel ter steenrotse af ? En, evenwel bewaart
De losse star, van 't West in 't Oost, haar streek envaart,
Of snelst of trager, naar den hoefslag, daar de zeven
Een hooge of lager wijk en wachthuis wierd gegeven
Veel honderdduizenden van mijlen wijd van een.

—iii. 987, &c.

P. 129. Hier moet Hevelius geen verrekijker leenen,
Om sproet en vlek en licht, in 't aanschijn van de maan,
Te zoeken met den bril, en aarde en Oceaan
In zijne manekaart te malen.   —iii. 968, &c.

ADAM IN BALLINGSCHAP.

P. 140. Ik, eerst geheiligd om de kroon van 't licht te spannen,
En nu van 't eeuwig licht in duisternis gebannen,
Kome uit den zwavelpoel opdondren van beneên,
En, zonder mijnen ban en banpaal t'overtreên,
Hier boven spoken ; want hoe gruwzaam en verwaten
D'Erfvijand mij misschiep, nog wordt me toegelaten
Met u, mijn Helleraad ! gedagvaard hier ter vlucht,
Te heerschen over zee, het aardrijk, en de lucht,
Dat past den Grootvorst van de wereld en zijn luister,
Afkeerig van den dag en krachtiger bij duister :
Waarom hij ook den nacht tot dezen optocht kiest :
En schoon de nanacht nu allengs het veld verliest,
Nog kan de hater van het licht in schaduw duiken
Van nachtspelonk of haag of lustbosch, boom en struiken
Waar ben ik hier ? men hoort den schellen nachtegaal,
Den voorboô van de zonne en heldren morgenstraal.
'K Hoor deven wekker met een morgenkoelte opkomen,
En lieflijk klateren door klatergoud en boomen.
Men hoort vier sprongen, uit één bron en waterval,
Van eenen heuvel zich uitspreyen overal.
Dit tuigt ons klaar genoeg, wat bodem wij betreden :
Hier vloeit d'Eufraat. Hier bloet de hof in 't Oostersch
    Eden.

Het rijk van Adam en zijn gade aan hem getrouwd.
Hier most ik schuilen, met mijn schildwacht in een woud
Of donker lustprieel of myrthegalerije,
Dan achter uitzien, dan van vore, dan ter zije,
En letten, hoe men best berokkene eenig kwaad ;
Want ik, veraard van 't goed, dien vloek der vloeken haat,
En wensche Hem, wiens niets kan in zijn wezen deeren,
In zijn geschapenheên te schenden en schoffeeren.
Zoo wordt het Helsche rijk van Lucifer gebouwd,
Dat eeuwig duren zal.   Geen aanklacht is te stout
Voor mij, die niet ontzag den Hemel aan te randen ;
Zoo neemt mijn wraakzucht al de wereld op haar tanden,
En rukt dit groot heelal uit zijnen winkelhaak,
Dat's hemels as nog eens van mijne heerkracht kraak'
Het lust me hem voortan gedurig werk te geven,
En, schoon de bliksem mij ten troon hebbe uitgedreven,
Te laten blijken, wat ik, na dien val, vermag.
Al schoot ons macht te kort daar boven ; 't hoog gezag
Moet aanzien, dat ons nog die macht is bijgebleven,
Zijn willekeure in al zijn werk te wederstreven.
De naam van almacht is een titel zonder daad,
Een krachtelooze klank van roemzucht.   Wist hij raad
Om eenig wezen gansch van iet tot niet te brengen,
'T was uit met mij ; men zou me in wezen niet gehengen,
Min laten in 't bezit van's Afgronds heerschappij :
Daar legt zijn macht te laag, al schijnt mijn macht in lij
Te leggen.   Loeft men aan, gewis, het kan niet feilen,
Wij zullen in den wind dien hoek te boven zeilen,
En drijven dan ruimschoots de rijke haven in,
Waar naar men stevent.   Al 't geluk hangt aan 't begin ;
Aan d' uitkomst hoeft men niet te twijflen door mis-
     trouwen.
Laat vrij al 't hemelsch hof van zijne tinne aanschouwen,
Dat wij niet slapen, als er roof te halen is.
Hij zette uit achterdocht, om 't rijk der duisternis
In toom te houden, hier een schildwacht uit van Englen,
Die zouden Adams hof beschutten en zich menglen
In onraad en gevaar ; dies dienen wij bedekt
Te werken, eer men hen tot tegenstand verwekt.

De koning van den hof, onnoozel, zonder wapen,
Mag op deze Englewacht gerust en veilig slapen.

— i. 1, &c.

.   .   .   .

P. 144. Doch dit's een poos te vroeg. Men moet den tweeden
    sprongk
(Want d'eerste is ons mislukt) zoo renkeloos niet wagen,
Maar zachter toetreên, en gelegenheid belagen
Van waar en hoe men best den schepper bij den dag
In eenig schepsel, groot of klein, bestormen mag
Alle afbreuk strekt tot winst. Men moet allengs bij
    trappen
Beginnen, en van laag op steigeren en stappen.
Wie statig steigert raakt ten leste daar het stuit,
Een rijp beraad draaf voor ; dat wint een slag vooruit.
Laat zien, wat kans, wat stof d'opgaande dag wil geven ;
De zon, aan 't rijzen, zal den lusthof verf en leven
Bij zetten, Adam en zijn gade, hand aan hand,
Door wandelen den hof, die, heerelijk geplant,
Hen luttel min ziet dan aerts englen begenadigt
En uit Gods vollen schoot, naar lijf en ziel, verzadigt.
Men sla het onderling gesprek van verre ga,
Bespiê wat middelen den schepselen tot schâ
En afbruck dienen ; lett' in eenen hoek gescholen,
Wat hun verbaden werd en wat hen wordt bevolen
Op lijf en ziel straf ; want Hoogste is niemands vriend,
Dan die zijn hoovardij ten roem en aanwas dient ;
Eene oorzaak, waarom gij mijn Hemelsche eedtgenooten,
Als weder spannigen, ten Afgrond zijt gestooten.

— i. 71.

P. 148.   Ben ik uw vleesch en been
Zoo draag u, als een man, en laat ons lotgemeen
Te gader leven 'k noode u Gods eige gaven,
Zoo zal uw kennis trotsch tot aan de staaren draven ;
Zoo wordt gij in wetenschap en wijsheid God gelijk.
Gebruik uw vrijen wil, en toon mij de eerste blijk
Van liefde, in 't volgen van mijn aller eerste bede.
Zij lijdt geen weigeren. Gevolgzaamheid baart vrede.

— iv. 1322.

P. 149. O welk een strijd ! Hier staat het vrouwen beeld, daar
        God
        Hier vleit me hare beê, daar dreight me een streng
          verbod ;
        Zal ik de liefde en gunst van mijne vrouwe ontberen,
        Of de opperste genade in ongenâ verkeeren ?
        Een onweêr barnt er in mijn geest.
                                      —iv. 1338.

P. 150. Een andre ribbe legt u nader aan het hart,
        Dat d'opperste u een vrouw, naar uwen zin, bootseere.
                                      —iv. 1383.

P. 150.   Wij scheurden
        De witte zijde van hunne eerste onoozelheit.
        Dat zijn de slippen, ruil van stof, en rood beschreid
        Van slijk en sprenglen bloeds. Zij jammeren en krijten.
        Men hoort ze elkandre de schuld der misdaad wijten
        En vloeken. Eden galmt van jammerlijk misbaar.
        Mistroostije Adam krapt zijn aanzicht, rukt het haar
        Met lokken uit zijn hoofd en wekt de hofgeschallen,
        Uitschreeuwende : Waartoe, war ben ik toe vervallen !
        Ik gaf mijn bruid niet, maar mijn vijandin gehoor.
        Mijn vleesch heeft mij verraân. Ik volgde een heilloos
          spok.
        Een vuile snoeplust was de pijl, die Eva griefde
        En mij al teffens. Och! dit komt van vrouwen liefde !
        Ik ben van mijne ribbe en eigen vleesch verraân ;
        De vroweliefde komt mij al te dier te staan.
                                    —v. 1485.

P. 152. De hovaardij heeft mij bedorven en bekoord.
        Het spook des Afgronds klampt mij met geweld aan
          boord,
        Ik voele en voere alreê een oorlog in mijn leden ;
        Het vleesch wil anders dan de geest verstand en reden
        En wil, geteisterd van dien onverwachten smak,
        Gevoelen al te spade een vreeselijken krak
        K gevoel de jammeren van buiten en van binnen.
                                    —v. 1502.

P. 153.   *Ev.* Zoo schuift ge uw eige schuld alleen op mijnen
hals.

Ad. O oorzaak van mijn val en zooveel ongevals,
Hieruit te spruiten ! och dit komt van echtgenosoten !
Op zulk een voorwaarde is ons huwlijk niet gesloten.

   Ev. Het voegt den man zijn vrouw Godvruchtig voor
te treden.

   Ad. Laat dees gevloekte boom getuigen, wie eerst
Eden

Durf schenden, en zich aan 't verboden ooft vertast.

   Ev. De zwakke vrouwe kunne is van een lust verrast.

   Ad. En uw vervloekte lust mij bitter opgebroken.

   Ev. Het voegt een manshoofd zich te houden onbe-
sproken,

En stand te houden, zoo het vrouwebeeld bezwijkt.

P. 154.   Dus sleept de wellust van een oogenblik, eene uur,
Een lange keten na van rampen en verdrieten.
Het lust me langer niet, het leven te genieten.
'K verbeeld me, waar ik ga en sta, een bange dood ;
Zij grimt me leelijk aan.   Och, open uwen schoot,
Ontvang me o aarde ! want de lust is mij benomen ;
Ontvang me wederom, ik ben van u gekomen.
Dit lichaam komt u toe.   De ziel verhuize en zoek'
Een heimelijk verblijf, daar een verdiende vloek
Haar benevoere ; want zij heeft des Hoogsten zegen
Misbruikt wat toeft de dood ? het leven is me tegen,
De nare duisternis veel liever dan de dag.
Mijn schande legt te naakt.   Zoo 't mij gebeuren mag
Ze sterven, keer het niet.   Laat u mijn doot behagen.

SAMSON OF HEILIGE WRAAK.

P. 172.   Wat mensch zit in dien eik dus eenzaam en alleen ?
Het schijnt, hij bidt ons om een aalmoes, gansch verlegen
Van bittere armoede.   —ii. 184.

P. 172.   God hoede ons allen !   Wat verschijnt ons !   Och ! wat
raad ?   [duwen ?"
Och, och ! hoe kunnen wij dit schikken ?   Dit ver-
ii. 196.

'K heb vele maanden lang, gesloten aan dees keten,
In't molentuchtuis hier mijn tijd bedroefd gesloten,
Zoo blind, gelijk ge ziet, geslagen en begrauwd.

ii. 204.

P. 173.

Sam. Toen door God's kracht een bron uit egels tanden
     sprongk,
En ik verhit van slaan, het hart verkoelde en dronk
Bekwam die wonderbron mij dus in mijne smarte
De hemel zegene u voor uw meêdoogend harte.

Rei. Prins Samson, vrome prins ! wat is het ons een pijn
U hier te vinden, in dien jammerlijken schijn !
Wij zijn Iodinnen, hier vergaard van west en oosten,
En komen op dit feest u zoeken, u vertroosten,
Naar tijds gelegenheid, maar niet naar onzen wensch.
Geen onbeschaamde dier, dan een ondankbar mensch ;
Dat weten uij, u dienst en hulp en eere schuldig
Verdadiger des volks, och ! draag uw smert geduldig,
Totdat het God voorzie. O hartewee ! O smart !
Al weigert u de zon haar licht, God kan uw hart
Verlichten met een glans inwendig, die de stralen
Van duizend zonnen dooft. Wie kan de macht bepalen
Der Alleroppersten ? Die u zoo wonderbaar
Begaafde met een kracht, verbogen in uw haar,
Is machtig, als het Hem belieft, in u te werken
Ook zonder haarlok u te wapenen en te sterken.

—ii. 261.

P. 176.   Och ! waar Ik schuw geweest van Filistijnsche vrouwen,
           Bedrieglijk in den aard ! Mij mag de dag wel rouwen,
           Dat ik bij Sorck lest verliefde op Dalila
           Lichtvaardig, liefdeloos, en gierig. Op genâ
           En ongenade van een boelschap los te drijven,
           Is op een stille zee, in nood van eens te blijven,
           Zich reukloos wagen. Zie, die op beloften zag,
           Door's vijands geld bekoord, hield aan mij, nacht en dag,
           Te vergen het geheim van mijne kracht te melden
           In 't heetse van den gloed der minne ; een zielstorm,
            zelden

Van mannen wederstaan. Had toen! helas! mijn geest
Zoo sterk van krachten en geweld als 't lijf geweest
'K had dicht gebleven, mij gehoed dit klaar te zeggen.
Noch wist ik 't driewerp haar met eenen schijn t' ont
    leggen.   —ii. 237.

P. 178.   Maar 't ongenadig lot, dat hem ten deele viel,
          Het licht t' ont beren, in een nacht van duisternissen
          Wat is dit anders dan het halve leven missen?
          Hij leed een halve dood, toen hem, van kracht beroofd,
          De vijand boorde bêi zijne oogen uit den hooft.
                        —ii. 484.

          Geen mensch, geen vorst kan mij mijne oogen wedergeven.
          Ik mis mijne oogen, och! dat 's meer dan 't halve leven.
          De dag ging onder, eens voor eeuwig. Ik verwacht
          Den opgang nimmermeer. Het is hier eeuwig nacht;
          Nog mogen in der nacht alle andre dieren slapen
          En rusten; Samson ziet geen rust voor hem geschapen.
                        —iii. 871.

P. 180.   Dees ongelukkige, verkloekt, verrast, gegrepen,
          Berooft van 't hemelsch licht, met ketenen genepen
          Gedoemd ten arbeid, op 's aanklager's straffen eisch.
                        —ii. 569.

P. 180.   De Goden leverden dien vijand in ons hand,
          Door kracht van uw gebeên. Nu wenschen al de Heeren,
          Dat Samson onder dit zeeghaftig bankettcren,
          Die vijand, onlangs nog onoverwinbaar sterk,
          Op een triomftooneel, mocht spelen in de kerk,
          Tot prijs van Dagon en tot blijschap van hun allen.
                        —iii. 756.

P. 180.   Laat Samson inkleên. Laat de schowburg open zetten.
          Wij zegenen het spel, God Dagons naam ten lof!
                        —iii. 774.

P. 181.   Mijn Engel Fadäel kwam heden
            Mij noch vertroosten, daar Ik zat
            En op de kniên om sterkheid bad;

Toen steef een nieuwe kracht mijn leden,
Gods geest, die mij, van kindsbeen af
Tot hooge daden heeft gedreven
Gebiedt mij rustig door te streven
Bereidt me een heerlijk vorstengraf.

—vi. 1077.

P. 183.   Nu den grooten ommegang
Eens gevierd met spel en zang,
En in Dagons naam begonnen
Die den vijand heeft verwonnen.
Laat de schutterij vooruit
Henetreên, op bom en fluit,
Festbazuinen en trompetten.
Laat zich Gods gewijden zetten
In hunne orde, paar aan paar,
Met een statig kerkgebaar
En, gekranst met eiken blåren,
D'eer van 't hooge feest bewaren.
Laat koralen hunne keel
Mengen met schalmeye en veêl.
Samson trede op hun gezangen,
Met een braven stoet behangen.
Dan de torts, dan 't wyrookvat.
Dagon, 't Heiligdom der stad,
Volge, op eenen stoel gedragen.
Wij, gereed op zijn behagen,
Volgen hem, en op dien trant.
Al de Vorsten van het land
En Vorstinnen en de Grooten
Met den stoet van 't hof gesloten.
Gij, koralen ! zingt ons voor
Op dit zegenrijke spoor.   —iv. 1379.

P. 184.   Groot is Dagon, 't hoofd den Goden
Die Gods vijand onverwacht
Heeft geleverd in ons macht,
Voor wiens kracht de reuzen vloden ;
Die alleen zoo veel vermocht,
Zonder zwaard op zie te gorden,

Als een heerkracht in slagorden
Op een vorstelijken tocht.
Groot is Dagon, 't hooft der Goden,
Die Gods vijand lèide aan band,
En hem leverde in ons hand,
Tot een schimp der blinde Joden.
Ziet, hoe is hij nu verneêrd
Tegens wien nooit Filisteenen,
Ongekwetst in 't veld verschenen
Ziet, hoe Gaza triomfeert !
Groot is Dagon, 't hoofd der Goden,
Die Gods vijand, overal
Zoo ontzaglijk, brocht ten val,
Haalt uw hart op, gij genooden,
Die ten offermaaltijd zult
Samson zelf, op treur tooneelen,
Zien zijne eige treurrol spelen.
Schrikt niet, zoo hij briescht en brult.
—iv. 1405.

P. 186.

Rei. Genade, o God ! genade ; o help ons, help ons heden !
Vertroost ons in dien nood. Wij schreyen van beneden
Naar uwen hoogen troon. Wats' dit een overval !
Waar zijn, waar staan wij ? Dit afgrijselijk geschal
Verdooft onze ooren. Al dit stof verblindt onze oogen
Wij stikken. Wij vergaan van stof. Het puin gevlogen,
Gestoven door de stad, vervult de ruime lucht.
De stad is vol geschreis, vol jammers Het gerucht
Het huilen, het gekerm verspreidt zich door de straten.

. . . .

Wij durven, en 't is best, niet uitzien naar bescheid.
Wij duiken stil een wijl in deze kerkhof hagen,
Hier komt er een, verbaasd, verbijsterd, en verslagen
Laat ons vernemen, hoe het staat, hoe 't is vergaan.
Ai ! hoveling ! belieft het u, ai ! blijft wat staan.
Verhaal ons toch, hoe 't legt geschapen en geschoren.

Bode. Hebreeuwsche joffers, och ! heel Gaze is nu verloren,
Al 't Filistijnsche land in zijnen hoofsten nood

Rei. Hoe ging 't met Samson, is hij levendig of dood ?

Bode. Al dood en koud. Och, waar hij tijdig dood gesmeten,
In steê van blindeling, gebonden aan een keten,
Mishandeld, omgevoerd, verbitterd, en verstokt!
Nu heeft hij in zijn wraak zich zelven in gebrocht.

Rei. Zoo missen wij Hebreên voor eeuwig onzen rechter
En landdeschermer. Och, dit's jammerlijk! Maar echter
Verhaal ons, stuk voor stuk, al wat gij hoorde en zaagt.
—v. 1460.

P. 189.

Bode. Wij zagen Samson eerst den ommegang geleyen
Voor Dagon's Heiligdom ten toon treên op schalmeyen,
Op snaar en zegezang en vrolijk feestgeluid.
Hij stond den schimp en smaad des geduldig uit
En mak, gelijk een lam, en hiel zich in getrokken,
Maar kauwde midderwijl de heimelijke wrokken
Zoo raakte d'ommegang van Dagon aan zijn end;
Het offermaal begon, gelijk men is gewend,
Doch heerlijker dan ooit, uit blijschap, dat de landen
Den grootsten vijand, nu gevangen in hun handen
Vast ringeloorden, in zijn blindheit en verdriet.
.   .   .   .
—v. 1492.

De Kerkgalm bauwt hen na. Men hoort de galmen klatren,
Die groeyen bij den wijn. De groote kelk ging om
Op d'eer van Dagon, en het gansche godendom
Men zou, tot slot van 't feest, ten spele zich bereiden
De blinde Samson zegt: Ai, tuchtknaap! wil me leiden
Daar dit tooneel aan bêi de hoofdpilaren leunt
En 't schrikkelijk gevaart van al de kerk opsteunt.
—v. 1525.

G. BRANDT'S ACCOUNT OF VONDEL'S LITERARY METHOD AND STUDIOUS HABITS.

His industry and power of work were well-nigh incredible, knowing, as he wrote in a certain letter, "that he who ascends the heights of Parnassus all panting and perspiring, mounts by slow degrees, and that study and vigilance sharpen the under-standing." All his extant writings, more than thirty plays, besides his other great works, and such a multitude of poems of every description, are witnesses of his industry. His avidity for information was intense, and he availed himself of every possible means for acquiring it. In order, upon every subject and topic, to find the right expressions, he inquired from every class of men what Dutch words each made use of in matters relating to their work, business, or art. The country people he asked how they spoke about agriculture, and how they named and expressed everything connected with it. Concerning house-building he questioned in like fashion the carpenters and masons; con-cerning navigation and ship's tackle, the sailors; concerning the art of painting, and whatever related to it, the painters; and similarly concerning every other business, science, or art. This served for the building up of the language, and helped him to express whatever occurred to him in words which were appro-priate to the matter in hand. — *Leven van Vondel,* p. 100. *Nederlandsche Klassieken door Dr. Verwijs,* vol. iv.

THE END.

PRINTED BY BALLANTYNE, HANSON AND CO.
EDINBURGH AND LONDON.